For Melodie —

In the hope that
soon you'll be autographing
one of your books to
me — All best —

Ralph M. Surrey

D1266731

Books by Ralph McInerny

The Noonday Devil   1985
Connolly's Life   1983
Romanesque   1978
Spinnaker   1977
Rogerson at Bay   1976
Gate of Heaven   1975
The Priest   1973
A Narrow Time   1969
Jolly Rogerson   1967

The Father Dowling Mystery Series

Getting A Way with Murder   1984
The Grass Widow   1983
A Loss of Patients   1982
Thicker Than Water   1981
Second Vespers   1980
Lying Three   1979
Bishop as Pawn   1978
The Seventh Station   1977
Her Death of Cold   1976

The Noonday Devil

The Noonday Devil

Ralph McInerny

Atheneum   New York   1985

Library of Congress Cataloging in Publication Data

McInerny, Ralph M.
    The noonday devil.

    I. Title.
PS3563.A31166N59   1985   813'.54   84-45042
ISBN 0-689-11488-5

Copyright © 1985 by Ralph McInerny
All rights reserved
Published simultaneously in Canada by McClelland and Stewart Ltd.
Composition by Maryland Linotype Composition Company,
Baltimore, Maryland
Manufactured by Fairfield Graphics, Fairfield, Pennsylvania
Designed by Mary Cregan
First Edition

For Connie
sicut erat, nunc et semper

The Noonday Devil

Prologue

THE MAN in the light topcoat came onto the roof of
a building on the Via Parioli and squinted against the
Roman sunlight. He had the thin, ascetic face of an El
Greco saint, and his deep-set eyes seemed in search
of some ideal not to be found this side of the grave.
His watch read half past two. He was exactly on schedule. He took the .45 from his pocket. When he started
across the roof its heft seemed to pull him forward, as
if the gun were using him and not the reverse.

Only a ledge separated the building he was on from
the next. He paused and looked up the erratic arc the
rooftops made as they followed the curve of the street
below. The sound of afternoon traffic and the voices of

children lifted to him. He swung his leg over the ledge and moved swiftly across the next roof. His destination was the fifth building up, and when he got to it the roof door was marked as it was supposed to be: a pink plastic bucket with a few dry rags and a brush in it. He opened the door and, holding the .45 in his left hand, started down the steps.

The ambassador's apartment was on the top floor. The stairs led him down into a darkness relieved only by a sliver of light at the bottom of the door. Before he grasped the knob he inhaled. He turned and pushed. Nothing. The door must open toward him. He pulled. It was locked. He hesitated only a moment. His decision had been made earlier, when he had run through the procedure in his mind and confronted this possibility. He returned up the stairs to the roof.

At the rear of the building, looking down at the balcony, he uncoiled the nylon rope from around his middle. He gave it several test tugs after securing it to a water pipe, then backed to the edge of the roof and went over. The balcony doors were open and a panel of white curtain emerged ghostlike from within. When he was on the balcony, he got out the .45 again.

Jorge Silva-Mateos, the Salvadoran ambassador to the Holy See, sat at his desk facing Monsignor Alfredo Paredi and Bishop Garcia-Gomes. To his right, forming a third point of this triangle, sat Cardinal Fergus, the archbishop of New York, come these thousands of miles on short notice in the remote hope that the affairs of the Church in Central America might achieve stability with honor. The cardinal's profile could plausibly have emerged from the helmet of a combat infantryman, as indeed it had, in his youth. The cardinal was visibly controlling his impatience. Paredi's expression was that of the veteran diplomat, showing neither approval nor disapproval of this mad bishop from elsewhere with his preposterous proposals for bringing peace to his troubled country. The ideas of Garcia-Gomes had the simplicity of the Gospels. Sell off the riches of the Church and use the proceeds to help the poor. What would be done when the money was gone and the poor remained? The bishop's smile was beatific. An impoverished Church could then act as a symbol.

When the figure appeared in the balcony doorway, blotting out the sun, the ambassador had the fleeting impression of a winged thing. Coattails whipped in the wind as the man entered the study. Silva-Mateos rose behind his desk as if to welcome the slug that slammed into his face, slapping him back into the chair, which toppled under his dead weight.

The man in the topcoat shot the clerics next, observing the ecclesiastical order as he did so, moving from lower to higher rank. Paredi retained to the last the noncommital expression of a Vatican diplomat. His hands opened prayerlike and he was shot twice in the chest. The bishop fell to his knees and began to pray aloud. He said only *"Nunc Dimittis"* before a bullet silenced him. The prayer was one a priest says at compline every day. The cardinal was echoing the prayer as he sprang at the assassin and tried to get hold of the gun. If the bishop had prayed in the certainty that this was the world's last night, Cardinal Fergus meant to contest the matter. Nonetheless the Lord dismissed his servant when one bullet tore through the cardinal's heart and another through his head.

Señora Carman Silva-Mateos sat in a brocade chair in her room, the crystal beads of a rosary slipping through her arthritic fingers. Her eyes popped open

5

at the shots. Jesus, Mary, and Joseph! She got to her feet, oblivious of the pain the sudden movement cost her. She pulled open the door of her room and looked into the hallway.

A man with a gun came out of her husband's study. His face was impassive when he lifted his left hand and aimed. The terrible noise, the sharp pain in her shoulder, seemed the realization of her darkest fears. Her hand gripped the knob of the door when she fell backward, pulling it closed. Habit persisted at the heart of horror. She tried to turn the key in the lock but her fingers would not close on it. The second shot splintered the panel of the door and sent her reeling back across the room.

She did not realize that she had been screaming steadily since her first glimpse of the gunman.

He opened the shattered door and looked down at the crumpled body. The beads of her fallen rosary caught the glint of the sun. She had stopped screaming but she was whimpering, the sound pitiful. He entered the room, gun still in his hand, and crouched beside her. Her lips quivered, she might have been trying to form words, and her eyes rolled upward leaving only the whites, which gave her the milky look of the blind. Her mewling had the sound of a prayer. He extended his right hand over her and started to make a gesture but the rings on her gnarled fingers stopped him. The dying woman was of the rich. He put the gun to her temple and fired again.

In the study he stopped at Paredi's body and took a key from his pocket. Not three minutes had passed since he entered the apartment. When he came out onto the balcony, he found himself looking directly at a girl.

She was twenty-five yards away, on a diagonal, standing on the balcony of another building. Her lips were parted and her eyes were wide as she leaned toward him, puzzled, frightened, fascinated.

He went to the balcony railing and she stepped back into the shade. She must not go away. He smiled and beckoned her with his right hand. She stepped into the sunlight again, drawn toward him as he had expected she would be. He knew the power of his smile. The look of fright had left her face and there was a suggestion of complicity in her manner. He lifted the .45 and shot her between the eyes.

The nylon rope still hung from the roof above. He pocketed the gun, grasped the rope, and handed himself up the wall, a spider devouring its thread, his vulnerable back atingle.

On the roof, he felt a sudden impulse to lie flat, to become invisible, to be somewhere miles away. He pulled the nylon rope up after him but left it on the roof. The sound of the sirens did not bother him. Not nearly enough time had passed for them to be for him. He moved rapidly across the roofs to the door from which he had originally emerged.

The door would not open. It could only be stuck, not locked, but pull as he would it refused to open. The pulse of fear began, but it was weak, hardly sufficient to cloud his mind. He looked back the way he had come, counting the ledges. Of course. He had another roof to go.

Once inside again, he descended swiftly, his rubber soles silent on the marble steps that led him down six flights to the street. He unbuttoned his topcoat, revealing a Roman collar. The skirts of his cassock had been rolled up and secured at the waist. He undid them and

7

the black garment dropped to his ankles. He left the
.45 in the pocket of the topcoat, which he removed and
folded over his arm.

On the street floor he emerged from the building to
find the portièra sweeping the sidewalk. Wizened simian
face, gray hair knotted behind her head, she bowed as
he went by. When he entered earlier, he had put a
hand to his breast in explanation of his reluctance to
speak. She had read the sign as he hoped she would. The
priest was bringing the sacrament to someone in the
building.

Now, after the priest had passed, the portièra put a
finger below her eye and tugged downward. She was
glad to see him go, a tall figure in black, beret pulled
onto his shaved head, coat over his arm, cassock whip-
ping at his legs.

There was a bar directly across from the entrance to
the Salvadoran ambassador's building. The man in the
cassock crossed the street, went into the bar and ordered
a coffee. He lit a cigarette as he waited and glanced
across the street.

By the time he finished his cigarette and coffee, the
street was filled with the wail of sirens. He went outside
and looked up at the top floor of the ambassador's building. Then he turned and walked slowly to where Paredi
had parked the car with Vatican City plates. He opened
the door, got behind the wheel, and started the motor.
In the rearview mirror his eyes looked back at him.

"Bless me, Father, for I have sinned."

He said the words aloud. In English. His eyes crinkled
when he smiled.

Book One

Part 1

D O L A N , having ascertained that the lunch was on the *Times,* insisted that they meet at the Algonquin, a place Hanratty abhorred. In the lobby faded figures talked too loudly to one another, the suggestion of celebrity in their tone, their restless eyes seeking recognition. Has-beens, all of them. "In the room the women come and go, speaking of Michelangelo." Hanratty murmured these lines as they waited to be seated but Dolan did not take the bait. He was already salivating in anticipation of crab legs.

Hanratty ordered seafood bisque and a salad. He seldom ate lunch and when he did he was content with

Chock Full O' Nuts. Here they were surrounded by monied whispers. Lawyers, agents, actors, visiting firemen: the clientele was drawn from that segment of society whose taxes, in Hanratty's estimation, should at least be tripled. It was his cross that he himself was one of them. Unlike Dolan. Perhaps he should not begrudge the editor this treat.

"Is the subscription list still dropping?"

Dolan shrugged. "Yes, but we're still read."

"Better read than dead."

Dolan gave him a little smile, contemplated the crab meat on his fork, and dunked it in butter. His lips were already oily from excess. Dolan was seventy, a member of the second generation of *Commonweal* editors, surrounded now by much younger people who had little sense of the magazine's noble tradition. Dolan brought his fork toward his mouth, then arrested it, a whimsical expression on his oval face. "Do you know, Matt. I liked it better when we were fighting the bishops, not allied with them."

"You still have the cardinal archbishop of New York as foe."

"Ah, the eminent Fergus." Dolan continued with his crab.

"I plan a series on the Church and Central America and I want to pick your brain."

"Pick away."

Dolan himself continued to pick away at his crab. Hanratty, anything but a gourmet, marveled at Dolan's delight in the crustacean. Perhaps his own taste buds had atrophied during the three years he spent discovering he was not meant to be a monk. Thoughts of the Kentucky hills never failed to fill him with a delicious sense of loss. Our Lady of Gethsemani, a few miles out of Bardstown, an historical center of mid-American Catholicism, had been made famous by Thomas Merton. Hanratty, caught up in peaceful protests during the Vietnam War had made a journey to see Merton in his hermitage. Even before he met the monk, Hanratty had the eerie feeling that he was coming home.

The monastery buildings were ugly, the landscape bleak, the food in the guesthouse heavy and indigestible even to him. But the first time he knelt in the visitors' gallery and looked down at the monastery church and saw the ghostly monks drift into vigils, Hanratty longed to take his place in choir. One of Merton's oddities was that he had sought permission to live apart from the monastery. Hanratty sat with him on the porch of the hermitage from which they looked down a vista of fields flanked by woods toward hills that were almost mountains. This was the scene Merton saw daily from his writing desk inside. The monk wanted news from the outside world and Hanratty obliged, but with the feeling that he had already put all that nonsense behind him.

"I want to stay here," he said finally.

Merton looked puzzled. He had a flat face, a round mouth, a heavy upper body. He had been in the monastery since 1941 and still looked youthful.

"I want to be a monk," Hanratty explained.

Merton looked disappointed. "That's a common feeling among visitors."

"You had it yourself, I remember." Merton had said as much in *Seven Storey Mountain* and in the *Secular Journal*. What is it like to have your personal life a matter of public record?

"Talk to the abbot."

Of course there was the impediment of Hanratty's

failed marriage. He had been a junior at Notre Dame when he met Jane. She was a student at Saint Mary's across the road. Saint Mary's had traditionally supplied spouses to Notre Dame men. His relationship with Jane followed the usual pattern. They had a gloriously bourgeois wedding in Lake Forest and he went to work at the First National Bank in the Loop. There had been no children: just a fact, not a policy. They lived in an apartment near the Water Tower and he felt his life grow schizophrenic. On the one hand his life in the bank and with Jane, on the other his deepening involvement with the antiwar movement. It became unwise to go to Lake Forest where arguments with his father-in-law were inevitable. After his second arrest he lost his job and then his wife. Jane stayed put with her parents the afternoon Hanratty unleashed an impassioned indictment of the life they led. There was a discreet divorce after an unsuccessful attempt at an annulment. Incredibly, Jane had remarried. She still lived in Lake Forest with her second husband and their two children. The abbot frowned when Hanratty told him all this.

"You could never take vows."

"Just let me stay."

"Come back in three months."

He came back in two weeks. He haunted the guest-house. He pleaded with the abbot. Merton convinced him that his own intercession would be a negative factor. But then the author monk seemed not to approve of Hanratty's vocation.

"You're doing important work outside."

"Protesting the war? Speaking out for peace?" How idiotically childish all that suddenly seemed.

Eventually he was admitted to the monastery as an oblate. Without vows or the prospect of them. He could walk away whenever he wanted. At the time it seemed impossibly unfair: he wanted to bind himself to that austere life with hoops of steel. At last he knew what really mattered. God, silence, sacrifice. He was certain that if this life were known people by the thousands would descend on the monastic redoubt demanding entry.

Three years later he walked away from it. By that time he had come to see monastic life as culpable self-indulgence. Such news as reached him from the world suggested that the apocalypse was at hand. Peace and prayer and silence—God seemed somehow absent now —were luxuries. He rose at three in the morning, his diet was vegetarian, he worked like a serf, he had no time to call his own, and his life seemed one of impossible luxury.

Back in the world, he began to write for *Commonweal*, submitted elsewhere, writing, writing, his output the product of the diligence he had learned in the monastery. He sold three pieces to *The New York Times* magazine and was hired as religion editor. Religion editor! They wanted a Catholic. There seemed no need to mention that he had lost his faith.

You can take the boy out of the monastery but getting the monastery out of the boy proved impossible. Hanratty wore what was left of his hair close clipped. His indifference to food and a passion for cycling kept him lean. His large, accusative eyes looked out at the world and found it wanting. Just so he looked around the restaurant of the Algonquin.

"What do you think of the draft pastoral on the Third World?"

Dolan thought there were some good things in it.

"How could there not be? It is one hundred and

seventy pages long. Long enough to contain a lot of crap too."

"Matt, a document that thoroughly pleased you could never be passed. It probably could not be written."

"I'd settle for the removal of the section on liberation theology."

Dolan raised his brows. "I thought it was remarkably tolerant."

"Tolerant! That is exactly the word. The one version of Christianity that truly speaks to the times is tolerated."

"Don't forget the pope."

"I like the pope," Hanratty said, too loudly. Other diners looked at him. Human respect. To hell with them. Nonetheless, it was an idiotic remark. What difference did it make whether or not he liked the pope? "The pope is a juggler."

"Our Lady's juggler." Dolan laughed at his own joke, a habit of his. "I'm going to have another Manhattan."

"Go ahead."

Hanratty did not drink. It did not attract him despite the fact that he was undiluted Irish. If he had been attracted, memories of his father would have deterred him. His mother's cross, an Irish drunk. And one of the finest men Hanratty had ever known. His mother had been a saint and his father had not, but if he could have ten minutes with either of them now he would pick his father. Dolan reminded him of his father. Sort of.

"Publish Haley's piece on Guatemala."

"It's scheduled."

"Move it up. You're right. People still do read *Commonweal*. That article will cause a splash."

This was the real reason for the lunch. Bishop Haley's

affirmative appraisal of liberation theology, if only as a Latin American solution to the Church's difficulties with modern man, was one of several articles Hanratty was shepherding into print. There was also Boyle's three part series in the *National Catholic Reporter.* That would be less effective. The *Reporter* had lost all sense of moderation and its readers were largely flakes. Monsignor Wimple's column would appear in two thirds of the diocesan papers and Hanratty had talked Andrew Greeley into doing five thousand words for the *New York Review of Books.* Hanratty thought of these other things as an escort for Haley's article, and it was important that Dolan not bury it away in a special issue.

On his third Manhattan, Dolan promised that Haley's article would appear in two weeks.

"That's perfect, Pat. I'll hold you to that."

"You have my word." His slurred word, as it happened. But Hanratty would send off a memo to Dolan as soon as he got back to his office.

In the lobby, as they went out, an actress who had a minor role in a daytime serial was signing autographs.

They parted in the street and Hanratty set off into the brisk October breeze. It was not until Broadway that he became aware of the Extra. The *Post.* "Cardinal Fergus Assassinated." Hanratty was wary. The story was all inside and it might turn out that it was Fergus's reputation that had been assassinated. But the story was true to the headline. Fergus dead! Hanratty began to jog toward his office. Thank God he was alone when he heard the news. Even Dolan might have been scandalized by the smile Hanratty was unable to suppress. Words he would shortly write formed in his mind as he moved along the afternoon sidewalk.

The New York archdiocese was open!

MYRTLE LEFT THE OFFICE and the incessantly ringing phone and scooted over to Saint Patrick's where she sat in a pew halfway up the nave and let the tears come.

Outside, the cathedral was dwarfed by the surrounding buildings, but inside it was huge. Tourists wandered up and down the aisles, a brisk business was conducted in the shop at the rear of the church, but it remained a house of prayer. Scattered through the nave were others on their knees, saying the rosary, asking favors, thanking God for favors received, or just paying Him a visit. No one would notice her crying here, or if they did, they would not find it odd.

Myrtle Hanley Tillman was fifty-nine years old. She had been Kevin Fergus's secretary since he was the youngest auxiliary bishop and she was twenty-nine. Thirty years. Longer than she had lived before coming to work for him. So many of her days had been spent typing his correspondence and memos and drafts of sermons and talks, the familiar voice speaking into her ear intimately as the voice of conscience. He dictated everything, using a portable device no bigger than the palm of his hand, recording on microcassettes.

"And it is American made," he had said with satisfaction.

Well, it was an American brand but it turned out that it was manufactured in Hong Kong. Monsignor Barrett had told her this, taking great pleasure in the information. Why did they all kid the cardinal so? Hong Kong or not, it was a great improvement over the belts he had recorded on for years, though Myrtle felt a bit like an astronaut wearing the all-but-invisible headset, a clear tube running to her ear. She had actually been listening to the cardinal's voice when she got the dreadful news.

Monsignor Barrett came in and stood before her desk. She looked up, continuing to type, and said nothing. He was not wearing his usual devilish grin. She stopped typing.

"The cardinal has been shot in Rome."

"My God." Her shock was at what she took to be a horrible joke. He couldn't be serious. But he was.

The cardinal, the bishop of San Salvador, the Salvadoran ambassador to the Vatican and his wife, a Vatican diplomat, and a neighbor woman had all been killed. But it was Cardinal Fergus who made the big news. Monsignor Barrett seemed to think she would be consoled by that. And then the phone began to ring. She was asked if the cardinal had received threats on his life. Had the cardinal lived in fear of such an attack? Inane questions, stupid questions. Myrtle wanted to ask questions, not answer them. The story was still so vague. But the reporters who phoned did not want to answer her questions. After fifteen minutes of hell she escaped to the cathedral.

Myrtle tipped her head back and looked with tear-blurred eyes at the ribbed ceiling high above her. Gradually she lowered her chin and her eyes rested on the red hats suspended from the ceiling above the sanctuary. They would hang there until they turned to dust. Cardinal Spellman's, Cardinal Cooke's and, by comparison bright and new, Cardinal Fergus's. He would turn to dust before his cardinal's hat did. Myrtle drew her lower lip between her teeth. Dear God, how sad it was. The cardinal was nearly a decade older than she, but he had reason to expect more active years, years he could spend trying to reintroduce sanity into the American Church. The words were his. Familiar words he had used in dozens of the speeches she had typed. The Cold War Cardinal. That was what he had been called. The bishop nostalgic for the times of Senator McCarthy.

"McCarthy," the cardinal had said, shaking his head. "How old do they think I am?"

McCarthyism. The Cold War. For most people, they were mythical evocations. But the truth was that the cardinal considered the cold war to be going on apace.

"Who declared it over? Of course the Soviets wanted us to think that an era of cooperation had dawned. The Helsinki Accords, Salt I and Salt II. More agreements for them not to keep. No one seriously thinks they abided by any previous agreements. It is always the next treaty that is the important one. Well, you cannot be for peace if you are willfully ignorant of the dangers to it."

Myrtle never commented on such remarks; she wasn't expected to. She was not the real addressee. In truth, she didn't really know what she thought of the controversies he had been embroiled in since he first became bishop. All she knew was that he seemed to be cutting himself off from any possible advancement. He had thought so himself.

"If I'm lucky, they'll pack me off to Ogdensburg. Or Walla Walla."

That was before the election of John Paul II. Fergus's stock had risen immediately. On the pope's visit to the United States, twenty minutes had been set aside for a tête-à-tête between the pontiff and auxiliary bishop Kevin Fergus. From that point on, he had been given dozens of confidential assignments, most of them unheralded. (John Paul II created Fergus a cardinal in his first consistory.) There had been some who suspected he was sent on secret missions. Matthew Hanratty of the *Times* was one of them.

"Are you ashamed of it?" the reporter had asked, fixing her with his strange eyes.

"Ashamed of what?"

"Of Bishop Fergus's special standing with the Vatican."

Myrtle just looked at him. Any answer to such a question would be a betrayal, she wasn't quite sure how. Hanratty ran his hands down his face. How sunken his cheeks were. The man looked as if he had not had a square meal in his life. Perhaps he was ill. It made it easier to talk with Hanratty if she imagined that he had a terminal illness and was wasting the last hours of his life in pursuit of clerical gossip.

Hanratty said, "It is well known that Bishop Fergus has been given a number of special assignments, some coming from the apostolic delegate, some directly from the Vatican."

"If you know all about it, why are you asking me?"

"So it's true."

It was stupid to have answered. She kept her face expressionless, at least she tried. Hanratty was a journalist she did not like, perhaps because of Fergus's opinion of him.

"He exemplifies Andrew Greeley's rule. The way for a Catholic to make it in the United States is to be an anti-Catholic. Hanratty had adopted a completely secular attitude, yet he insists on calling himself a Catholic. If a non-Catholic wrote of the Church the way Hanratty does he would lose his job." Fergus had groaned his way through Hanratty's book, *A Concerned Catholic's Look at His Reactionary Church.* Hanratty urged the Church in the United States to give proof that it had emerged from its McCarthyite period.

"He needs McCarthy the way the Democrats need Nixon."

It was good to know that all Hanratty had were suspicions and she could conceal the cardinal's unpublicized efforts for the pope. Myrtle was not sure that her attitude toward Hanratty was completely Christian, but it would have been treacherous to discuss her boss's secrets with the reporter.

"You should speak with His Eminence," she was soon able to advise him.

"When can I have an appointment?"

"I will bring it up with him."

"On the phone, he tells me he is too busy."

"That's true enough."

"He can't duck the press. You should tell him that."

"You can tell him. When he gives you an appointment."

Hanratty retaliated by writing a column about bishops who refuse to make themselves available for questioning. By the laity. By the press. He meant by himself.

When Myrtle told Fergus of Hanratty's efforts to interview her, he accepted her loyalty without praising it. He expected it. After all, the pope himself was involved, at least indirectly, and he hoped he did not have to tell her that confidences involving the pope were in a class all by themselves. For Myrtle, a confidence was a confidence.

What she had never been able to understand was the hatred her boss attracted simply by talking about the world the way it was. He insisted on the incompatibility of Marxism and Christianity. He counted it a blessing to live in the free world and felt that the Church in the United States had a global role to play. Nor would he let people forget what Russia had done in Cuba and Afghanistan and Poland. No one could deny the truth of what he said, yet many were infuriated. And not just non-Catholics. Catholics, particularly Catholics, criticized him, and some of those Catholics were his fellow bishops. Myrtle found it all very confusing.

Sitting in Saint Patrick's, crying softly, thinking of Cardinal Fergus as she might an older brother, she realized she should have known that violence would be done him. Had she ever really worried about it? Even after the pope was shot, and the president, had she ever seriously thought that anyone would try to harm her employer? As a cardinal he seemed to assume the eminence of his title. Your Eminence. She had found it easy to call him that, a man she had called just bishop when she first met him.

Whenever he spoke of the possibility of death he seemed to have in mind illness or accident. As for illness, well, he had been healthy as could be. Accidents? Why think of it? He had never had a serious one in thirty years. Yet now, after the horrible news, Myrtle felt that he had had a premonition of what would happen.

"They are ruthless, Myrtle. A pope, a president, what do they care? They don't have to worry about public opinion, at home or abroad. That is the real tragedy. The free world press protects the Soviet Union."

He was convinced that the KGB had been behind the attempted assassination of the pope, and despite his own theories he had expected a worldwide outburst of indignation. But the story had been killed with a thousand qualifications. Everything was alleged. Denials got twice the coverage of accusations. And readers grew bored with the story. Finally Fergus decided he was not really surprised by the reaction. Or by the shooting.

"It's a risk we all run."

He said that solemnly, and she had thought he was being melodramatic. She had never really worried about him, his physical safety. His reputation, yes. Other bishops, singly and in groups, had begun to criticize him more and more sharply. It diminished a bit after he was made cardinal but then took on new life.

The tourists in the side aisles moved from altar to altar. Myrtle got up and went to the altar of Saint Anthony of Padua. Cardinal Fergus had had a special devotion to this saint. Myrtle stood there with her eyes closed, trying to pray. That is when she remembered the tape.

"I want you to keep this is your safety deposit box, Myrtle. Don't keep it here in the office."

The microcassette he handed her was like dozens of others he brought back from any trip. She put it in her purse and forgot it. Two days later he asked about it and she said she was taking it to the bank on her lunch hour. The tape might have stayed in her purse for weeks if he hadn't reminded her.

"Think of it as my last will and testament."

Cardinal Fergus smiled as he said this, but a moment later she looked up to find that he was staring past her, a remote look in his eye. The cardinal was frightened and it frightened her to realize it.

When she left Saint Patrick's she went to her bank and signed a slip for admission to the vault. She removed the microcassette from her safety deposit box and put it in her purse.

Now that she had it with her, she felt vulnerable.

3

AUSTIN CARDINAL CAREY, archbishop of San Francisco, kept one day free every two weeks. In order to get the most out of this respite from his unending series of appointments, he liked to leave the city. A favorite spot was Saint Mary's College in Moraga, which was both close and secluded. The Christian Brothers gave him a guest room in a residence that housed elderly members of the order and this gave the cardinal seclusion within seclusion, out of the campus mainstream. On his day off he drove himself; that was part of the therapy. Riding in the back seat of the archdioceasan Cadillac always made him feel that he was a ceremonial figure being wheeled from confirmation to luncheon to conference, a prisoner of his schedule. When he himself was behind the wheel he could imagine that he might turn right or left, go anywhere he wished, simply get lost for the day. But he always ended up at Saint Mary's.

Thus it was that the cardinal, wearing khaki pants, loafers, and a dark, short-sleeved turtleneck, left the city at the wheel of a five-year-old Datsun and started into the foothills toward the Napa Valley. The inbound traffic was brisk at nine in the morning but outbound he was able to get into the right lane and hold it at fifty, already beginning the relaxation that was the point of the day.

Carey's name seldom appeared in the press now without the standard rider: leader of the progressives among the American bishops. The description was exact. Carey did not believe in false humility. Neither was he overwhelmed by the significance of the leadership role ascribed to him. He had quite openly run for the presidency of the National Conference of Catholic Bishops. Camacho, his predecessor, had been the unworthy beneficiary of misguided affirmative action. He was archbishop of Detroit, conservative, cautious, and, luckily, inept. A week or two after the fact, Camacho would figure out that he had been manipulated. As in the successful effort to keep Kevin Fergus off the Latin American Committee. Well, off its chairmanship anyway.

The throwbacks in El Salvador had sent frantic wires to Camacho; it was clear that Fergus was their man. Small wonder. Like them, Fergus thought you could turn back the clock in Central America. Align the Church with the landed gentry, placate the peasants. Camacho, to the degree he thought at all, probably agreed. The difficulty was that he agreed with whomever had last spoken to him.

Well, they had prevented Fergus from becoming chairman of the committee and that was a whole lot better than nothing. The chairman, at least if it was Fergus, would try to turn the United States Catholic Conference staff into errand boys. There would have been a riot. So they put Liberati in as executive secretary and the USCC retained freedom of maneuver. Liberati had sent Carey a box of havanas—and not the kind made in Miami.

Carey realized that few grasped the distinction between the NCCB, the National Conference of Catholic Bishops, and the USCC, the United States Catholic

Conference. The first is specifically clerical and episcopal; the second is the bureaucracy the bishops officially created in 1966. Liberati, as the executive secretary, presided over various committees, each of which had a director, a small permanent staff, and a large group of consultants, experts, lay and clerical, Catholic and non-Catholic. Only a few bishops were directly involved with the USCC. The point of all this organization was to represent the Catholic viewpoint to congressional committees, to prepare reports, draft statements, and the like. For example, the pastoral on war and peace was written by staff members of the USCC for a committee of the NCCB. Until very recently, the staffs at the USCC issued papers without prior clearance by the bishops who ultimately had to accept or reject them. This chaos had been brought under some control, but of course they could still use a leak to suggest *the* position of the Church on any given issue.

A horn sounded behind him and an irate driver shot by. The speed of the Datsun had dropped to forty-five. So what? The left lane had been open. The rearview mirror showed him an all but empty road behind. Carey shook his head. The man might have been himself on any day but this. Rush, rush, rush. Thank God, he had established the practice of getting out of the race fortnightly.

Fortnightly. He smiled. That was not a word one heard much nowadays. When he was a kid there had been a fortnightly club in the parish, a men's club. He was diappointed when he found out it was largely an excuse to get out of the house and play cards in the parish hall. Which had also been the auditorium of the school. And the gym. The card tables were set up on the floor of the basketball court. At one end of the room was a stage. Exercise rings hung from the ceiling. An all-purpose place. Austin Carey had thought fortnightly meant something to do with the military. Bank night. Another forgotten locution. At the Leola Theater. His earliest memories were of the thirties. Light-years ago.

"Bimonthly?" Horvath had asked, when he told him the frequency of his free days.

"Every two weeks." Carey frowned as he explained. To him bimonthly suggested every two months. He looked it up and found that it meant either that or twice a month. He waited for Horvath to mention it again so that he could tell him of the ambiguity. But if Horvath had been in the habit of nettling the cardinal he would soon have had another assignment.

It was a menial assignment, master of ceremonies to a bishop, and it mattered little that the bishop was a cardinal as well, Carey knew. That was how he had started out himself. Back in Duluth. Duluth. From his present perspective, Duluth seemed ultima Thule and he marveled at the distance he had come. He had gone to Rome with his bishop during Vatican II and there had made the contacts that put him on his way. He had served seven years in Washington, which is why Liberati kept him informed. He was still one of the boys so far as Liberati was concerned. And of course the executive secretary saw Carey as his ticket upward.

Saint Mary's, chalk white against the still green hills, its central buildings and arcades covered with rust-red Spanish tile, never failed to delight Cardinal Carey. The brothers who ran the college were as efficient as the Franciscans who had founded all the missions whose architecture was mimicked here. Their vineyards in the Napa Valley provided an endowment whose dimensions not even Carey could learn. They talked poor mouth, of course; that went with the vow of poverty. The school was in jeopardy, enrollment was down and contributions (contributions!) had dropped off. They began a program in business, one of those ersatz graduate programs that had sprouted up on liberal arts campuses across the nation. Cater to the career orientation of students, as it was put, but only after they have received a liberal education.

Carey's attitude toward the college was realistic but affectionate. He liked Saint Mary's. He had not missed a commencement since coming to San Francisco and he hoped they appreciated it. All those vineyards . . .

He came up the drive toward the main building, swung to the left and shortly arrived at a graveled parking lot behind the residence. He put his car in a spot that would be shaded in the afternoon, and, briefcase in hand, got out of the car and slammed the door. As if activated by the noise, the door of the residence opened and Brother Benignus appeared. Carey had difficulty not seeing him as one of the seven dwarfs. It wasn't that Benignus was short. He wasn't. But he had an egg-shaped head, a ruddy complexion, fluffy white hair over his ears, and a bulbous nose. And he had a frown that cut deep furrows into his face. The deeper the frown, the happier Benignus was. Carey suspected the influence of French spirituality, Jansenism. Blessed are the miserable.

"Phone call for you, Your Eminence."

"Oh no."

"Father Horvath wants you to call him as soon as you get here."

"Some day off."

Benignus was visibly aware of the urgency of the call. Only once before had Carey been disturbed during his fortnightly and that was when his sister died. He had flown back to Duluth to say the funeral Mass and had been truly surprised by the nostalgia the hilly town over-looking Lake Superior elicited. Death, memories—he had indulged the thought that he would have been better off if he had stayed right there in Duluth. But he had visited a classmate or two and gotten over that. He would have withered on the vine just as they had.

Since there was no phone in the guest room, Benignus led him to an office that contained little more than a desk and chair and a bookcase whose shelves bowed in the middle though their burden was light. As he sat at the desk and drew the phone toward him Carey glanced at the shelves. Archbishop Goodier. *The Passion and Death of Our Lord Jesus Christ.* It was odd to think of a bishop writing a book. How times had changed. Now bishops formed committees that drafted pastoral letters on the problems of the world.

"Cardinal Carey's office." Horvath's voice was precise and unmodulated. He might have been a recording.

"You called me, Father?"

"Have you heard the news?"

"What news?"

On the other end of the line, Father Horvath drew in his breath, but he could not retain his calm when he spoke. "Fergus has been shot in Rome. He, two other bishops, three others."

"Shot?"

"Killed. All of them."

"Dear God. Give me the details."

Horvath had few details. But even as he listened, Carey's mind was spinning. A first reaction, quickly suppressed, was that a foe was gone from the field. But this was no heart attack or plane crash. Assassination carried unpredictable implications and Carey tried to sort them out.

"The radio reports have become repetitive, Your Eminence. There really aren't many facts."

Facts were the least of it. It was the interpretation that mattered. The fear grew in Carey that some idiot had turned Fergus into a martyr. Dying with the bishop of San Salvador couldn't hurt him.

"I'm sorry for breaking into your bimonthly like this."

"You were right to call me, Father. Thank you."

"Will you be returning tonight?"

"Perhaps earlier. I want to think. I'll let you know."

He put the phone carefully into its cradle. The windows of the room were closed and the air was stuffy. The sunlight, caught in the curtains, seemed solid, smokelike. From outside came the far off sound of young voices. Students. On the wall beside the door was a formal photograph of himself with a spray of palm behind it. His photographed self looked out at him from a severe black frame. How gaudy his cardinalatial getup was. He held the cape open as if to display the frilly surplice and the jeweled pectoral cross, the latter a gift from Pinelli when he was consecrated bishop. It was, according to Pinelli, a cross John XXIII had worn as patriarch of Venice. By contrast his ring looked modest, a flat wide gold band adorning his right hand like a continental wedding ring. He tried to discover in the photograph some inkling of what he had felt when he first donned the robes of a cardinal. The picture had been taken before he went to Rome to receive the biretta from the pope. The biretta, not the red hat. Fergus had been one of the last to receive the flat red hat to hang high in his cathedral.

Kevin Fergus dead. He picked up the phone and dialed o-202 and then the number of Liberati's office.

"May I help you?" an operator asked.

"Cardinal Carey calling collect."

She hesitated as if suspecting a joke. "Cardinal Carey?"

"That's right. I'm calling Monsignor Liberati."

Whose line was busy. He tried it again a few minutes later. Still busy. Well, he could imagine the excitement at the USCC. And in New York. He felt becalmed, out of it, sitting in a hot, airless room on a college campus in California. That had been a factor when the chance of San Francisco came up. It had seemed so far from the action. Now he was doubly removed from center stage. This was his day to think, to recharge his batteries, to pray. Pray. What is prayer? The lifting of the mind and heart to God. Kids no longer had those catechism answers in their heads. Belatedly he remembered to pray for the repose of his brother bishops, cut down by an assassin.

"May their souls and the souls of all the faithful departed through the mercy of God rest in peace. Amen."

He had not liked Kevin Fergus but he would miss him. Who would take his place as the head honcho of reaction? Deegen. Carey had the feeling that he had just won a major battle without firing a shot. A future with Fergus out of the picture was one in which the USCC could do whatever it wanted. Carey's eyes lifted once more to his photograph.

The first thing the National Conference of Catholic Bishops would want was to have a say in the selection of Fergus's successor.

Cardinal Carey picked up the phone and dialed Liberati's number again.

_____

THE PRESS CONFERENCE was scheduled for one
o'clock, and that was the first mistake. Reporters would
not like either postponing their lunch or hurrying
through it in order to get there. Setting up the bar on
the second floor came as an inspiration. Liberati took
the thanks but the suggestion had come from young
Father Lewis. Liberati only wondered if it should be
a cash bar.

"It has to be," Lewis assured him. His face was pale,
his eyes a faded blue. If his hair had not been khaki he
could have been an albino.

"We can afford it, Lewis."

"That isn't the point. Free drinks are like a bribe."

Liberati wasn't sure about that but he did not have
time to argue the point. He would leave the placating
of the press in Lewis's hands. He had to take a call from
California.

"Dreadful news," Cardinal Carey said, not bothering
to identify himself.

"Yes, Your Eminence. Have you spoken with the
press?"

"This is my day of retreat."

"I thought you might postpone it."

The silence seemed to chide Liberati. He ignored it.
Was Carey trying to pass himself off as a charismatic or
something? But Liberati remembered Carey's odd remark on being named cardinal. "I want to spend the
rest of my life growing closer to Jesus," he had said
unctuously. One wondered what he had been doing up
to that time.

"Later today I will issue a statement," Carey said.
"Now, about the news conference."

Liberati glanced at his watch. "It begins in seven minutes."

"I have a suggestion."

What Liberati must do, subtly, not insistently, was to let it be known that the nation's hierarchy would be playing a decisive role in the selection of Fergus's successor. The importance of the New York archdiocese, the new autonomy granted national conferences of bishops by Vatican II, and the American episcopacy's more intimate knowledge of possible candidates commended this relative innovation.

"Rossi isn't going to like that." Guiseppe Rossi was the apostolic delegate to the United States, the pope's representative to the American Church.

"I said do it subtly. If the delegate's name comes up you should add that the bishops will of course be working with him. We propose, the pope disposes."

"Who said that?"

"If you don't know, don't use it."

"Who do you think it will be, Your Eminence?"

Fergus's successor. Another silence. "It is far too soon to enter into such speculation, Monsignor."

Liberati stuck out his tongue at the receiver. One of the difficulties of his job was that he was still in theory a menial. He could be removed at will. That was the theory. In practice, it was he who led the bishops while speaking in their name. But without the support of such prelates as Carey that would be impossible, as Carey very well knew. That was why the San Francisco cardinal discouraged anything remotely resembling chumminess from Liberati. It was also why his suggestion was an order. Liberati assured Carey that he would insert the remark about choosing Fergus's successor into some response.

"That's right. Don't volunteer it."

"Good advice."

Carey ignored the praise. "Keep me posted."

Liberati sat looking at the phone. The conversation with Carey had put him into a bad mood and that was no way to face the press. Today there would be more than the usual crowd. The usual crowd was the Catholic press, a few stringers, and half a dozen others with dubious credentials. The first echelon would show up today. He had already seen Matthew Hanratty come in.

"Do you suppose he was in Washington?" he asked Lewis.

"He just got in on the shuttle."

That meant the *Times* religion editor realized that the place to follow the story on New York was in Washington and not Manhattan.

"If Carey hadn't called I'd have talked with Hanratty first, before the conference."

Lewis's expression was more than usually blank. "I talked with him."

"What about?"

"Procedure."

Lewis could be as infuriating as Carey and it did not help that Lewis was his subordinate. The young priest was from the New Orleans diocese; he had a Roman degree in theology, from the Angelicum, not the Greg. Did he share the ultramontanism of the archbishop of New Orleans? Liberati could not figure him out. In his bleaker moods, it seemed to Liberati that he could not figure out half the people on whose cooperation his career depended.

Lewis added, "I couldn't just send him to the bar."

"I wish you'd sent him to me."

He pushed back from his desk and headed for the auditorium. He felt bracketed by insolence, Carey's and Lewis's. He was in no mood to hold a press conference.

But when he reached the podium and faced the audience, his demeanor masked his misgivings. He did not smile, of course, but neither did he look abject. Those already seated settled back but he waited for those still coming downstairs from the bar. He had not written an opening statement but it would be recorded. And Lewis would take it down as well. Hanratty sat in the middle of the fifth row, his eyes unblinkingly on Liberati. Browner from the *Post* was there as well as the man from the Moonies. Admirari from the *National Catholic Reporter* lounged in back while Lulu van Ackeren, the impossibly beautiful redhead from the *Register*, was the center of a group to Liberati's right. Lewis slipped into a seat at the end of the front row and Liberati began.

"The Catholic Church in the United States has suffered a severe blow in the death of Cardinal Fergus of New York. Cardinal Fergus was conferring with brother bishops from other countries when he, with several others, was cut down by an assassin. The bishops of the United States have lost an esteemed colleague, a wise counselor, a spiritual giant. Kevin Fergus was born in . . ."

For the bio, he referred to the entry from *Who's Who* that Lewis had Xeroxed for him. Nothing he said alluded to the fact that Fergus had increasingly isolated himself from the other bishops, inveighing against the direction their political activism was taking them, insisting that they at least meet with the clergy and hierarchy from Latin American countries before issuing statements about them. Fergus had headed a faction and when his cohorts diminished, retiring, dying, unwilling to take the heat, he had become a gadfly. Finally he had been made to seem a crank.

Liberati finished and said he would take questions.

He hoped Hanratty would raise his hand but it was Geach from the *Wanderer* who spoke up.

"Now that Cardinal Fergus has been murdered, who will speak out against communism in the American Church?"

"I was unaware that there was any communism in the American Church."

Geach made an impatient noise. "You know what I mean."

"The American hierarchy prefer to speak out in favor of things, not against them. Catholicism is not reactionary."

"Then why don't you speak out in favor of America the way Cardinal Fergus did?"

He was rescued by Admirari who wanted to know if Monsignor Liberati could give more details on the death of Cardinal Fergus.

He repeated what they already knew if they had read the wire dispatches. There had been a satellite transmission on Ted Turner's station but the major networks had added nothing to the first report. Hanratty waggled his fingers and got to his feet when Liberati acknowledged him.

"This may be premature, Monsignor, but would you review the procedure that will be followed in naming Cardinal Fergus's successor? I imagine the importance of the New York archdiocese makes an early appointment desirable."

Liberati agreed that it was indeed premature, shocked as they all were by the unexpected and brutal death of a much admired prelate. "Needless to say, the American hierarchy will give careful prayerful thought to the matter in good time."

"And make recommendations to the apostolic delegate?"

"Bishops propose, the pope disposes."

"But as a matter of practical procedure, anyone can make suggestions to the apostolic delegate, can't they? Bishops play no special role."

Liberati smiled. "The question suggests procedures of another era. Since Vatican II, national conferences of bishops have acquired increased responsibilities. The see of New York is, as you suggest, an important appointment. The Holy Father will want the advice and counsel of the American bishops in making it."

"Let me get this straight," Hanratty persisted. "Are you saying that the American bishops will convene to pick a successor to Cardinal Fergus?"

"They will consult with one another, of course." Liberati was beginning to wonder about the wisdom of introducing this matter now. Geach was waving his hand wildly and a dozen others were seeking recognition.

"Will there be an election?"

"Why don't we leave that subject, Mr. Hanratty . . ."

This turned out to be impossible. The next five questions concentrated on the means and method of choosing Fergus's successor. The Moonie seemed to think that what was being proposed was an infringement of the prerogatives of New York Catholics.

"Why can't they choose their own bishop?"

"That's not quite the way it works, Mr. Scheez."

Patiently outlining the procedure, Liberati had the distinct impression he was being sucked into a description that would sound Byzantine and monarchical to American ears. Scheez had a point, though it was doubtful he realized it. There had been growing demand for the popular election of bishops, something for which there was sound historical precedent. Hanratty's question had drawn attention to the procedure in a democracy like the United States. Catholic monarchies with a concordat had had the right to name candidates to open sees. Popular election had gone out with the patristic age. So the apostolic delegate, the pope's man, forwarded names to the Vatican. The whole process was wrapped in secrecy. It would have been impossible to say whether a selection represented a consensus or went contrary to it. Traditionally it had been assumed that naming bishops was a papal prerogative to be exercised in a more or less untrammeled way. Of course the thrust of Carey's suggestion was that they did not want another Fergus named to New York. The slain cardinal had been defanged over the years, but his seemingly beleagued status had enhanced his news value.

The conference went on for forty-five minutes and it was unexpectedly an ordeal. Liberati felt he had made a real mess of it despite the apparently sincere congratulations of Father Lewis. Hanratty came up to Liberati. "Monsignor, can you set up an appointment for me with the delegate?"

Lewis said, "I'll arrange it."

Liberati went upstairs in hope of a drink but the bar had been dismantled. He wanted a drink. For that matter, he wanted lunch. Neal Admirari had followed him, clearly sharing his designs on the bar.

"Going somewhere for lunch, Monsignor?"

"Is that an invitation?"

"Dutch treat."

"Good enough."

THE FREE WORLD POLICY CENTER was located on Connecticut Avenue not far from Dupont Circle in a building that overlooked a small park on whose benches secretaries and apprentices in the various lores practiced in the nation's capital ate their hurried lunches. Fellows and research assistants of the Center ate in one of its three restaurants, Alpha, Beta, or Gamma, depending on their grade. Like a number of other think tanks, FWPC was a conservative response to the nefarious influence on government planning and policy exerted by the Institute of Policy Studies.

Harold Packard, founder of FWPC, had had appointments on the law faculties of Columbia and Harvard before entering government service during the Nixon years. He had not been alone at the time in thinking that, with Nixon, conservatives had a second chance to accomplish what they had failed to accomplish under Ike. After all, Nixon was a Republican, a conservative, an anticommunist. The inauguration of 1969 was a time of euphoria only slightly dimmed by the fact that Kissinger would play a role in the administration. Would life be possible if we could read the future? If Harold Packard and his ideological kin had foreseen that Kissinger would end as secretary of state and that both Agnew and Nixon would be chased from office leaving Gerald Ford and Nelson Rockefeller in power, they would have demanded a recount and prayed that Hubert Humphrey emerged victorious. Far better to be out of power, still occupying the not uncomfortable role of critic and Cassandra.

Those dreadful consequences had occurred and Packard felt tarred by the brush despite the fact that even his most virulent enemies conceded he was a man of consummate integrity. Packard, they knew, would gladly have turned the key on Nixon himself. After some months of brooding, he concluded that the country was still unready to grasp the folly of its pre-Nixon ways. Education was necessary, above all the education of opinion makers and congressmen. He spoke with friends, he solicited the rich, he founded FWPC.

Laura Ramey came to work for Packard six months after the center opened. At the time of the founding of FWPC, she was still Sister Agnes Miriam. Her resumé had interested Packard—she had a Ph.D. in economics —but it was only during the interview that she told him she had been a nun. He could not hide his disapproval, though it was not the disapproval of a Catholic who misunderstood her reasons for leaving. Packard was influenced by the image he had formed of women religious from the press and television. For some years nuns had been going over the wall in spectacular ways, repudiating their pasts, blaming the Church for their defection. Increasingly, media nuns spoke the language of radical feminism.

"I left because the convent was no longer what it was when I entered. I accepted the changes inspired by Vatican II, but we went far beyond those. Everything has become politics . . ."

"Perhaps at bottom everything is politics."

"Religion isn't."

"The Holy Roman Empire?"

And they had been off on their first exhilarating discussion. They disagreed, their angles of vision differed, but a mutual respect sprang up quickly between them. Laura said that if she was going to be politically active, she would do so as a lay woman.

He glanced at her application. Was he calculating her age? "I am thirty-seven years old."

He nodded. "And I am fifty-seven." He looked at her and smiled. "One gratuitous remark for another."

She got the job. The first question was: what was the job? Packard already had a secretary. At first, Laura was called a coordinator and assigned the task of bringing out a monthly newsletter. At the time there was no monthly newsletter, so she had to initiate it. She also supervised the publications of the Center, a job that swiftly grew in scope and importance. Some of the publications were ephemeral, reprints of articles published elsewhere, sheets of data and statistics for circulation to congressmen, background for an impending vote. But there were also position papers by one or several hands, which ranged from sizable pamphlets to small books. Packard gave her the title of administrative assistant to the director. Now, six years later, she was associate director.

Her hair was still honey blond, her face was intelligently attractive, and though she was a trifle heavy in the thighs her figure was good. She was not obsessed with the way she dressed but she gave it thought. Listeners always respond far more to the speaker than to arguments and rhetoric, and this is particularly so when the speaker is a woman. It is the person one hears and the female speaker is never free of her gender. These were simple facts. Laura felt no rancor in recognizing them.

Harold Packard, it emerged, was a womanizer. There was a great turnover, apparently in several senses of the term, among his secretaries and immediate female aides. He had been married three times, was a poet of monogamy, decried the tide of carnality sweeping the country, and bedded every woman he could. He made a feint in the direction of a proposition one rainy afternoon but Laura's manner stopped him. Her all but uncomprehending terror came through to him as virginal disdain. For a week, in a small and remote corner of her heart, she almost wished something had happened.

It was, after all, one of the things that had crossed her mind when she pondered leaving the convent. She was released from her vows and that meant she was eligible. But most of the men she dealt with belonged to a woman already. She was admired for her mind, something every woman wants, up to a point. The lunches and dinners she had with men were appointments rather than dates. In one of its major promises, the world had proved a disappointment to Laura.

Perhaps in consequence she approached her job at the Center as a vocation, not merely a career, transferring the motivation she had taken with her from the religious life to the FWPC. It almost seemed that implicit in her decision to leave the Servants of Mary was the intent to defend what her sisters in religion seemed determined to bring down. Laura had been unable to adopt the anti-Americanism that had crept into the religious life, some said as a result of the Vietnam War. As Sister Agnes Miriam she simply had not believed that the United States of America was what was wrong with the world. As an economist, she was astounded by the receptivity to socialism among Catholic activists.

"As a system, it doesn't work," she pointed out. "It never has."

"Then it must be made to work."

"We already have a working system."

Her interlocutors were shocked. Did she seriously mean to defend capitalist greed?

Patience and argument had little effect on such people. She told herself that if the United States were a socialist country, they would be against socialism.

They were inspired by an odd death wish that, when wrapped in the remnants of religious belief—obscure references to the coming kingdom, for example—disarmed critics. Sister Agnes Miriam had watched her own order turn from its historic mission of educating young women to become a band of bachelor gals dedicated to enacting the liberal agenda. Leaving was like not leaving because what she left was so different from what she had entered.

In the years since she had left the religious life things had grown worse in the Church. Radical nuns were now allied with lesbians and their demands for ordination had become wholesale condemnations of the Church as a male-dominated institution. The vows she had taken were three in number, poverty, chastity, and obedience. Obedience! Affluence, sexual experience, and defiance now characterized her former sisters in religion. And priests were no better. Finally even the bulwark of the bishops began to go. The pastoral letter on war and peace, accepted in Chicago by a vote of 238 to 9 in May 1983, had been the beginning.

"The culmination," Cardinal Fergus corrected.

"How do you mean?" Packard asked.

Laura had brought the two men, her uncle and her employer, together in the cardinal's New York office.

The cardinal, her mother's half brother, gave a rapid sketch of what he clearly regarded as the downward slide of the National Conference of Catholic Bishops over the past twenty years. He hesitated when Packard asked if such a dramatic change of direction could be due to chance.

"A conspiracy?"

"I know the word has become equated with paranoid fears, but I use it in a precise sense when I apply it to what has happened in the World Council of Churches.

People of a quite particular stripe set out to make use of the churches to further their political goals. It was subversion even though it was overt, all but announced. The churches set up bureaus over which they lost control. Their agenda were applauded by the media and any criticism was subjected to the usual liberal vilification. Cowardly silence ensued. At first the Protestant churches were simply the instruments of run-of-the-mill liberal causes. Then they became radical. The Greek Orthodox withdrew over the issue of homosexuality."

Cardinal Fergus nodded. "And we have followed the same path. Our Washington bureaus can no longer be controlled. Religious orders have fallen apart. Seminary education has become a farce. We are being punished."

Packard lit a cigarette. The cardinal leaned forward and shook another free from the package on the table. "Camels," he mused. "I used to smoke this brand." He put the cigarette in his mouth and accepted a light from Packard. He did not inhale. Packard of course did, deeply. His words emerged as visible puffs.

"So that's your theory. Your church is being divinely punished. For what?"

The cardinal looked at Laura. "You must tell Mr. Packard about Fatima."

"Oh, I know about Fatima, Cardinal." When he had asked about the proper way to address a prince of the Church and Laura had told him, his jaw set. He was damned if he was going to call a fellow American Your Eminence. So he called him Cardinal.

"Then you know part of my answer."

"Only part?"

Cardinal Fergus did not respond directly to the question. It hadn't mattered. As Laura had expected, the two men got along. They were particularly of one mind on Latin America.

Cardinal Fergus put out the cigarette after barely tasting it. "You mentioned what has happened to the word conspiracy. It is already sufficient to label something a conspiracy theory. Even when conspiracies are proved. Hiss. The Rosenbergs."

"Especially when they are proved. The liberal is willfully obtuse."

"Domino theory is another. The more often it is proved the more it is maligned. El Salvador follows Nicaragua and Honduras. Yet this is taken to disprove the domino theory."

From that meeting on, Cardinal Fergus received all the papers and books published by FWPC.

And now he was dead.

The numbing news seemed something Laura had expected, though she could not recall ever consciously forming the thought that her uncle might be assassinated. Packard came to give her the news and then stood in silence for several minutes before leaving her office. He had no words for such an occasion. Forever lamenting the waning influence of religion in American life, he himself believed nothing. Not that faith made such a horrible moment easier. Laura herself had nothing to say. She prayed for his soul, not thinking her uncle really needed her intercession. She could not rid herself of the thought that the Church in the United States was approaching a supreme crisis. And not only in the United States.

The forces her uncle had opposed were in the ascendancy, and there no longer seemed to be anyone to oppose them.

T H E R E W E R E more than fifty bishops in the sanctuary of Saint Patrick's cathedral for the funeral Mass of
Cardinal Fergus. The celebrant was Cardinal Carey of
San Francisco, the eulogy was preached by Bishop
Rogers, an auxiliary of New York. Laura was lucky
to get into the cathedral and she would have been
content to remain standing in the back, near the bust
of John Paul II, but Myrtle spotted her and she was
led up the long aisle to the front pew on the right. The
two of them were family for the occasion.

Laura had not been drawn to the funeral by the tug
of blood or grief alone. She had come to know her uncle
much better after introducing him to Harry Packard,
but even then her training did not permit her to cross
an invisible line of reserve.

"I want to talk to you after the funeral," Myrtle had
said on the phone.

Laura seemed to have no choice, but she agreed
readily. It was like being asked to console the family.

"There's something I have to pass on to you."

"I see."

"From the cardinal."

"Pass on to me?"

"I think Mr. Packard should see it."

Laura's curiosity was piqued but when she told
Packard he shrugged. He was probably right. It could
be anything. Nonetheless, whatever it was, it had the
mysterious allure of a communication from beyond the
grave.

On the flight to New York, Laura had the strangest
experience. Seated by the window, her companions
buttoned-down types who immediately opened their

briefcases and went to work, Laura opened a biography of Saint Catherine of Siena, but the last minute appearance of Matthew Hanratty in the company of a young cleric put an end to her reading.

She recognized the *Times* reporter right away; he had attended a FWPC conference the year before and had written several slightly debunking articles about it. Though their eyes met as he went past, no sign of recognition appeared on his face. The two men took seats in the row directly behind Laura's and in what was obviously the continuation of a previous conversation talked in tones it would have been difficult not to overhear. After she had listened a bit Laura would have found it impossible to ignore what they were saying.

"The delegate refused to see me. Obviously it was no accident you couldn't make an appointment for me over the phone."

"He's not known for talking with the press."

"It's not the press. My God, I'm the *Times*. It's got to be me personally. Apparently I'm being punished for things I've written."

"Have you ever written about Rossi?"

"I've mentioned him from time to time, not much more than that. I think it was my story the day Fergus died that did it."

"I don't recall it."

"I wrote of the necessity for Fergus's successor to be chosen by Americans rather than Italians. That was before Liberati's press conference. His words were music to my ears, not least because of the consternation they sowed among our reactionary brethren. Rossi must have taken umbrage at my remark that the Vatican can no longer regard the Church the United States as a colony with the delegate as satrap."

"I'd forgotten you'd said that." The young priest

sounded as if he might just have heard Hanratty's words for the first time.

"Will the bishops stick to their guns on this?"

"All there has been thus far is Monsignor Liberati's statement and that was in answer to a question."

"And your own glorious archbishop's statement. Deegen pleads with the Vatican to appoint Fergus's successor without delay so that the crusade that brought the palm of martyrdom to Kevin Fergus can continue. Does Deegen have his eye on New York?"

"Archbishop Deegen is totally devoid of ambition."

"Ha! If that were true, he would be a parish priest today."

"A seminary professor. . . . No, it's true. He will do whatever he is asked to do, but he would never seek advancement."

"How loyal you are, Father Lewis."

"I hope so. But that's the simple truth."

"I won't argue the point. But if he did want a transfer to the Big Apple he couldn't go about it more shrewdly. If the appointment is left in Vatican hands, that is."

"Even if the bishops decide to take a more active role in the process, they cannot appoint the next archbishop of New York."

"But they can tie the pope's hands. Look, it's a simple scenario. They hold a meeting. Say in New York, at the Waldorf, and the press covers it like a blanket. There is open discussion, nominations, a vote. The whole world knows what happened. Now, do you think the Vatican would dare overturn a vote like that?"

"You may be right."

"You know I'm right. So the question remains, do the bishops have the guts?"

The man beside Laura continued his paper work, wholly absorbed. The very audible voices behind simply did not interest him. Well, why should a businessman or lawyer or whatever he was care about such churchy gossip? She herself was fascinated to witness how events could be arranged. Here was the religion editor of *The New York Times* sketching the process whereby the next archbishop of New York could be named. The reference to Liberati and the identification of the young priest as Father Lewis enabled Laura to place him. The USCC.

Now, seated in Saint Patrick's, she shifted her weight and looked at the solemn prelates in the sanctuary. She wanted to think them incapable of the kind of media event Hanratty had described to Father Lewis. There was no doubt that if the bishops did take matters into their own hands they would not choose anyone at all like Cardinal Kevin Fergus. It would be someone progressive and one more major see would pass into the control of those who had turned the bishops' conference into a political body. With Cardinal Fergus gone, one had to look to Archbishop Deegen of New Orleans to find a man with a mind of his own and some sense of what activities are appropriate to bishops. Like young Father Lewis, however, Laura found it a remote prospect that Archbishop Deegen would be transferred to New York.

Honestly, it would be so easy to despair of the Church. Laura had been a young nun when Vatican II drew to a close and she had felt the excitement of its challenge. Aggiornamento, as they had learned to say, updating, letting in fresh air, thinking anew the old task. The renewal of religious orders had begun at once, and young as she was Laura had been elected a delegate to the provincial chapter that would deal with the matter. Inevitably, perhaps, the first item on the agenda was the traditional habit. That it would be discarded went without saying; the question was an acceptable substitute. There had been an interval of nearly two years when they wore a hybrid outfit, neither habit nor secular dress. It was a hideously designed jumper sort of business that had stopped between the ankles and knees. They had still worn a veil with it. Laura had not been among those who resisted the suggestion that they go the whole way and simply dress tastefully in the style of the day, but later events were to prove the importance of distinctive dress to the religious vocation.

After the habit had gone most of the traditions of the Servants of Mary. It was heady to realize that virtually anything could be questioned. Discipline went. Community went. Small groups moved out of the convent and into apartments. Experimenting was the rage. And the flood of departures began. The nuns who stayed were either saintly elders or tough cookies with chips on their shoulders. For all the talk of dialogue, there was little tolerance for criticism of the way things were going. When Laura left, she felt she was being forced out.

Sorrow at these changes, so very few of them for the better, combined with the funeral liturgy to make Laura's eyes brim with tears. If she cried, she cried for herself as well as for her uncle. She was one of the casualties of the changes he had fought against.

Cardinal Fergus was laid to rest in the crypt of the cathedral in the company of his predecessors. When Cardinal Carey came to shake her hand, Laura tried not to think of him as the enemy. He seemed just another Irishman rendered momentarily somber in the presence of death.

"And what do you do, Laura?" When she told him she worked at the FWPC, there was only the slightest flicker of his eyelids. "Is Harry here?"

"He is terrified of funerals."

"Poor fellow. But who can blame him?"

Outside, she went with Myrtle in the direction of Madison Avenue. Myrtle was saying how glad she was that the burial was in Saint Patrick's and not in a cemetery.

"What's the difference?"

"Have you ever seen a New York cemetery?" Myrtle shuddered. "They're enough to make you favor cremation. Bodies jammed in, headstones looking tipsy. They remind me of stalled traffic. A cemetery should look like Arlington."

"What is it you have for me?"

"A typescript."

"Of what?"

"You'll see. No one can say we weren't warned."

Myrtle's mouth was a thin line and she nodded once emphatically. The older woman had obviously been greatly affected by the cardinal's death and the way he had died only made it worse. Laura found her talk of warnings unnerving. A less sympathetic listener might suspect that Myrtle was unhinged.

The suspicions would have grown in the office. Myrtle locked the door after them, put a finger to her lips and stood in silence for a full minute, listening. Such silence invites a thousand sounds but none of them was the one Myrtle listened for. Finally she moved to her desk and unlocked the top drawer.

"This is the only copy. The tape is in my safety deposit box. You'll understand why I didn't want to have this with me in church."

Myrtle extended a sheaf of typewritten pages, but before letting them go she looked into Laura's eyes.

"This is a revelation of how the communists have infiltrated the Catholic Church in this country."

Part 2

_____

_____

RIDING DOWN FROM RYE at nine thirty in the morning, when he would have thought the drudges long since ensconced in their city offices, Philip Knight was forcefully reminded of why he had said good-bye to all that four years before.

Not that he had ever been a commuter. God forbid. Early and late he had felt only condescension for those who rode an hour or more at either end of their day, neither country mice nor city mice, hurry, hurry, hurry. He had had a client in publishing who raised bees on his farm far up the Hudson. The poor devil did not seem to know when he was in exile, on Madison Avenue or when busy with the bees. Knight had been a city man through and through.

He had been a poet of Manhattan, as only a midwestern transplant can be. Even after the first time he was mugged he dismissed it as a fluke. His apartment was ransacked and he moved, but it was as if nothing had happened. He was mugged again, at high noon, on a path in Central Park with dozens of potential witnesses within earshot. Even as his watch was ripped from his wrist, two kids went by on a bike. Knight was terrified. He was a head taller than his assailant, he was in excellent shape—in the evening he ran in that very park for half an hour—but the mad gleam in the mugger's eyes made him turn over everything in his pockets. Left alone he collapsed on a bench and cried.

He felt that he was weeping for a dying civilization. He looked around at the quiet paths, the trees, and in imagination stripped the island of all its urban increments. He was back in the forest primeval. Nature red of tooth and claw. Life is nasty, brutish, and short. He lived in a jungle and at last he was willing to admit it.

He became a bore on the subject. He collected atrocities: elderly citizens held hostage by gangs, greatgrandmothers raped repeatedly by young savages, on and on. But it was simply the daily fare of the newspapers. No one needed Philip Knight to tell them what the city was like.

"Why the hell don't you leave it if you hate it so much?"

"Why doesn't everyone?"

"Because they have to earn a living."

That of course was the point. Knight was a private investigator. He had a good reputation, a steady if unphenomenal income. How would he support himself if he left New York? Any city large enough to have a sufficient pool of possible clients had all the defects of New York. Sometimes more. What to do? The problem was further complicated because of Roger.

Roger was his younger brother, thirty-two, doctorate from Princeton. He was a doctor of philosophy in philosophy, and of course unemployed. Unemployable, more accurately. Roger had received his Ph.D. at the age of twenty-one. He had been a prodigy and perhaps all prodigies are a bit mad but Roger was unusually eccentric. Knight attributed this in part to the fact that their parents had died in a plane crash when Roger was ten years old. Up to that time, he had been regarded as more or less retarded. In school he was dumb. In the wake of the tragedy, receiving special attention from concerned teachers, Roger revealed himself to be in truth a genius. Previously he had been bored. He finished high school at thirteen, was graduated from Yale at seventeen, and joined the navy. Ours. His naval career had been three years of contretemps. Scores of chiefs and officers had tried to find a niche in the navy for Roger. He was sent to electronics school, to ordnance school, to navigator school, it was suggested that he apply for Annapolis. All to no avail. Roger spent what was laughingly called his active service lolling in the base library reading his way through its contents and gorging himself on junk food. He passed on to the public library in downtown San Diego. When he was honorably discharged at the age of twenty, he weighed 183 pounds and was accepted in the graduate school at Princeton. After one semester he took the candidacy exams and was awarded a doctorate the following May on the basis of a seventy-five-page memoir on Gödel's theorem. Such swiftness was unfortunate. Roger longed to dwell forever in academe. Why did Princeton not hire him? Why did not some other school? No one who knew Roger posed such questions. To eccentricity had been added avoirdupois. Those who had thought Roger retarded as a lad seemed vindicated, and those who now mistook him for the village idiot were not without reason. He was enormous. Brilliance, genius, a sparkling intellect, are not everything. If he had had to fend for himself, Roger would have starved. He became his older brother's ward.

It wasn't as if the boy were company. His schedule was as eccentric as everything else about him. He would stay awake for thirty-six hours, for forty-eight hours, then fall into a comalike sleep from which only the pangs of hunger would make him stir. And, dear God, his appetite. Roger now weighed 275 pounds and he was five seven. Knight considered caring for Roger a debt to their dead parents. He had never married, a eunuch for Roger's sake. That potential wives might react with revulsion to Roger seemed a certainty. But, trial that he was, Roger from time to time had been of help to him on a case. To put it mildly.

Roger had never been mugged. Like drunks and other idiots, he led a charmed life. When Knight explained that they were moving to Rye to get away from the concrete jungle, Roger had no reaction.

In Rye Knight found a fine brick house on three quarters of an acre, surrounded by cyclone fence save for a stone wall where it faced the road. They had two English setters which went off like alarm clocks when anything larger than a squirrel appeared on the horizon. Knight felt safe. Roger adjusted to the new surroundings; sometimes Philip wondered if his brother even realized they had moved. But Philip went off on cases in the confidence that his redoubt in Rye awaited him when he was through.

He had never been particularly adventurous, but now he was even more careful of the jobs he took. He ran an ad in the yellow pages of the seven largest cities in the country. An 800 number, call toll free, operators await your call. (Actually a recorder.) This wider net introduced variety into his cases, taking him into strange territories. But for the care he exercised in accepting assignments, it was like going off to war. After victory, there was Rye, in every sense of the term. Knight rewarded himself with a serious drunk after the successful conclusion of a case, when the check cleared. His practice had diminished since the move to Rye. But if his income was less, it had more purchasing power away from the bunker of Manhattan. Still, he worried. And alone. Roger had a Franciscan indifference to such worldly matters, as long as his supply of food was not affected.

Philip Knight had been inactive for two weeks when the phone call from Washington came. The Free World Policy Committee. Ms. Laura Ramey. She corrected him when he repeated her name. Miss. She asked if he were free to take on what might become an extended assignment. He said he was free to look into it. Could he come to Washington to discuss the matter? He could.

Thus it was that he was on this morning train to Manhattan. He would take a cab from Grand Central to Penn Station and ride Amtrak to Washington. He avoided flying whenever he could. Having been mugged and robbed and mugged again he did not want to press his luck and end up on a hijacked flight to Cuba. Not to mention a crash. Look what had happened to his parents. Besides, on the train he had time to review the material Roger had put together on FWPC.

Why a conservative think tank would need a private investigator, let alone Philip Knight, was one of the fascinations of the trip. Once on Amtrak, he was able to order coffee and that enhanced the taste of his cigarette. He pondered the material. From time to time, thanks to a tunnel, his window became a mirror and he caught glimpses of himself, slumped in his seat, smoking, thinking. Hardly the picture of a private detective. He had gotten the height in the family, six two, thick straight hair, graying on the sides, large lensed glasses surrounded by clear plastic. Tweed jacket, button-down shirt, tan slacks, black Rockport shoes in which he could walk for miles without pain. Besides cigarettes, his inside jacket pocket contained a dime store spiral notebook and a nineteen-cent ballpoint pen. Keep the overhead down. In New York he had had an expensive suite of offices, a secretary, a bookkeeper, messenger services, expenses, expenses, expenses. Cabs, bars, restaurants. The phrase "cash flow" had a tidal significance. All of it, well much of it, had been for show. Business is good, that was the message. And how many clients had he actually met in his office? It had been largely a waste. The move to Rye freed him from all that.

He fell asleep in the Amtrak car and lurched awake as they were pulling into Washington. He sat up and looked around. They must have stopped in Wilmington. Had he slept through it? How vulnerable, to be asleep like that. He would have checked his pockets if he had been carrying money. His bag was still overhead and his briefcase beneath the seat. Living in Rye had made him too relaxed. Nor did approaching a new job while asleep seem a good omen.

The cab dropped him off in front of a building on Connecticut Avenue. There was a security man in the lobby who phoned up to see if Philip Knight was indeed expected. Maybe it was the suitcase that made the man wary. When Knight entered the elevator he was confronted by his full reflection in a huge mirror that made up the back wall of the car. He looked weary, something of a vagrant, not the insouciant spirit he had imagined himself to be. Maybe—unsettling thought—Laura Ramey would find him insufficiently prepossessing to be hired by her think tank.

She came out of her office even as he identified himself to the receptionist.

"Oh good," she said. "You did bring a bag. I didn't know if I had made it clear that we will need more than today to acquaint you with the nature of the . . ." She paused. "Job?"

He smiled. Did she think he would refer to it as a caper?

"I called your office." She looked questioningly at him.

"It's my home."

"A man answered."

"And you hung up."

"No. He did. He would only say you were not there and when I tried to explain why I wanted to reach you he hung up."

"That's Roger."

She waited. Well, perhaps she deserved an explanation.

"He's my brother. And he's heavy. You have to forgive him. He's a prodigy. That is, he was. Now he is fat and lazy and highly educated."

"Your brother?"

Now she was simply being polite. She stooped to pick up his bag but he got to it first. He had not yet reached the stage where he wanted young women carrying things for him, or women his own age, for that matter. Miss Laura Ramey seemed to be the latter. He found her smile disarming. Her total attention was on him as he settled into a chair in her office. How would he like his coffee? She left him alone without apology when she went to get it. A good many pots hung from the ceiling and from them dangled a variety of plants he did not recognize. Roger would know them all by name, but Knight was content to think of them as growing things, obviously well cared for. They made the office seem less an office. The drapes at the window were unofficelike too. She came back with the coffee, sat behind her desk and watched anxiously while he tasted it.

"Is it strong enough?"

"Just right." He was not used to being fussed over.

"Good. I smell tobacco on you. You may smoke, if you wish."

"Do you?"

"No." She took an ashtray from her desk and passed it to him. "Now then. I assume you already knew about FWPC or have informed yourself about us since my call."

"The second."

"Your sources are probably hostile. We are conservative but not reactionary. We think of ourselves as champions of the values that made this country great and still hold it together." She spoke in matter-of-fact tones, home truths. "Where do you locate yourself on the political spectrum?"

"I don't."

"That's impossible."

"Politics bore me. Politicians disgust me. Pundits enrage me. I avoid keeping up with the news except in the line of duty."

"My." She turned her head slightly to one side and looked at him with a little smile. "Above the fray, is that it? What if everyone felt like that?"

"They don't."

"And it's a good thing. Not that I dispute your estimate of politicians. They are indeed a mischievous bunch. Contempt of Congress, according to Mr. Packard, is a test of rationality. That is why politicians cannot be ignored."

"Miss Ramey, if you are looking for someone who agrees with your political views, I'm not your man."

"Do you disagree with them, presuming you have the clairvoyance to know what they are?"

"Put it this way, I wouldn't take a job at the Institute of Policy Studies. I don't know what you have in mind, but the fact that my head isn't cluttered up with a lot of political opinions might prove an asset."

"What we have in mind is quite outside our own line. Do you have any religious views?"

"No."

"None whatsoever?"

"Not that I know of."

"Don't you believe in God?"

He hesitated, not liking being quizzed. "Yes, but I wouldn't want to get into a discussion of what that means."

"You don't belong to any church?"

He might have told her that Roger took care of that sort of thing, but he did not. He was more surprised than annoyed by the questions she was asking. She noticed his surprise.

"I said this was outside our usual line. We have made inquiries about you, of course. Your answers do not surprise me. You get high recommendations. Do you have any views about communism?"

This at least was predictable. "The same as yours."

"Meaning that you will adopt our views?"

"That's right."

She watched him light a cigarette with such interest that he offered her one. She refused. "Mr. Knight, on the basis of our conversation thus far, what is your guess as to the nature of the task we want you to take on?"

"I haven't the faintest idea."

"Religion and communism," she said helpfully.

"Could equal many things."

"If you followed the news you would know there has been increasing criticism from Christians because of the political involvement of their churches."

"The Richard Neuhaus and Peter Berger group?"

"So you know of them?"

He recited. "Church staffs are in the hands of liberals or worse and they are aiding and abetting revolutionary movements whose compatibility with Christianity is questionable. The World Council of Churches is accused of arming terrorists. Methodists and Episcopalians . . ."

He paused but she waited for him to go on so he did.

"The FWPC has had several seminars on this general topic and published a collection of papers. Why do you say this is outside your usual line?"

"Hiring a private investigator is already outside our usual line."

"What is the job?"

She glanced at her watch. "Look, it's nearly three o'clock. I've booked a room for you at the Wilson, a quiet little residential hotel in the neighborhood. Why don't we take you over there and get you settled? I'll leave some material with you and you will have time to read it before you and I and Mr. Packard meet for dinner. Is that all right?"

"You're the boss."

"If you're hired Mr. Packard will be your boss."

"When will I know?"

"At dinner."

.   .   .

The Wilson was a diminuitive building, six stories high. In a little room off the lobby elderly citizens formed a half circle before a television set. Their heads swung in unison toward the desk when Laura Ramey and Knight arrived. The man behind the desk wore what looked to be a bellboy's uniform but he was as old as those in the television room.

"A reservation for Mr. Knight," Laura said.

The ancient boy thought about it for a moment, then bent over and brought out a small, green metal box from beneath the counter. He opened it and ruffled through the cards.

"With a *k*," Knight said.

"Here it is." He plucked out the card as if success had been rare in his life. "Philip Knight." When he smiled his teeth had the look of meerschaum.

"Bill that to the Free World Policy Committee," Laura said.

A registration form was produced and Knight proceeded to fill it in.

"I'll leave you," Laura glanced dubiously at the clerk. "I'll be back to pick you up at six thirty." She asked the clerk, "Is there a bar in the hotel?"

His mouth flew open and he shook his head slowly back and forth before his eyes drifted toward the television room. He leaned forward. "Wine is served with meals. The restaurant opens at five."

"We won't be eating here."

"Most of our guests are permanent." It might have been an explanation.

"I understand."

"Will you be staying just for the night, Mr. Knight?" Again the honey-colored teeth appeared.

"I'll let you know later."

Laura left him. Knight refused the clerk's help with

his bag but he had to be shown to his room. That was the Wilson policy and doubtless had been since its namesake was president. The elevator would have been claustrophobic for one. It rose with infinite patience to the third floor while the clerk whistled through his stained teeth. He preceded Knight down a low-ceilinged corridor to 313 and had trouble unlocking the door. Before pushing it open he looked slyly at Knight.

"I could bring you a bottle." He might have been offering the sinful delights of the orient.

"It doesn't matter," Knight lied.

He waited in the hall until the ancient bellboy came out of the room and shuffled off toward the elevator. The room was what he might have expected. The bed was high off the floor and covered with a tufted spread of pink and white. The woodwork was stained dark and the ceiling light consisted of four bulbs in milky white tulip-shaped shades. Only two of the bulbs lit up when he flicked the switch. The table lamp beside the bed had a shade that was still encased in cellophane. The brownish shades were drawn two-thirds shut and flanked by dark green drapes. An easy chair of leather had flat wooden arms. A Morris chair? Dear God. It was like being in a time warp.

Had Laura Ramey any idea what the Wilson Residential Hotel was like inside? The suggestion that he settle down here to read had conjured up the image of a considerably different room. Ah well. He sat at the desk and took from his briefcase the sheaf of typewritten pages Laura had given him.

Dictated August 15

There is no surprise with respect to the Russian Orthodox Church. It is obvious that the best way

6 4

for the Party to control the Church is to control the Church. And not simply from without. They put their people inside, seminarians, priests, bishops. In how many countries behind the iron curtain is it the same? Perhaps everywhere but Poland. There, scrutiny of seminarians is constant. They never relax their vigilance. There are Polish accommodationists, no doubt, but there is no danger the Church will be subverted from within. All this seemed to be a problem for the Church only under communist regimes. No one seriously thought it need worry us.

We were wrong. It is clear that there was a steady influx into the missionary orders, and for obvious reasons. When did missionary activity come to be likened to colonialism? Preaching the Gospel was said to be the dissemination of bourgeois western imperialist values. The new task of the missionary was to listen to the people, to adapt to their needs. How quickly this was transformed into revolutionary talk. The coming of the kingdom, overthrow of wealthy landowners, reform, power to the people. Liberation theology is the apotheosis of all this. American missionaries desert their priesthood, go native, marry, stay on in the country to which they were sent as clerics. Now they are revolutionaries. Terrorists. Their faith is in this world, their hope is for a future they themselves will not see. But why are moments in the future to be preferred to moments in the present? Why is the present generation to be sacrificed to a later one? They do not know. They are ideologues. Perhaps some of them become communists only in the field, but there is no doubt that others entered the seminary with subversive intent. Under orders they studied to receive Holy Orders. Without faith. Imagine the daily routine of the seminary, Mass, meditation, the study of theology, spiritual conferences. And the daily reception of Holy Communion! All that without believing a bit of it.

It is the same modus operandi as in the political order. Underground people, moles, latent in society, submerged in the sea of the people, awaiting the order to emerge. But then everything is politics to the Marxist. So what if he must wait in the disguise of a priest and she in that of a nun? This has been going on for years undetected. And now it may be too late.

I do not mean that this was confined to missionary orders. It is just that they threw off the mask first. The priesthood of the nation contains a fifth column. Subversives. And not only priests. A month ago I spoke with the Holy Father about these things. He answered my suspicions with facts. He has reason to think that at least one bishop in the United States is an agent of the KGB! He does not have his name. "Your Eminence," he said to me, "I want you to find out who he is. Prudently. I must know his identity."

His knowledge answered my own suspicion, yet disbelief was strong in me. Even as the pope spoke I found myself thinking how much in the grips of anticommunism he is, an old cold warrior. It is impossible for an American not to feel a kind of shame when he speaks of the communist menace. How did that come about? Any politician who champions American strength, who worries about our position in the world, immediately becomes a figure of fun in the press, a threat to the peace.

That is what has happened to me and not only

in the secular media. The Catholic press is worse. And some of my fellow bishops. Not only the Judas among them either. If I am right in thinking I know who he is, he has whispered words of sympathy in my ear. When the Holy Father spoke of this, he looked me deeply in the eyes. *"Vigilate et orate,"* he said in a hoarse whisper. What knowledge he must have, how visibly it weighs him down. We spoke of his visits to the United States. He retains a middle-European view of the West. It is dying from within because of self-indulgence, luxury, sensuality, corruption. Why should God stay the hand of destruction? Well, one cannot expect this pope to see the West as the good guys and the East as evil. That is a Manichean view in any case. But I am an American and I know the goodness and decency there still is here. A struggle goes on within the West and not merely between us and the East. It is true that there is a constant attack on every aspect of personal and public morality, a rampant sex madness, a loathing for the normal, for the family, parents, and children. And abortion. Dear God, that endless slaughter of the innocent, drowning the country in blood. Still, that is not the full story of the West.

Nonetheless, I am first a priest, and it is the danger within the Church that must be my primary concern. The pope gave me that assignment and I have brought it almost to completion. I think I know who the traitor is. I will not speak his name until I am certain. *Vigilate et orate.* That is what I will do. Watch and pray. And I must do it alone. To tell other bishops what I know would be to open myself to more mockery. Nothing is confidential anymore. The USCC is a sieve. Watch and pray.

Knight had taken a cigarette from his pack but held it in his hand unlighted while he read this extraordinary document. His initial reaction was that he had been admitted to some kind of paranoid wonderland. When he had finished reading, Knight lit his cigarette and settled back in the uncomfortable chair, exhaling contemplatively.

There were two possibilities: the cardinal had become unhinged and more or less imagined the things he was so concerned about, or else it was all true. Either way Fergus would have been in a spot going public. True or false, he would look like an ass. Russian boats in our coastal waters, Russian aircraft overhead, KGB agents crawling all over Capitol Hill and infesting the United Nations. Common knowledge, yet nobody gave a damn. To give a damn was to be relegated to the lunatic fringe.

Cardinal Fergus had given a damn. He had also given his life. That somber fact lent an authority to the pages Knight had just read. There had been a slaughter in Rome, taking the lives of Fergus and several other churchmen. In Italy, three different groups had by now claimed responsibility for the massacre on the Via Parioli. The president had offered the services of the FBI and the CIA and had been somewhat starchily refused by the prime minister. Interpretations in the press of what had happened were confusing. A conservative cardinal, a revolutionary bishop, and a Vatican diplomat did not point in a single direction, but any of the terrorist groups who took credit for the grisly murders were irrational enough in their ideologies to have regarded all the victims as enemies. Which of the claimants had actually done it? Fortunately for the harried newsmen, these dreadful events were soon overtaken by others no less dreadful, and the story faded from the screen. Presumably, the official investigation went on. Presumably, too, without results since no announcements had been made, no arrests or indictments announced.

Knight got up, put the typewritten pages back into his briefcase, took off his jacket, loosened his tie, and lay upon the bed. He tried to make his mind a blank. Anticipating the conversation he would have with Laura and her boss was not helpful. It could go in many directions. At the moment Knight was disinclined to take any job with the FWPC that had as its basis Cardinal Fergus's memorandum. One way or the other, it would involve the internal affairs of the Catholic Church and that was terra incognita to him despite the years he had spent in Italy. Maybe because of those years. There had, in fact, been two separate years, with an interval of four between them. Roger had received a fellowship at the American Academy and later another from the National Endowment for the Humanities. More than enough of a stipend to keep them both. He felt Roger owed it to him. He himself had loved Rome. Roger gave it a week or two of attention, then got lost in his books. He might have been in Topeka. Except that he seemed to pick things up by osmosis. That is what the statue by Michelangelo in the church of Saint Peter in Chains said. Osmosis. *Ise Moses*. Roger loved to fashion such outrageous puns. Did Laura and her boss imagine Knight an expert on the Roman Church because of those two years beside the Tiber?

There was another reason too, why not admit it to himself? He could not afford not to take a job, not just now. But he was painfully aware that in working for the FWPC he would be a vigilante in the pay of vigilantes. He would be linked with the right wing and he knew what kind of a press that would give him. And it

6 9

didn't matter a damned bit that Laura was such a nice person.

He closed his eyes and was soon asleep. Some time later he came awake, but kept his eyes shut. There had been a sound outside his door. He opened his eyes as he swung his legs off the bed and got silently to his feet. He pulled open the door to find himself facing the elderly bellboy. Startled, the man backed across the hall, displaying his distinctive teeth.

"What do you want?" Knight demanded.

The man put a trembling hand inside the jacket of his uniform and produced a small bottle of Scotch, the kind available on airplanes. He thrust it at Knight. "This is the best I could do."

Knight took the bottle, thanked the man, closed the door of his room. He wished he knew whether or not there had been a knock on his door. It was absurd to feel such apprehension. He studied the bottle of Scotch but decided against drinking it. He really did not care for Scotch.

Back on the bed, he consulted his Timex then closed his eyes. *To sleep, to dream and by a sleep to say we end the heartache . . .*

He drifted back into sleep with a smile on his lips. Roger would be proud of him.

2
———

KNIGHT HAD BEEN a disappointment but Laura saw no reason to say so to Packard. Let him make his own judgment. Perhaps she was wrong. She hoped so.

She devoutly hoped so. What she feared was that Knight would read the transcript of Cardinal Fergus's tape and conclude that the archbishop of New York had had some sort of nervous breakdown. Packard said, "He will almost certainly not take the thing seriously."

Laura looked at him. He continued to surprise her. Normally Harry Packard took acknowledgment of the communist conspiracy to be a test of sanity.

"You understand that I myself have not the slightest doubt of the truth of what Cardinal Fergus said. He is simply reporting what the pope told him. That is not the kind of thing the pope would say without meaning it. But that does not mean Philip Knight has to believe it. We can, however, make use of Mr. Knight without enlisting his credulity. Indeed, if he did accept Cardinal Fergus's last will and testament at face value I would say we had been badly advised."

"He says he will accept our view of such matters if you hire him."

"Fair enough."

Laura did not agree. What Cardinal Fergus had said was of such seriousness that she did not want anyone taking it only as an interesting hypothesis.

Laura went to the Wilson. The man at the desk assured her that Knight had had no visitors. "Phone calls?"

He shook his head and she told him to ring Knight's room.

When they arrived at the restaurant, Harry was already at table. He did not get up, only extended a hand when she introduced Knight. He might have been royalty. Or a bishop. Kiss my ring. But Harry Packard was devoid of religious belief and a foe of aristocracy to boot. "You live in Rye," Harry said to Knight when their drinks had come.

"And on it."

Packard smiled grudgingly. "Have you read the extraordinary document Laura gave you?"

"Yes."

"It is the transcript of a tape made by the late Cardinal Fergus. The only transcript. It was passed on to Laura by the cardinal's secretary."

"Why?"

Laura said, "She thought Mr. Packard should see it."

"Have you heard the tape?"

Harry had sent her to New York for it but Myrtle agreed only to let her hear it. They had gone to a sleazy electronics store on Forty-fifth Street where Laura put on a headset and listened. There was no doubt the voice was the cardinal's. The transcript was accurate. Laura had followed along on the page as she listened.

"I have not listened to the tape," Harry said.

"Do you doubt its authenticity?"

"No. But I want to know if the charges made are accurate."

"You doubt the pope?"

"I want the name of that bishop. I want you to identify him for me. Do you think you can?"

Knight finished his drink and half turned in his chair to catch the waiter's eye. He looked at Packard. "I'll try."

They actually shook hands on it. Laura felt gloom rather than relief. This was a game to Harry and he had enlisted Philip Knight. Did either of them understand or care what it would mean to the Church if the accusation was true? Oh, she did not doubt its truth. That would have meant doubting Cardinal Fergus and the pope. But in Harry Packard's hands the information would be a weapon in a secular battle.

"How will you go about it?" she asked Philip Knight.

He looked thoughtful for a moment and when his

eyes met hers they were cool and remote. "How would you?"

"I haven't any idea."

"How long have you had the transcript?"

"Four days. This is the fourth day."

"Whom do you suspect?"

"Me? Don't be silly."

"You must have wondered about it. You couldn't read that transcript without considering who the traitors might be."

"There's Haley," Packard said. "Anyone would think of Haley right off the bat. Isn't that right, Laura?"

"Tell me about Haley," Knight said.

Bishop Haley was a Maryknoller who had spent three years in a Guatemalan prison. He had escaped and come home to a hero's welcome and just a year ago had been named titular bishop of Tarsus and assigned to the USCC in Washington. He made frequent appearances before congressional committees, was a fierce, uncompromising foe of American foreign policy in Latin America and a leader of the peace movement. He went everywhere in his cassock, a simple black cassock, wearing a pectoral cross, a ring, and the red zucchetto of a bishop. ("That's a beanie," Packard explained.).

"For three years I was denied my identity as a priest. For three years I was not allowed to say Mass. Now I will make up for those years."

Clerical clothes were all but unknown among the lower clergy now and bishops wore street clothes in their public appearances. Not even in Europe were priests seen on the street in soutanes anymore, but Bishop Haley was never seen in anything else. The darling of the media, he was something of a pariah among the other bishops, even those who shared his views. Cardinal Carey had been his patron, getting him the Washington assignment, but on occasion even he seemed less than pleased with his protégé. Haley did not see himself as anyone's protégé. He was a loner.

"He doesn't sound like an infiltrator," Knight observed.

"Too obvious?"

"Don't you agree?"

Harry Packard nodded. "Haley is out."

Laura objected. "Don't try to be so subtle. Look at the priests in the Sandinista cabinet. A point is reached when dissembling has served its purpose and one can come into the open. Haley has certainly gained a following by speaking and acting as he does. He has more influence than some archbishops. And not just because of his connection with the USCC."

"Do you understand the make-up of the bishop's bureaucracy?" Packard asked Knight. "If you don't you should. In large part it suffers from the classic pathology of any bureaucracy. The story of the sorcerer's apprentice. Just as the Congress is so busy it cannot possibly do well the limited work constitutionally assigned it, necessitating the creation of huge committee staffs with undefined autonomy, agencies, bureaus, the whole subculture of unelected and unmonitored but effectively ruling people, so too the bishops, if on a smaller scale. The federal bureaucracy has effectively become a fifth branch of government."

"Fifth?"

"Yes, joining the executive, judicial, legislative, and journalistic."

It was one of Packard's complaints, and not an original one, that the press had managed to constitute itself a branch of government, taking the First Amendment to be in effect the constitutional establishment of the press as the critic of the other branches of government.

The fact that *The New York Times* and the *Washington Post* were instances of private enterprise seemed not to disturb the public view that they occupied some neutral Olympus. It was important to steer Harry Packard away from his tempting target.

"Pathological or not," Laura said, "bureaucracies can be good or bad. They are tools."

"Which swiftly get out of control."

"Harry, my point is simply that Cardinal Fergus would not have objected to the USCC if it took a more balanced view. It was the bias of the USCC that annoyed him. They make it sound as if a Catholic has to be a political liberal."

"Laura is a Catholic," Packard explained.

Laura said to Knight, "I'll give you Brian Benestad's book."

How could he do the job successfully, knowing as little as he did about the Church? Later, when she expressed this doubt to Harry, he dismissed it. "The less he knows the better. You want Knight to think the Church is a unique organization. I want him to approach it as a political entity."

Maybe that was wise; Laura didn't know. Certainly a Church that had a KGB agent in its hierarchy was not the Church of her youth.

3
_____

SOMETIMES, in reflective moments, Matthew Hanratty would tell himself that resentment is the fuel of journalism, which also encourages a number of other unattractive vices: slander, gossip, revenge, a pervasive misanthropy. And no wonder. Dear God, the obsequiousness needed to gain an interview, to make contacts, the dissembling and wheedling and lying one had to do to get the truth out of fractious politicians and churchmen. That sonofabitch Rossi had given him the runaround in the noble Roman manner. The apostolic delegate subject himself to the quizzing of a scrivener? My dear fellow! Thus resentment built until it gained its outlet at the typewriter. The typewriter as weapon. The word processor mightier than a missile. At his writing machine the journalist was king and all the mighty quaked in their boots wondering what story would emerge.

Cardinal Fergus had been buried on Tuesday, Monday having been devoted to letting the simple faithful file past the closed coffin to pay their last respects to the slain prelate. Rossi, who had dodged Hanratty in Washington, dodged him again in New York, although in the second instance he was dodging the entire press corps. Archbishop Rossi did not want to be maneuvered into a discussion of how Fergus's successor would be chosen.

In the meantime, Hanratty—and he was not alone, though no one else spoke with the authority of *The New York Times*—kept up the steady drumbeat. New York was an appointment so important to the American Church that it could not be decided far off in the Vatican where there was an imperfect grasp of the peculiarities of the New World situation. Hanratty likened the situation to the inability of the Romans to understand the vast system of higher education Catholics had built up in North America. There was nothing like it anywhere else in the world. Ted Hesburgh of Notre Dame had made that point to him and Hanratty used it again and again. His prose became mellifluous and benevolent as he absolved the Vatican bureaucrats of any ulterior motives in the matter. They simply did not understand the way the Church had evolved in the United States of America. How then could a key appointment like that to the vacant see of New York be entrusted to such bureaucrats?

Monsignor Liberati phoned to say that the Hanratty stories were causing a stir.

"Where?"

"Where it counts."

"So what are they going to do?"

"Well, Matthew, as you know, slow is fast in ecclesiastical matters. *Festina lente*, as one used to say."

"Bullshit. You're going to be preempted before you figure out whether to buy a helmet or pith in it. You can move plenty fast when you want to. People who are motivated by principle can always move fast. Remember *Humanae Vitae*." In 1968, a statement signed by almost a hundred people had been put together overnight and released to the press at the same time as the encyclical in which Paul VI tried to put the clock back in the matter of birth control. Hanratty had a way of referring to this episode as if he had taken part in it. During the good years of his marriage he and Jane had struggled almost nightly to reproduce themselves, to no avail. Birth control to them was as sunglasses to a blind man.

"Matthew, I am the servant of the bishops."

"So serve them. Do you want me to phone Carey?"

"Cardinal Carey is in Washington."

"Where?"

"This is not for public knowledge. He's holed up in one of the USCC residences."

"I'm coming down."

77

"He won't see you."

"Oh, I think he will."

Hanratty banged down the phone. Carey owed him, and the cardinal knew it. So did Liberati for that matter. At least the monsignor had let him know Carey was in Washington. On a skeptical impulse, Hanratty put through a call to San Francisco and asked to speak to Cardinal Carey.

"The cardinal won't be in today," Father Horvath said.

"This is Matthew Hanratty of *The New York Times*."

There was a satisfying sound of surprise imperfectly muffled three thousand miles away. "Mr. Hanratty, this is the day the cardinal makes a private retreat. He can't even be reached by phone on such occasions. I can give him a message as soon as he returns."

"He's out of the city?"

"In a religious house."

"And he'll be back tonight?"

"He always is."

Hanratty was still smiling after he hung up. Ah, the disingenuousness of the clergy. Horvath had not said anything explicitly untrue, but his whole response was misleading. He had given absolutely no hint that Carey was a continent away. When he talked with Carey he would congratulate him on his secretary.

Two hours later Hanratty disembarked at National Airport and was surprised to find Monsignor Liberati waiting for him. The executive secretary looked like someone out of *Going My Way* in traditional street clothes. All he needed was a straw boater, but it was after Labor Day.

"I got through to the cardinal and he suggested I bring you to him."

Hanratty nodded. One must never acknowledge a favor from a news source.

Liberati led him across the parking lot to a nondescript but spanking new American-built car. Before getting into the passenger seat, Hanratty looked at the silver Metro cars poised and waiting: he had intended taking the Metro into town and felt almost cheated. He had been told that the Washington Metro was reasonably safe, at least during daylight hours. And clean.

He did not speak until Liberati had maneuvered them into the flow of traffic. The monsignor's driving skills seemed minimal.

"Why is Carey in Washington?"

"A few minutes more and you can put that question to him."

"When is the next meeting of the bishops scheduled?"

Liberati's smile seemed smug. Although he was balding on top, he had a heavy beard. Curious. "The next *scheduled* meeting is November fifteenth."

"Ah."

"I've told you nothing," Liberati said, his smile radiant. Hanratty looked out at the city. Games clerics play.

Carey was in shirt sleeves and slippers in a guest room of the residence. He swung away from the desk and looked up with a friendly frown when Hanratty came in.

"Good afternoon, Matthew."

"Your Eminence."

His eminence stood and surveyed the room. "Let's talk down the hall. There's a common room that should be free this time of day. Am I right, Monsignor?"

"It's all yours, Your Eminence."

"Is Father Lewis around?"

"I'm not sure."

7 9

"Tell him I want to see him."

"After your talk with Mr. Hanratty?"

"He can join us."

The common room was plush by contrast with the room they had left. A massive console television stood in the corner with all the chairs turned toward it. A wall of bookshelves seemed full of titles that had been pitched out of seminary libraries fifteen years ago. Hanratty actually spotted a Merkelbach. *Theologia moralis.* Ye gods. There was a wet bar as well as beer on tap. The cardinal drew a beer with a practiced hand. "Will you join me, Matthew?"

"Thank you." He didn't drink but he wasn't a fanatic about it.

"À votre santé," Carey said, lifting his glass.

"Olé."

Father Lewis had come in and was standing behind the cardinal when Carey announced, "I am calling a special meeting of the bishops. We will convene two weeks from today. The place of the meeting will be the Abbey of Our Lady of Gethsemani in Kentucky. The main order of business will be Cardinal Fergus's successor."

"The main order of business?"

"That's right."

"Will you gather names to forward to the delegate or . . ."

"We will take a vote."

"Bravo!" Hanratty brought the beer to his lips and actually drank some. The cardinal sat down and so did Hanratty, but Father Lewis remained standing. Carey said to the priest, "This is not a press release, Father. I wanted you to know that Mr. Hanratty has been informed." Father Lewis nodded and Hanratty remembered their conversation on the shuttle. It was pleasant to think that Lewis had been his instrument in bringing about this decision.

"Does Rossi know?"

"Thus far only you and I, Monsignor Liberati and Father Lewis know. I'm not worried about Rossi. But not all my brother bishops may agree that we should meet for such a purpose."

"What about Archbishop Deegen, Father?"

"I wouldn't presume to speak for him," Father Lewis said. "Is there anything else, Your Eminence?"

Carey let him go. What had been the point of calling in Lewis, to have a witness? Liberati would have served that purpose. Odd.

"Why a Trappist monastery?"

"I'm surprised you should ask."

Aha. Hanratty had alluded to the sumptuous surroundings in which the bishops habitually held their meetings: luxury hotels, spas, resorts. The spectacle of the successors of the apostles gathered in a ballroom glittering with mirrors and chandeliers, plump and ruddy and prosperous looking, suggested nothing so much as a meeting of business executives. Hanratty had proposed they meet where they could dress as bishops. His suggestion had been the National Shrine in Washington where he imagined the bishops filling the church as the council fathers had filled Saint Peter's at Vatican II.

"Gethsemani may be a little hard on members of the press," Carey said.

Touché. "When can I release this story?"

"I am relying on your integrity, Matthew. I will give you the word. I don't want bishops reading about this in the newspaper before I have contacted them."

"You say Rossi doesn't worry you. How about John Paul?"

Carey was silent for a moment. "We want to take a burden from his shoulders."

"Your Eminence, you will be doing something of tremendous importance."

"Let's hope so." The prospect of favorable publicity removed the frown that the mention of the pope had brought to Carey's brow. "Would you like another beer, Matthew?"

"No thank you. None's my limit."

4
___

CARDINAL CAREY did not need Matthew Hanratty to tell him he was playing for big stakes. The meeting in Kentucky would shatter precedent and that meant risk, but he had always despised prudent caution. That wasn't the way to have an impact on the Church and on the world. Fergus, benighted as his ideas might have been, had understood that. May he rest in peace. Carey could admire a man who fought for what he believed in. And Kevin Fergus had paid the price.

Reports out of Italy made little sense, one terrorist group after another claiming they had performed the massacre. Fergus deserved better than that. His death, and those of the others who had died with him, was being turned into a macabre joke. Not that there wasn't a terrible fittingness to the way Kevin had gone. Well, the time had now come to put Fergus's comic book conception of Good and Evil to rest and get someone into New York who would talk sense.

The trick would be to muster support for the meeting, and a candidate, without alerting Deegen and his crowd. Carey meant to present his enemies with a *fait accompli*. It would be devastating to take the risk of such a meeting and then have it disintegrate into internecine warfare. It had to go smoothly, a candidate had to be chosen who would command wide support. Once he was named, the ball would be in the Vatican court. No matter what happened then, the bishops of the United States would be seen to have minds of their own.

"Have you thought of going to New York yourself?" Father Lewis asked.

He shook his head. The fact that he had not even considered such a move made him feel impossibly innocent.

Liberati said, "It could be done."

"It never crossed my mind."

"Well, it crossed mine," Liberati said, and young Father Lewis nodded.

"No, I'm out. So who's it going to be?"

They were in Cardinal Carey's office in San Francisco, Liberati, Lewis, Horvath, and the cardinal. Horvath said, "Who is your candidate, Your Eminence?"

"Frank Haley."

Liberati nodded. Horvath repeated the name. Lewis said, "There would be opposition."

"Opposition with arguments, yes. The kind of arguments Fergus himself would have used. But you have to have another candidate to oppose a candidate. Who could they put up?" It went without saying that he meant by *they* Archbishop Deegen of New Orleans.

"Archbishop Toohy," Lewis said firmly.

"Toohy?" Liberati laughed. Horvath frowned. Cardinal Carey immediately saw the shrewdness of the suggestion.

Edward Toohy, archbishop of Dubuque, was a spiritual extremist. Years ago in the seminary he had been known as "The Scrupe" because of his punctilious observance of the rules of the house. His spiritual advisor had suggested the possibility of a monastic vocation, one of the sterner orders, perhaps the Carmelites, but Toohy, having listened politely, having prayed over the matter, shook his head. No, Father. He felt that he had a vocation to the diocesan priesthood.

He had been three years behind Carey at the Saint Paul Seminary and there had been members of his family in the clergy of the archdiocese for as long as anyone could remember. The Toohys were known as *bons vivants*, good companions, great card players, golfers, serious social drinkers. Edward did not fit the Toohy mold. He was obviously using the seminary years to become holy.

On ordination, he was sent as assistant to Joe Green, the one black priest in the archdiocese, whose parish, Saint Benedict the Moor, was the poorest in the Twin Cities. The neighborhood was squalid, the living conditions on a par with those of the parishioners, the pastoral problems immense. The first time Edward Toohy heard confessions he had to deal with two murders, adultery, theft, incest, and the loss of patience. Perhaps the archbishop thought Toohy needed toughening; perhaps he thought the assignment would either break the young man or turn him into a typical Toohy. Young Father Ed became a legend among his black parishioners. Green spoke of him in superlatives. "The kid's a saint." That kind of talk can be the kiss of death, but Toohy survived it. He was moved to the cathedral rectory so the archbishop could get a closer look at his Francesco Borgia. Urban renewal had turned the area around the cathedral into a moonscape. Poverty and all the other ills that flesh is heir to throve there. So did Father Edward Toohy.

The archbishop became convinced that Toohy was the real thing. It seemed a favor to the family to move him out of town. He went on loan to the newly formed USCC where his reputation for sanctity and zeal among the poor increased. He was named the first bishop of Crawfordsville, Indiana, and went on to Dubuque when it fell open. His clergy were less enthusiastic about Toohy's holiness than those who could admire it from afar, but his record in Iowa was superb.

He was completely apolitical. He simply could not be drawn one way or the other when disputes raged in the NCCB about Latin America. As a result he was made a member of the three-man delegation to San Salvador where he was such a success that he was invariably put on tough committees. Everyone trusted Toohy. Lewis was right. Toohy could be a formidable candidate.

"Maybe we should put his name forward," Horvath said.

"There's Smitty," Liberati said.

Indeed there was. Aloysius Schmidt, bishop of Fort Elbow, Ohio. A maverick. As a chaplain Schmidt had gone on a bombing raid over Hanoi, been shot down, and spent nearly five years as a prisoner in North Vietnam. At first his captors assumed his credentials were phony, but when they were able to verify that Schmidt was indeed a Roman Catholic priest they set about trying to reap propaganda advantages from him. There was continuing dispute as to whether or not they had succeeded. On the one hand, Schmidt was wheeled out whenever Jane Fonda or Daniel Ellsberg came to town to lament their country's savage aggression. Schmidt was quoted as agreeing with them. At the same time, however, he criticized the Hanoi regime. Why did his captors tolerate such criticism when they could get pure, undiluted anti-Americanism from their celebrity visitors? Some said Schmidt had been taken in order to chide those Vietnamese insufficiently enthusastic about Ho Chi Min. Schmidt became an expert on this smooth, relentless, Paris-educated revolutionary, even met with him several times. When the prisoners came home, there were those who wanted Schmidt's head.

He offered it to them. He formally requested an inquiry into his behavior as a POW. His fellow prisoners came to his defense. Few had known of his appearances at propaganda events; what they knew were his heroic exploits in the prison compound. The notion that he had been given favored treatment was put to rest by tales of the torture and punishment he had borne. He had offered Mass for his fellow inmates and sustained them spiritually. Was he a hero or a traitor? He had certainly become a pacifist.

He was one of the first members of the hierarchy to join Pax Christi. He opposed registration for the draft. He opposed nuclear weapons. He opposed all weapons. He marched, he spoke out, he seemed to be everywhere. But no group could count on his total support. He lamented the group immorality of the peace movement, but he was for unilateral disarmament.

When he was named bishop of Fort Elbow, the *National Catholic Reporter* was jubilant. The *Wanderer* appeared with its front page edged in black.

"So we have three candidates," Horvath said.

"If you nominate one, the other two can be put in nomination, and the meeting might end in an impasse." Lewis spoke without emotion. Carey found the young priest uncanny at analysis but deficient in moral support. It was chilling to think that Deegen too could call on Lewis for advice. Carey realized that he would not want to ask Lewis how he might respond to such a request from the bishop of his home diocese.

"I wonder if any one of those three would accept nomination," Liberati seemed to take comfort from the doubt his question involved.

"They should be visited," Lewis suggested. "Soon. And discreetly. If it is explained to them how they can be used . . ."

"They would both back Haley," Carey said confidently. He was sure he could count on the support of Toohy and Schmidt.

"The meeting has to be announced soon," Liberati said. "Hanratty is chomping at the bit. He's afraid word will get out."

"If it does, it will come from him." Horvath meant that apart from those in Cardinal Carey's office, only Hanratty knew of the planned meeting. Perhaps it was the idea of a responsible and loyal Hanratty that galvanized Cardinal Carey. He dispatched Lewis to talk with Bishop Schmidt and Liberati to speak to Haley. He himself, presuming on their seminary days, would telephone Archbishop Toohy.

Meanwhile he would tell Matthew Hanratty to begin dropping hints in the *Times*. The religion editor sounded upset. Carey asked him what was the matter.

"The FWPC has hired a private investigator." The remark was spoken in such a way as to suggest that it was the answer to many riddles.

"Have they?" Cardinal Carey wondered if the reporter was losing his grip.

"Cardinal Fergus's niece works there. Laura Ramey. Fergus and Harry Packard were thick as thieves. Something is afoot."

Cardinal Carey was pardonably more interested in the matter he himself was setting afoot. In saner mo-

ments Matthew Hanratty would understand that the
archbishop of San Francisco would scarcely be excited
to learn that the FWPC had hired a private investigator.

"It's a free country, Matthew."

"Sure. But for how long?"

5

ROGER TOOK WELL the fact that his brother had
assumed an all but impossible job. It was not crystal
clear that he understood what Philip had said.

"A red bishop," Knight repeated.

"I thought they all were." Roger's face, never pretty,
became grotesque when he smiled.

"I don't know where to start." What on earth had
possessed him to take on this sisyphean task?

"Sisyphus defied the gods. You are merely defying
common sense."

"Shut up and listen." The silly fact was that he had
taken the job because he sensed Laura Ramey did not
think he could do it. I'll show her, he had in effect
growled. Playground stuff. Packard on the other hand
treated the job as merely routine.

"It is," Roger said. He was having his midafternoon
treat, soda crackers and milk, the two mushed together
in a big bowl. Never exemplary, Roger's elocution was
now a soggy insult. "All you need is the data."

"All I need is the data! Of course, that would make it
routine. But where the hell is the data?"

"There is the *Annuario Pontificio* published each year
by the Vatican. It lists all the dioceses and all the bishops
in the world. There's the *Catholic Almanac,* the *Catholic*

88

Directory, and the *Catholic Who's Who*. We can cross check their entries once we get the whole mess into the computer."

"I can't take books like that out of the libary. Provided I find a library that has them."

"Go to Manhattanville. Mother Gladys Canby will let me have them for a finite period of time."

And indeed the nun, when Knight found her in the college library, was more than helpful. Called a Madam of the Sacred Heart, she was not in full sympathy with the reforms that had put her unattractively into a baggy wool suit.

"You should have seen our habit, Mr. Knight. It was glorious. Half my vocation was due to the attraction of that habit. Now look at me."

"Wasn't it awful about Cardinal Fergus?"

She closed her eyes. Knight guessed her to be sixty. Was she praying or feeling pain? A wisp of gray hair lay across her wrinkled forehead. She wore a veil far back on her head. "May he rest in peace." So she had been praying.

"I wonder who will succeed him."

"That's up to the pope, no matter what you read in the *Times*. So why am I worried? Have we ever had such a wonderful pope? I only pray he gets good advice and acts on it."

Roger set about entering the data from the reference works into the personal computer Philip had bought him half fearing, half hoping he would get hooked on video games. Roger designed a format for the entries, using the *Catholic Directory* as his basic text, coding in a number of key words at the end of each entry. What was the point?

"Say you want to know how many bishops were born in the midwest, have studied in Rome, hold degrees in theology, belong to Pax Christi and have been bishops longer than five years. Just an example. What we would like to ask the computer is how many bishops are commies, lost their faith in the seminary or before, and have recently been in touch with a KGB control."

"Not much of that in those books."

"No. We have to supplement them. I need a list of the bishops who belong to Pax Christi. I want the voting records of their recent meetings. Get me those and then I want to be left alone."

"Any idea where I can get those?"

"Harry Packard." He was right. Laura said she would send the information up by special messenger.

"I want to talk to Cardinal Fergus's secretary. The one who gave you the transcript."

"Myrtle? Oh good!"

It was the first time he had pleased her, and it pleased him more than he would have guessed.

Laura made the date for him and he took the train to the city to meet Myrtle Tillman. She did not want him to come to her old office at the chancery so they met in a tea shop in the Village. God, how that setting brought back memories, few of them welcome. The shop was hardly more than a storefront, and exotic aromas greeted him as he entered. A woman in a turban and floor-length dress floated toward him, drifting among tables the size of checkerboards. Of course she knew Myrtle. She escorted Knight to the corner where a small, steady-eyed woman awaited him.

"Thank you, Bonita," she said, but the woman waited to take their order. Knight, asked to choose from a bewildering number of unknowns, selected orange pekoe and was regarded by the two women as though he'd flunked a test.

"Have you moved out of your office?" he asked when Bonita withdrew.

"Some would like me to, but I'm leaving everything right where it is until there's a new archbishop. I can stay on, even if he doesn't want me for his secretary."

"Who do you think it will be?"

"I've no idea. Wait until there's a new archbishop."

Had she thought he meant the new secretary? Well, everyone has his own perspective on the world. "Any idea who *he* might be?"

"Only fears."

Their separate pots of tea arrived and he reached to pour but she stopped him. "It's not nearly ready yet. It must steep. Would you like some buttered toast?"

Bonita too awaited his answer. Her freckled arms were ringed by half a dozen cheap plastic bracelets. Suddenly the thought of hot buttered toast was like ambrosia.

"With cinammon and sugar," he said, making up for the orange pekoe. Myrtle put her hand briefly on his arm, an absolving gesture. This small, birdlike woman had typed the transcript he had read in the Wilson Residential Hotel in Washington. Before asking who she feared might be appointed to New York as Cardinal Fergus's successor, he wanted to talk about the cardinal's taped memorandum.

"Were you surprised when you first listened to it?"

"I was frightened, but not surprised. I had worked for the cardinal much too long to be surprised."

"You mean he suspected some of his fellow bishops were . . ."

"No! Not that. I meant that he was convinced the Russians would do anything. After the shooting of the pope he said he really believed that anything at all was possible."

"Including his own assassination?"

She shook her head. "I doubt that occurred to him. He wasn't worried about himself. It was the Church and the country he feared for."

"Did you ever speak to him about what was on that tape?"

"No. I didn't even listen to it until after he was dead."

"He never alluded to what was on it?"

She shook her head. "I'm sorry. I'm not much help."

He switched the topic back to her fears about Cardinal Fergus's successor.

It was late when he got back to Rye and his return was announced by the joyful barking of Either and Or, the English setters, so called because Roger claimed he could not tell them apart. The only light was in the back room where the computer was set up. Roger was printing out when Philip came in and the two brothers waited for the clacking to stop. Roger tore off the sheet and handed it to Philip. There was three names. Haley, Schmidt, Toohy.

"I can print out their entries."

Philip shook his head. "Not now."

"I suppose you want to know how I arrived at those names."

"It's a funny thing, Roger."

"What?"

"Myrtle Tillman mentioned these same three names."

"On what basis?"

"Apprehension. Hunch. I don't know."

"Well, that may be as scientific a method as mine. In any case, I'll take her apprehension as confirmation of my method."

Haley, Schmidt, and Toohy. Philip recited the names dreamily.

"Which one is it?" Roger sighed.

"Eenie, meenie, minie . . ." Philip's voice drifted off.

6

MATTHEW HANRATTY was seriously convinced that what Cardinal Carey proposed to do was one of the most innovating moves in ecclesiology since the Council of Trent. It was hard to have such a story and hold it back. On the other hand it gave him an advantage analogous to omniscience. Knowing what was planned for the meeting in Kentucky, he could repeat his generalized advice that the bishops convene in more appropriate places. He could express the wish that the appointment of Cardinal Fergus's successor take into account the needs of the American Church. *And* that the American bishops have a say in that appointment. The closer he got to saying what he knew, the edgier he became. He could not forget that the FWPC had hired a private investigator.

He considered asking Miss Barry, his secretary, to be on the alert for suspicious types, but that would have been to invite her derision. Early in their relationship he had made the mistake of asking her what she thought of something he had written only to learn that she despised his style. She described it as fruity, she called it unctuous. "You know, like Uriah Heep."

"Thanks a heap."

"Read Hemingway's journalism. Read *Death in the Afternoon.*"

"Hemingway! You're dating yourself."

She gave him a look of pure hatred. "It's better than never having loved at all."

She was five feet high and five feet wide, Miss Five by Five in the title of a song that dated Hanratty. Why was Ms. Barry so cruel to him? He in turn was cruel to her. The thought of being nice to her was like a Lenten penance. If Harry Packard had hired a detective to find out what Hanratty knew of the upcoming episcopal meeting, Barry could easily be enlisted in any plot against him. That was why he had composed his story about the surprise bishops' meeting only in his head. He felt he was being followed. He could never turn fast enough to surprise a tail but wasn't that the whole point of it? He distracted himself by imagining who would be named at the Kentucky meeting as the bishops' choice to succeed Fergus.

Liberati had an absolutely buttoned lip on the matter, refusing even to speculate with Hanratty on the phone. The executive secretary sounded sorry that Hanratty knew of the meeting at all.

"I'm for Haley," he told Liberati.

"Hmmm."

"I realize he isn't Italian."

"Are you sure?"

That stupid retort had led to a wasted couple of hours spent trying to track down possible Italian forebears for Haley without letting his secretary find out what he was doing. Had Liberati been playing a deliberate trick? What did the executive secretary really think of the religion editor of *The New York Times*?

There were times when Hanratty wished he had gotten as far from the Church as possible after coming out of the monastery. Two vocations had ended in failure, not that he really blamed himself for either of them— Jane had given him the shaft and he never had a full shot at becoming a monk—but it did prey on the mind that he had wasted years traveling roads that had turned out to be culs-de-sac.

He had toyed with the practical order when he was a junior banker, marching, speaking out, protesting, all of it symbolic. As a Trappist he had tried to see life as something controlled from within, the inner and outer fused. When he left he wanted something as direct as Dorothy Day's soup kitchen. When you hand a hungry person a bowl of soup you have done something real.

"Sure," Bishop Haley had said. "But you have to do it over and over again, every day. It solves nothing."

"How about hunger pangs?"

"What is the difference between a man who has just received a handout and a man consuming a portion of what he grows? The second man has solved the problem of hunger in a way the first has not. So too with a bed in a flophouse and owning the roof over your head. Don't confuse charity with justice, Matt."

"All solutions are temporary."

"Sure. So is life. But some things are more temporary than others."

It was Bishop Haley, oddly enough, who convinced Hanratty of the importance of the intellectual life. He spoke of the apostolate of the intellectual. Hanratty felt he could level with the Maryknoller.

"I don't have the faith I once had." Looking into Haley's eyes was like confronting someone wearing mirrored sunglasses. "Some eyes are like mirrors: when a monkey looks in no apostle looks out." He had used that variation on Lichtenberg in the profile he had written on Haley.

"What do you mean?"

"I could not recite the creed with conviction."

"Do you believe in God?"

"I'm not even sure of that."

"How long were you in the monastery?"

"Three years, give or take."

Haley squeezed his elbow and grinned. "Give it a little time. And for God's sake don't agonize about it. Remember the real test. I was hungry and you fed me, naked and you clothed me, lonely and you visited me. That's the only test of having lived well and it isn't very heavy with dogma."

"And you want me to be an intellectual."

"There are many kinds of hunger, many kinds of nakedness."

"Where does it say that?"

"You're agonizing again."

"What are you, my spiritual director?"

"If that's what you want."

Haley had not been shocked when Hanratty told him he had lost his faith. Had Haley lost his? Did men like Fergus and Carey and Liberati and all the others really believe that one day the graves would open, a New Jerusalem descend from on high and the good guys live happily ever after? Did they really believe that Jesus would come down out of the clouds?

Hanratty thought of signs nailed to trees along the back roads of his youth. "Jesus Saves." "Jesus Died For Your Sins." "Christ is Coming." Hanratty knew what the bishops thought of Jerry Falwell, the Moral Majority, all that. They were embarrassed to be likened to him and that sense of embarrassment as much as anything else accounted for the lopsided vote in favor of the pastoral letter on war and peace. Fundamentalists had an unnerving way of being against abortion, but they weren't very likely to come out against military might. Signing on with the peace movement had given the bishops a little space between themselves and the evangelicals. But did that get them away from those signs nailed to trees? One of the acclamations of faith after the consecration of the bread and wine at Mass was "Christ has died, Christ is risen, Christ will come again." Did Haley really believe that? Did Carey? If they did, there wasn't a dime's worth of difference between them and Jerry and they should face up to it.

Hanratty himself had stopped believing that sort of stuff. Oh, he knew of the nonliteral ways he could understand the creed. He knew theologians who regarded this as a time of transition, man passing out of his theological phase. Anyone who took the trouble to think about it would know that faith can't withstand the scrutiny of reason. But we can still hang on to the language. Maybe in the future religious language will completely disappear, but in this period of transition we can go right on talking like our parents and grandparents. We just won't mean what they did.

It was Hanratty's suspicion that this was the theology of some American bishops, maybe even many of them. If it was, then they were different from the Trappists in whose monastery Cardinal Carey proposed to bring them together. Peregrine, the new abbot of Gethsemani, had entered as the greenest of the green, was now head honcho, having all but dictatorial authority over the monks. The novitiate they had gone through together was somewhat on the order of Marine boot camp. Peregrine had spent a lot of time kneeling in penance for minute infractions of the rule. In the guesthouse, before starting the novitiate, they had talked, and Hanratty could not believe the other man when he said he did not know who Thomas Merton was.

"Haven't you read him?"

"What has he written?"

It had to be a leg pull but it wasn't. Merton had been

such an important part of Hanratty's own interest in the Trappists he could not believe anyone would come to the monastery by another route. He gave him some Merton to read, some of the late stuff when the influence of Zen was clear and Merton's militant pacificism and antinuclearism had come to the fore.

"That's what I want to get away from."

"Me too," Hanratty agreed, surprising himself only a bit. The monastery was the big escape, like dying, only you weren't really buried.

Peregrine had stayed and been elected abbot at an age when he could look forward to a long reign. With the other monks he would believe that every article of the creed was literally true. What sense would his life make otherwise? His faith was indistinguishable from that of the twelfth century Cistercians, from that of De Rance who at La Trappe had reformed the order. Hanratty had witnessed burials in the monastery. Never had a corpse looked more like a corpse. The no longer living thing clad in the robes of a monk was put in a hole in the ground where it would return to dust and likely be scattered as the years passed. Yet that very dust would rise again. Every one of the monks believed that to the bottom of his sandaled feet. In such a setting the bishops of the United States would meet and try to force the hand of the Vatican in the choice of a successor to Cardinal Fergus. What would Abbot Peregrine make of it all? What would they make of Abbot Peregrine?

Matthew Hanratty did not wholly enjoy his own sense of impending drama. But the meeting could be as dramatic as it liked so long as Bishop Haley emerged the choice of his fellows.

Neal Admirari called and, because he had picked up the phone himself, unwilling to sweat out his secretary's indifference to its ringing, Hanratty had to suffer the annoying breeziness of his colleague.

"Matt, does Carey have a secret meeting afoot?"

"I can give you his number," Hanratty said dryly.

"Funny. I am picking up rumors of a meeting."

"Who from?"

"You don't know her. Fergus left a statement." Hanratty listened with narrowed eyes. Honest to God, Fergus would be as much of an embarrassment dead as he had been alive. He made the trade with Admirari. He couldn't get through to Carey himself, so he sent the story on without telling the archbishop of San Francisco that the religion editor of *The New York Times*, for reasons beyond his control, could not keep his promise of silence about the meeting in Kentucky.

Part 3

I

TO SAY THAT CARDINAL CAREY felt betrayed
when Matthew Hanratty jumped the gun on the announcement of the Kentucky meeting would have been
only partially accurate. How could he not enjoy the
paean of praise that came his way as a result of what
was invariably called his bold initiative? He counted on
that favorable publicity to diminish the annoyance his
fellow bishops would feel on learning of the meeting
from the newspapers. But he had no illusions that Archbishop Deegen would be mollified. Quite the contrary.

Queried by knowledgeable reporters with an eye to
drama, the archbishop of New Orleans dismissed rumors

of a special meeting, saying pointedly that the president of the NCCB did not communicate with members of the hierarchy via the newspapers. Nor of course was there any question of the American bishops presuming to select the next archbishop of New York. That was the job of the Vatican and the pope. Carey groaned and reached for the phone.

Hanratty blamed it on his secretary but there was no note of apology in the statement. He chuckled when Carey mentioned Archbishop Deegen's reaction.

"You'd be better off if he boycotted the meeting."

Carey shuddered at the thought. The last thing he wanted to do was to create the public impression of dissension in the ranks of the bishops. That would diminish the impact of any nomination he might be able to engineer.

"Cardinal Carey, you have the nation with you." Hanratty spoke as if he had just delivered the fifty states to the cardinal archbishop of San Francisco. "You couldn't buy the favorable publicity you're getting."

Carey managed to end the conversation without thanking Hanratty. If the reporter had kept his word, gratitude might have been in order but he could scarcely thank Hanratty for the way he had handled the scoop with which he had been entrusted. His next call was to Washington. Father Lewis answered.

"I was just about to call you, Your Eminence. In light of the leak, I thought I would fly to New Orleans and talk with Archbishop Deegen."

The gratitude Matthew Hanratty had sought in vain was given spontaneously to the young priest. It was suddenly clear to Cardinal Carey that Father Lewis was as bright a light as there was in Washington. But then a cloud passed across the sun.

"Can you persuade him to come to the meeting?"

"I will try to put it in such a way that he will persuade himself."

"What will you say?"

"That the only way he can oppose you is by attending the meeting."

That was true enough, and Cardinal Carey could not think of another tack that Father Lewis might take with Deegen. It was a trade-off. Either he let Deegen torpedo the meeting or he encouraged Father Lewis to get his major adversary (now that Fergus was dead) into the arena with him. Better dissension within the walls than a public split in the ranks. He told Father Lewis to go ahead.

Less than a week later the Louisville airport was crowded with men in black suits and Roman collars as bishops and their aides arrived on flights originating all over the country. Greetings were exchanged with expressions grim or smiling as the prelates indicated their feelings about this hastily called special meeting. Buses awaited them outside but one or two eschewed this alleged convenience and piled into taxis for the expensive ride to the abbey via Bardstown. It had been by cab that Cardinal Carey and Father Horvath traveled to Gethsemani the night before. An anticipatory meeting involving Carey, Liberati, and Lewis, together with a half dozen bishops who would keep the meeting moving in the appropriate direction, had been held in the motel across the road from the guesthouse. Matthew Hanratty had already checked into the guesthouse but he had the discretion, thank God, to let the preliminary discussions take place without importuning Carey. The cardinal would make certain that Matthew was thoroughly briefed by either Liberati or Lewis before the sun set on their preparations.

When Archbishop Deegen strode across the airport terminal in Louisville, he gathered other bishops as he went. Some wanted to participate in the strength of his convictions; some were as strong-willed as Deegen but less influential, less charismatic; others were plying this side of the street for the nonce and would shortly work its opposite. The minibus was chock-full as the driver directed it along the narrow, winding country roads toward Bardstown.

Deegen made it clear that he was attending this meeting only because he thought it would be more irresponsible to avoid it.

"You may have read the statement I gave the press."

He half turned in the uncomfortable seat and directed his flushed face at the other bishops. Short, tall, hairy or bald, smoking cigars if they smoked at all, the chains of pectoral crosses cutting laterally across their chests, suggesting a coat of arms, they nodded. Deegen was their leader; they were his men. Who had not heard of Deegen's press release?

In it Deegen had said that after studying chapter four of part two of the *New Code of Canon Law* he failed to find in the discussion of episcopal conferences any suggestion whatsoever that they were competent to select replacements for vacant sees. He went on to say that he envied his brother bishops whose dioceses were in such apple-pie order that they had time to usurp the activities of the pope. He was happy to learn that all the stories he had heard about weird novelties parading as basic Christian doctrines were apparently unsubstantiated, leaving the cardinal archbishop of San Francisco free to fish in troubled waters. The organization of homosexual priests in that fair city could doubtless be trusted to look after things in the absence of their ordinary. As for himself, it was only with the greatest reluctance that he left his archdiocese, with all its problems, to attend yet another meeting of the episcopal conference. The trouble was, he had no idea what mischief his fellow bishops might be up to and he intended to go to Kentucky and prevent them from making asses of themselves.

"I used strong language and I wish I didn't have to but, gentlemen, things are getting entirely out of hand. If we don't stop it once and for all it is going to get worse. This meeting was in effect planned at *The New York Times* and I for one do not regard that rag as the font of anything but confusion. So let's have our special meeting, and let's have some special nominating, and electing too."

There was fire in the eye of Archbishop Deegen as he turned to scrowl at the gentle Kentucky landscape. He had spent some hours with the head canonist of the New Orleans archdiocese, and Deegen thought he had a surprise or two up his sleeve for Cardinal Carey and company.

At that precise moment, Cardinal Carey was in Abbot Peregrine's office. The word austerity took on new meaning in such a monastery and things did not improve when one got to the abbot's office. There was a desk on which was nothing at all, not even, so far as Carey could tell, the little memento mori of a speck of dust. The chair he sat in was identical to the one in which the abbot sat: studies in the geometry of right angles and maximum discomfort. On the chalk-white plaster wall behind the abbot a modernistic crucifix, vividly evocative of Christ's suffering on the cross,

1 0 4

seemed to give the reason for this life, this decor, these silent men. Peregrine had a Modigliani face. He sat very upright, arms folded, hands up his sleeves. Was he ashamed of the abbatial ring? Were the folded arms a way of concealing his pectoral cross, another sign of office? The abbot's expression was one of utter serenity. It was as if time stood still and the two of them were held in a moment that was in one-to-one correspondence with eternity. It must be a memorable experience for one of Peregrine's monks to sit face to face with him like this. For that matter, Cardinal Carey felt a bit in the dock himself. He was dressed in his cardinal's robes. He had never felt them to be vulgarly ostentatious before but he had the sense that Peregrine was amused by the worldliness of the garb of a prince of the Church. Carey felt, not so faintly, foolish. He had gone on a bit about how grateful he was to the abbot for providing them with a place in which to meet. His answer was that serene smile.

"I'm particularly grateful that you will let us hold our meetings in the abbey church. We will be sure not to interfere with the liturgical hours."

Peregrine nodded. What an exasperating man he was. But then a chatty Trappist would have been an anomaly.

"This is a special meeting," Carey went on inanely. He wanted to impress this monk with his own importance, with the importance of the national bishops' conference, with the historical importance of this particular meeting. He babbled on, speaking of Fergus, of the opening in New York, of Vatican II's desire, underlined by subsequent synods, that the bishops of a country take on fuller responsibility for the Church in their land.

"Cardinal Fergus sometimes made his retreat here."

"Did he really?"

"I don't imagine another man like him will be found."

"How do you mean?" Was Peregrine's tranquillity slightly jarred by the question?

"We have a very imperfect knowledge of what goes on outside. I meant that Cardinal Fergus was a very spiritual man."

Spiritual? Fergus? He must have stepped completely out of character when he made his retreat. Well, who doesn't? Peregrine's claim of total unworldliness had a hollow sound.

"But surely you have to travel, don't you, Father Abbot? Your life as abbot must be quite different from that of the ordinary monk."

"It is a major cross of the job that the abbot must frequently be away from the monastery. We have a number of sister abbeys, places that spun off from this one during the golden years of the fifties."

"You weren't here then, were you?"

The question might have seemed ridiculous, but Carey had been astounded when told the age of the monk who attended to them across the road in the monastery's motellike addendum to its guesthouse. That apparently youthful monk had been forty years in the monastery and he had entered as a priest. He had to be in his late sixties at least, probably seventy or more.

"I entered in the sixties. The late sixties."

"How long have you been abbot?"

"This is my third year."

"It is a great honor to have been elected so young."

Peregrine smiled slightly. "I did not feel I was doing the person I voted for an honor."

Carey did not even acknowledge this pious bushwa. He would wager that he would have Peregrine talking like a human being before the meeting was over. "You must have been the youngest abbot this place ever had."

"How old were you when you became bishop?"

Carey did not find the switch of topic to himself unwelcome, and he sketched his career in some detail until he realized that he had brought back the abbot's serene expression. It verged on the complacent, Carey thought. The whole notion of wanting to dress up in red, to wear a ring and pectoral cross, to be ogled and fawned over and fed too well wherever he went—all that seemed suddenly childish. It appeared to amuse Peregrine in somewhat the same way a tourist is amused by Roman traffic cops, carabinieri, Swiss guards.

Still, when the cardinal rose to go, Peregrine came quickly around the desk, genuflected, and kissed his ring. Carey was about to stop this obeisance and help the abbot to his feet when it occurred to him that he should not deprive Peregrine of his act of humility.

"Thank you for your time, Father Abbot."

"Our days are full yet we have little sense of time here."

"I feel a bit of that myself," Carey said. A courtesy to his host. Already the rustic atmosphere of the abbey was giving him the willies.

"Where are you from, Father Abbot?"

"My native city is Superior, Wisconsin."

Carey, at the door, wheeled, a smile on his ruddy face.

"Superior! I come from Duluth."

The abbot seemed to be practicing custody of the eyes. He leaned forward, studying the toes of his heavy, black shoes.

"I suppose Duluth sounds as remote from you now as Superior does to me."

Was Peregrine suggesting he was glad to be out of that hick town and into the sophisticated cosmopolitan atmosphere of the Trappist monastery?

"What was your name before you entered the order?"

"The same as now." A suggestion of annoyance appeared on the abbatial countenance but was quickly gone.

"Peregrine what?"

"I was known as Perry Green. My novice master had a sense of humor. Or perhaps he saw that I should keep the same name. Peregrine means pilgrim and I have always been that."

"Haven't we all?" Cardinal Carey said. He was tired of the abbot's tireless virtue. When he entered the office he had felt in the presence of a saint. Maybe he was a saint but Abbot Peregrine was also a bore.

Later that night, having a Scotch and water while Matthew Hanratty drank Perrier—why was he always ending up with teetotalers?—Carey described his visit with Peregrine. They were in the reporter's diminutive room in the guesthouse. Carey did not want to be buttonholed by either friend or foe before the meeting.

"You have to understand what the outsider looks like to a monk. Here one spends all day pondering the state of his soul. It is a relentless task, constantly reminding yourself of the presence of God, seeing every natural impulse, every ordinary motive, as an obstacle of imperfection, something to get rid of. One is wholly absorbed in lifting the soul to God. And then *we* come in, visibly concerned with a million comparatively trivial things. We look shallow. I know. When I was here I found it a constant temptation to smugness to notice those who came for a visit. For the few days they were here, they were, by their own lights, fervent. Full of resolutions. But the shallowness remained. If only because they were here as tourists. A taste of the religious life. Get up at three and come to office, be stirred by the chant and the spectacle of the monks filing in in the semidarkness. How thrilling. And they promise themselves that their lives will never be the same again. When they leave, they don't turn on the car radio right away, not wanting to violate the inner peace they have attained. By Louisville it is gone. A traffic jam, some jackass on the highway; inadvertently they flick on the radio, and it's all gone. That happened to me and I had resolved to come here and stay for good. Good turned out to be three years."

Cardinal Carey sipped his drink and nodded. Hanratty's had to be the most chronicled nonvocation in the history of western man. He had written it up any number of times; whenever he was interviewed the subject of his lost Trappist vocation arose. It had been suggested that Hanratty saw himself as a kind of twisted Thomas Merton, the failed form in which news of the spiritual life could be brought to Americans in the eighties. Carey had not read Hanratty's book on the subject, *Asleep in Gethsemani,* but he had been given the gist of it a number of times. The disciples fell asleep in the Garden of Gethsemani while Christ wept for the poor and downtrodden. Hanratty had likened the monks to the sleeping disciples. He himself had awakened from his dogmatic slumber and gone out to do something Christlike for the outcast poor. There was more, much more. Monasticism had grown up in feudal society, preurban let alone preindustrial. Hanratty likened it to a farm co-op movement that, in its time, had performed a useful function. The Trappist reform of the Cistercian life was already a nostalgia trip, he argued, but for men to try and live a twelfth-century life in the twentieth was cause for real sadness.

"What kind of reception do you get here now?" Cardinal Carey asked the reporter. He was bothered by a resemblance between Peregrine and Hanratty.

"Fine. I admire Peregrine. Genuinely. An institution can be outmoded but nonetheless an individual may live within it seriously. Did he give you the line about not knowing what's going on outside the walls? Don't believe it. He's as well-informed as anyone I know about what's going on in the Church. Since he's been abbot he's brought in a fair number of new theologians to address chapter. I've talked to the monks twice myself. I guess that's an indication that I'm not resented for my views."

"What was your topic?"

Hanratty smiled. This involved a kind of collapsing of his face. "The last time I spoke on the strengths and weaknesses of the American bishops."

"I've heard you on the weaknesses."

"Ho ho. Tell me, Cardinal Carey, what do you know of Kevin Fergus's will?"

"What have you heard?"

This sort of Ping-Pong could go on only so long. It turned out that Neal Admirari had made a remark to Hanratty suggesting that the late cardinal had left a testament saying dire things about the state of the Church.

"That sounds like any of his sermons."

"Admirari seemed to think it was more specific."

"Could he have been pulling your leg?"

Hanratty's expression suggested that he thought this all too possible. His visage became darker. "Harry Packard is sending his private investigater here, disguised as a journalist."

"He'll be wearing a dunce cap?"

Hanratty tried unsuccessfully to laugh. Cardinal Carey knew Hanratty thought Harry Packard was out to get him. But there were far simpler explanations for why FWPC would want an observer at this extraordinary meeting. Of course, there was no point in trying to make Matthew see that.

As if wanting to turn the conversation from his troubles to the cardinal's, Hanratty asked Cardinal Carey how he thought the meeting would go.

Father Lewis had passed on to Carey word of Deegen's plan to subvert the purpose of the meeting. Scarcely news, but then Father Lewis spoke as if he were simply confirming the already known. Deegen was an ace parliamentarian—the talent of small minds—and could prove to be troublesome. Soothed by Scotch, aided by his natural optimism and confidence in his own ability to deal with opposition, the cardinal pushed these thoughts from his head.

"According to plan."

Hanratty lifted his mineral water in a toast. "But whose plan?"

2
———

IT WAS QUITE DARK when Liberati went out between the two rows of parked cars, the only sound that of his walking. What a din his shoes made on the blacktop. He stopped, and total silence enveloped him. The universe stretched away infinitely above him, punctuated by stars whose individual enormity was dwarfed and whose collective infinity was mocked by a space that had no limit in any imaginable sense of the word. The entire firmament might have been created in the instant he stopped to look upward; equally, it might be billions of years old. Young or old, the universe was dying, like every living thing in it, disintegrating like every object it contained.

Liberati felt almost dizzy. He had not had thoughts like these since his second year in the seminary when he had been accused of having a bent for philosophy. "Bent but not broken," was the way he joshed about it later, truly grateful to have escaped the trap of academic life. But the pleasure of unanchored thought was fresh in him now, standing just beyond the range of the light over the monastery gate, at the end of the parking area for guests.

To his right, the traffic light suspended over the county road blinked yellow. It might have been a lesser star, emitting the message of its existence to whom it may concern. In the daytime, keeping his eye on the task at hand, Liberati, like everyone else, lived in an egocentric universe. It was a cosmogony indifferent to geocentric and heliocentric blather. The world wheeled around the projects, hopes, disappointments, joys, and sorrows of his day. This might have been culpable if there were any alternative to it. Now, standing in a darkness that began to seem its own kind of light, peering into the uncountable miles of space as if he were seeking the bottom of a barrel, Liberati had a profound sense of the inconsequential nature of his life. This sentiment was all the more disturbing because it included the judgment that all other human lives are inconsequential too. Liberati was not failing at something where success was possible. Life is a dying fall. What does it all mean?

Adolescence is the time for such metaphysical angst. Liberati had avoided that kind of rattling of the floorboards of his life for years, even on retreat, particularly on retreat. He did not seek such somber thoughts now. He had come outside for a smoke and some solitude, not wanting to be available should Carey or Lewis have one more bright idea about how to ram through a nomination in the meeting tomorrow. He was thoroughly weary of the machinations and politicking that made up his life. Suddenly seen in an unwonted cosmic perspective, it seemed worse than trivial. What the hell difference did it make, from any sort of perspective at all, who was the next archbishop of New York?

Liberati remembered the list of the bishops of Milan carved in stone in the Duomo of that city. The church there had been started by Saint Barnabas the Apostle and the first bishop dated from something like 50 A.D. There they all were, hundreds of them, columns of them, practically all the early ones called saints. Saint Ambrose and Saint Charles Borromeo caught the eye, as well as the two recent ones who had become popes, but Liberati had been struck by the shortness of their reigns. The same could be said of the bishops of Rome. Every once in a while there was an anomaly, someone holding the job for thirty or forty years, but by and large they got only a few years. Nowadays the normal attrition was aided by the rule of retirement at seventy-five. Measured against the eons since the big bang or whatever the genesis of the universe had been, those few years did not even register. Their finaglings, ambitions, projects, were all rendered silly by such thoughts. And Liberati had the self-serving notion that he had been dragged against his will into this scheme to wrest from the Vatican the prerogative of selecting American bishops.

Father Lewis had passed on to him a background paper prepared by one of the staff theologians pointing out that Rosmini in the midnineteenth century, in his *Five Wounds of the Church*, had urged the popular election of bishops, by clergy and by lay people. Liberati had filed it away. The theological brief would have little interest for Cardinal Carey. He had no desire at all, Liberati was sure, to put something so delicate and important as the selection of bishops into the hands of the laity.

All the gabbing about lay participation had brought to the fore some of the funniest ducks imaginable, spoiled priests, male and female, dying to get into the pulpit as lectors or to distribute communion as special ministers. The same types showed up on every parish council and in any given parish the same dozen pains in the neck were on every committee. Most priests kidded about it. But were the bishops any less silly, trying to have a say in naming Fergus's successor?

Deegen was right about one thing: every bishop in the country had more than he could handle in his own diocese. But those local troubles were all tar babies it would take courage of the first order to confront. Take nuns. No, leave them. Liberati was tired of thinking. He drew a cigarette from the pack in his shirt pocket and was about to light it when he realized there were voices coming toward him from the direction of the county road. He could have alerted the walkers by lighting his cigarette, but he chose not to, stepping swiftly off the road and standing beside the trunk of a giant tree. His reason for doing this, had he been asked for one, would have been that he did not want to chase away the metaphysical melancholy he had been enjoying.

The first voice he heard was that of Archbishop Deegen. Perhaps he thought he was speaking in a whisper. Perhaps he had no idea how sound carried on the chill Kentucky night air. Perhaps he didn't give a damn whether he was heard or not, although that possibility, when Liberati attended to what the archbishop was saying, seemed unlikely.

"The only way to fight is with our own candidate and

that is what we're going to do. Carey still means to put up Haley?"

"That's right, Archbishop."

The second voice belonged to Father Lewis, and Liberati was shocked by such treachery. Lewis was his assistant and in effect worked for Carey and here he was divulging the combined USCC and NCCB plan to the enemy. But then Deegen was Lewis's archbishop, so where did his primary loyalty lie? Still, it was sneaky no matter how you looked at it.

"I have a little surprise for them then."

"The assumption is that you will put up either Bishop Toohy or Bishop Schmidt."

"How the deuce did they find that out?"

"The way you knew they would put up Bishop Haley. By logic."

Was Lewis covering his tracks? Of course it did not take much mulling to figure out that Haley was the sort of person Carey would want to replace Fergus.

"Logic my eye. I think our two choices are subtle ones. Who would suspect that I would put forth either Toohy or Schmidt?"

"Cardinal Carey."

Deegen seemed reluctant to grant Carey any deductive powers at all. The two men had stopped in the road. Liberati could smell Deegen's cigar and he felt an over-powering desire to light his cigarette. But there was no way he was going to make himself known now.

That resolution entailed a fifteen minute wait there by the tree where he had taken refuge. The chill night air was uncomfortable and Liberati feared catching cold. And he had to go to the bathroom.

How oddly alike Deegen and Carey sound, he thought. All the appeal to principle and to differing ecclesiologies seemed to come down to a will to power. More deep thoughts in the silent night. A silent night that for a few minutes had seemed a holy night as well but was now aroar with all the schemes he had just seen as cosmically insignificant. He looked up at the sky but the tree obscured his vision; he could not consult the stars and thank God he was not like the rest of men.

Where did all this work and scheming and scurrying about lead to? Of course Liberati had his own ambition. He hoped to be named a bishop one day, and he had good reason to think he would be. All his predecessors in the job, since the formation of the Conference, had ended up as bishops. The desirability of being made a bishop was not something Liberati questioned. Normally. But tonight the last thing in the world he wanted was a diocese. He would never again be able to call his soul his own. It would mean an endless round of appointments, confirmations, graduations, jubilees, you name it: a bishop leads an all but totally ceremonial existence.

Like most priests who taught or worked in offices, Liberati dreamt of the pastoral life he really wanted. His own parish, far from the hue and cry, good Catholic families, docile, generous, respectful of their pastor, deserving in their turn his respect. In Liberati's imagination this ideal parish was located in a small midwestern town, its streets shaded by huge and healthy elms, unaffected by the blight; his rectory had a screened porch and he would sit there in the evenings, smoking a pipe, greeting the parishioners as they went by on their evening stroll. His life would be an idyllic round of Mass, parish activities, golf. And he would be generally respected in the town.

Standing in the now cold Kentucky air, jiggling to ease the pressure on his bladder, wishing Deegen and Lewis would get the hell inside, Liberati knew his dream

parish was only a dream. The pettiness of life could not
be escaped by seeking a lower station. Deegen continued
to orate in the dark. Did the universe seem simply a
more adequate cathedral to him?

"There won't be a hundred bishops here, Father.
Carey cannot possibly get a majority of the votes."

"Can you?"

Deegen did not answer immediately. "It really doesn't
matter if all I want to do is stop him." He seemed to be
trying the thought rather than endorsing it. Surely he
did really want the names of Toohy and Schmidt to go
forward. But that was the trouble with these games.

"You would have to come up with a surprise candidate."

"But who?"

Deegen began to move toward the monastery, and
soon he and Lewis came into the light over the gate.
Liberati left his tree and started toward the road. Suddenly he became aware of another figure in the darkness
and fear leapt in his throat.

"Who's that?"

"Fear not, it is I."

Liberati flicked his lighter and in its jumping illumi-
nation the gaunt face of Abbot Peregrine emerged from
darkness.

3

THE KNIGHTS drove from Rye in the van, Philip at
the wheel, Roger in the back, strapped into the swivel
chair in which he could revolve like a gunner though

mainly he slept, looking like a baby. Talking to Laura about Roger had broken the ice between them. In anecdotal form, Roger's antics seemed the lovable foibles of a domesticated bear.

Item: the paperboy came to be paid; Roger asked him to wait while he went for Philip, on the way picked up a book, got lost in it, and the poor kid stood on the doorstep for half an hour, Roger too immersed in his book to notice the doorbell ringing. Item: intrigued by a story in the *Times* about an archeological find in the Baths of Caracella, Roger put through a call to a friend at the American Academy and chatted for several hours. The person he called formed the impression that Roger too was in Rome and while surprised by the length of conversation did not dream it was long distance. Knight received an astronomical phone bill. It went on. Overflowing bathtubs, TV dinners cooked to ashes, Bach suddenly dispelling the nighttime quiet when a restless Roger decided to put on a record at the highest volume. Knight, levitating from his bed at the roar of sound, resented having his wrath construed as an antipathy to Bach.

Laura loved it.

"He is also the family Catholic."

"Oh?"

"He converted after reading the *Summa* of Thomas Aquinas and a church history by Jedin. He waddled down to a Manhattan church and told the priest he wanted to be baptized."

"What proof did he find convincing?"

"None. He says that if proofs were convincing the Church would not be what she claims to be."

"I'd like to meet Roger."

And then she told him Harry wanted the Knights to

attend the bishops' meeting that had just been announced. As journalists.

"You're kidding."

"You will represent our monthly magazine *Revelations.*"

The drive from Rye had been grueling yet somehow refreshing, the terror of the traffic balanced by the opportunity to let his mind wander untended over the terrain of the task given him by Harry Packard. He imagined people who would be stupefied by the thought of Philip Knight on his way to a Trappist monastery. He thought of the near impossibility of himself, an outsider, managing to flush from his episcopal incognito a buried agent of the KGB. He thought of Laura. When he finally entered Kentucky he found the countryside attractive and distinctive, the occasional horse farm giving just the right touch. Bluegrass all the way.

His mood of insouciance left him when he entered Bardstown and was only miles from his destination. If it was pleasant to control his own travel, this gave the possibility of changing his mind at any point, reversing direction, getting the hell out of there. What business did he have nosing around a meeting of the Catholic bishops of the United States? It didn't matter that he had a perfectly legitimate cover. In the back seat Roger slept, his lips fluttering as he exhaled, having seen all he cared to of the Kentucky countryside.

In Bardstown, at a circular intersection, Knight spotted a tourist information office and kept going around the circle until he could pull up in front of it. Parked, the motor turned off, he waited for Roger to awaken and wonder where they were. But the sonorous sounds continued. Knight got out of the car, slammed the door shut, and went into the information office. At

1 1 9

the counter he turned to see Roger, his fat face rising like a moon into wakefulness, look around, unkempt, unattractive, unhappy to have been banged back into consciousness by the slammed door.

The woman behind the counter was bright as a penny. Her identification badge informed him that she was Marjorie and a member of the Junior League of Bardstown.

"How do I get to Gethsemani Abbey?" he asked Marjorie.

She had been smiling when he came in and she was smiling now. Her face looked as if it had been sprayed to retain the smile the way her hair had been sprayed to keep the bouffant superstructure that added another-half-head to her height.

"You wanna go to the Trappist monastery? That's how we all talk about it here. What you said? We never call it that. It's just the Trappist abbey locally."

Either she suffered from a dearth of customers or she was just naturally loquacious. Knight leaned on the counter and urged her on from irrelevancy to irrelevancy. Suddenly Marjorie's smile cracked and began to fade. She was looking beyond him with something akin to horror. Knight turned to see Roger trying to get through the door. His efforts, and falling asleep in the car, had twisted his enormous trousers one way while somehow, topside, he was twisted the other. He looked like a bloated corkscrew.

"This is only Bardstown," Roger announced. He repeated it insistently as if Marjorie and the whole Junior League had been misrepresenting their location.

"He's with me," Knight explained to Marjorie. She whipped out a copy of a cutesy map of the region that looked like a place mat from an inexpensive restaurant.

She plunked it on the counter and drew a route in a bold line with a felt-tip pen.

"You just go right around the circle again and head out here and you can't miss it. It's maybe twelve miles." She pressed the map into Knight's hand, a woman who might never smile again. Roger had gotten through the door and was looking around for a place to sit.

"Get back in the car, Roger. We'll be on our way in a minute."

Roger could not be accused of disobedience. He rotated slowly and began again to negotiate the door. Knight turned back to Marjorie who was watching Roger in horrified fascination. "He's not a carnivore," he whispered.

Marjorie nodded nervously at this precious information. "I didn't think he looked like one."

"Looks have nothing to with it. I'm a carnivore."

Marjorie backed away from the counter and her eyes were fearful. "It's a free country," she said with a total lack of conviction. And, since Knight was by now headed for the door and Roger was already outside, huffing and puffing and staring at passersby, she added, "We don't have much of that sort of thing around here."

"You will," Knight said cheerfully. "Don't worry."

He could have found the monastery without Marjorie's map. He had given that to Roger, appointing him navigator, and so was subjected to a continual commentary from behind as he drove.

No horse farms around here. The road rose and fell, the houses became smaller and happier. He was clocking the mileage, and when he passed twelve miles he was sure Marjorie had got it wrong. But then they came to a rise in the road and on the left were the monastery buildings, looking like nothing so much as a state prison;

and directly ahead a yellow light flashed in the bright afternoon. Knight slowed, hung a left at the intersection, then another, and headed toward the monastery gate and the parking area. Journey's end.

It had not started so smoothly. Roger had packed everything but clothes, something Knight luckily discovered in his final inspection before leaving Rye. They had stopped one night on their way. Knight got Roger a separate unit in the motel. A mistake. Roger never looked at television but he had spent the night watching in his motel room, the volume turned up full. Other guests phoned the office, the office phoned Roger and Roger of course did not answer. Eventually Knight was wakened and the manager let him into Roger's unit. The noise was so deafening that no amount of knocking would have gotten Roger's attention.

Roger was spread over both the double beds, which he had shoved together. Pop cans, at least a dozen, were scattered around the room. Roger wore only the bottoms of his pajamas, enough material to sheet the Spanish Armada. He still wore a shirt and tie. He must have turned on the set in the midst of getting ready for bed.

"There are thirty-four channels on this thing," Roger said. "Two of them pornographic. I had not realized the practical effect of cable." On the screen an episode of "Father Knows Best" blasted inanities into the room. Knight turned down the volume. It must have been his imagination, but he thought he heard a collective sigh. Or perhaps it was the manager's way of saying thank you and good night. The door had closed.

Roger's appearance in the Bardstown tourist office was thus simply one more episode causing Knight to think he had made the mistake of the half century in bringing his brother along. Getting him into the guesthouse attracted the help of several monks whose shaved heads and black-on-white habits fascinated Roger as much as they did Knight. A wheelchair was brought out from the little shop next to the gate. Knight shook his head. Even if he needed it, Roger would not have got one bun into the chair. Still, it was a pardonable error, thinking Roger was handicapped. He was backing out of the truck and his foot was groping in air. Because of his belly he could not look down to find the step. For Roger, walking was a kind of Braille. Knight took the gyrating foot and guided it to the step. He should have left Roger in Rye where he was perfectly content and had more than enough to occupy himself during Knight's absence. His relative immobility would prevent him from seeing much of the monastery personally. Though he had been good company on the road, Knight admitted, when he wasn't asleep. Or reading Chateaubriand's work on De Rance, the father of the Cistercian reform.

The distance from the van to the entrance of the guesthouse was perhaps thirty yards, a trip they made in something like a quarter hour. By that time it was clear to Father Hyacinth, the guest master, that it would be a misdeed for which he would be eternally answerable if he put Roger on the second floor. So they were both given rooms on the first after two bearded adolescents were displaced and sent upstairs. When Knight saw the narrowness of the rooms he again wished he had left Roger in Rye. Each room was scarcely wider than the single bed that was its chief item of furniture. In the remaining aisle of space a chair and a small desk with a humming electric clock prevented passage to the window. With arms extended Knight could touch both walls. If Roger were shoehorned into such a room he might never get out again. He went next door where Hyacinth was helping Roger.

To his immense surprise Roger, having scooped in air

1 2 3

and held his breath, got into the room and professed to find it just right.

"I'm afraid they're all the same size," the monk apologized, and he sounded genuinely unhappy. "Actually I think our cells may be slightly larger."

"This is great," Roger roared. Did he fear being assigned to a cell? A cell could not be more austere than the guest rooms in Knight's estimation. Thank God his experience at the Wilson in Washington had prompted him to bring along a supply of rye. He had the feeling he would need it.

"Have the other reporters arrived?" he asked Hyacinth.

The monk was as tall as Knight. His head looked like five o'clock shadow, his body seemed to be making a perpetual bow and he spoke as if he would literally have to give an account of every word that issued from his mouth.

"Matthew Hanratty came yesterday. His room is upstairs, nearest to the chapel. There is another just across the hall from him. Neal. I do not remember the last name."

That would be Neal Admirari, of the *National Catholic Reporter*. Knight decided to take the bull by the horns; he went upstairs and down the hall to Admirari's room. The door was open. The reporter lay on the bed, hands behind his head, staring at the ceiling. His eyes moved to take in Knight, then went back to the ceiling.

"I am lying in state," he announced. "The state of Kentucky. The land of bourbon. Do you realize that most of the countryside is dry."

"I brought something with me."

Admirari sat up like the son of the widow of Naim. "I will construe that as an offer." He went to the sink and picked up a glass. "I'll bring this. Where's your room?"

"Downstairs. My brother and I just got in."

"I thought there were no empty rooms down there. I'm Neal Admirari."

"Philip Knight."

Admirari went ahead of him down the hall. "I came by cab from Bardstown. I was lying there wondering how far I would have to go for a drink and how much it would cost. You here for the big do?"

"I write for *Revelations*."

Admirari looked over his shoulder with an eyebrow cocked. "Packard is covering this?"

"I'm new with him. Maybe he decided to start me off with something easy."

"This may be soporific. Unless you are well into churchy gossip that is. Frankly I am weary of it all. I feel like one of those poor devils who lurk in sacristies. Are we nearly there?"

They were there. Admirari overshot the room and caught sight of Roger. When the reporter drew back his head he seemed taller than his five foot ten. "My God, the Goodyear blimp is here too."

"That's Roger."

"He seems to be asleep."

"It doesn't matter. He doesn't drink."

In his own room, Knight gave Admirari the chair, which the reporter tipped back against the sink. Knight sat on the bed, lifted his glass, "Cheers."

"Chin chin. I didn't know Jack Daniels made a rye."

"Oh, yes. It's not bad."

"Hanratty is off brown-nosing Carey. I sometimes think that bishops bring out in him what screen stars do in adolescents. He is completely fascinated by the higher clergy. This might be understood in one who sees them only from afar, but Matthew has been rubbing shoulders and whatever with them for years and the old spark is still there."

"He strikes me as more critical than adulatory."

"That is his disguise. How did you come to work for Packard?"

"He called me up."

Admirari's mouth went down at the corners as he shrugged. If Knight didn't want to talk about it, to hell with it. "Who's Roger?"

"My brother."

"Are you being Christian or literal?"

"Literal. Same parents. He is a prodigy. He was a prodigy. He is very smart."

"What's he doing here?"

"He's on retreat."

"From what?"

"He's a Catholic."

Neal Admirari found that terribly funny. His laughter consisted in a progressive lack of oxygen and sounded like gasping.

"Apart from being soporific, what will happen at the meeting tomorrow?"

"We get a briefing tonight. I wonder how many of the brethren will be on hand. Happen? Why a gesture will be made, one that will be given whatever significance it has because we are here. Carey has become a specialist in media events. He is no more for the popular election of bishops than Deegen is. I suppose the thought gives them pause. Where would either of them be in a truly democratic church? No, Carey has the soul of a cleric. He doesn't object to the centralization of power so long as he is at the center."

"Packard thinks he wants someone well to the left in New York."

1 2 6

"As do we all." He flashed a brief but wicked smile. "Almost all. But most important is that it be *his* man who is in New York. Oh, I have watched the Most Reverend Austin Carey operate for years. He is a Machiavellian in the best sense of the term, if there is a best sense. The true sense. Power. *Numero uno.* That's Carey."

"You don't like him?"

"My dear fellow, I am one of his most ardent admirers. Unlike Hanratty, I am not a spoiled priest. I do not cover church events with the wistful sadness of an unrequited lover. I can understand people like Carey. It's Hanratty I can't fathom." Admirari tipped his chair forward and whispered confidentially. "I can't figure out these monks either and the abbot is the worst of the lot."

"I haven't met him."

"You will. He told me that he feels a spiritual responsibility for anyone who comes under his roof. Hyacinth puts it differently. It's part of the rule. The guest is to be treated as if he were Jesus himself."

"They intend to crucify us?"

Again the wheezing laughter. Admirari was either a good audience or he was starved for amusement. Knight poured the reporter another drink. Would Hanratty be so tolerant of an interloper in the ranks of the reporters? Admirari seemed singularly incurious about the fact that the Free World Policy Committee had sent a reporter to a bishop's meeting. Knight doubted Hanratty would be so irenic. Even so he was unprepared for what happened at the news briefing later that day.

The briefing was held at seven in the guesthouse library. There were six reporters—seven if Knight counted himself—and they made a surly group, having just learned that they faced a nonalcoholic evening at least. Neal Admirari gave Knight a smile of complicity as Liberati was harangued by Agatha Kakia, a free-lancer and a nationally feared feminist (Admirari's ironic description) and Peter Featherweight, British, an ex-Dominican, twice married, who had cast himself in the role of interpreting the Roman Church for those who had been outside it longer than himself and had made a rather good thing of it. Again, Knight's source was Neal Admirari.

"Couldn't they break out a little sacristy wine, Monsignor?"

"Get up, Peter," a photographer in the back called. "I want to get your picture."

"If Peter could get up it would be worth a picture. His first wife claimed he was impotent." Admirari spoke in a stage whisper.

"What does his second wife say?"

"I suspect she considers it a blessing—or whatever apostates call graces."

Agatha Kakia said it was her understanding that Trappists were known for their beer. Liberati said she was thinking of Belgian Trappists. Agatha asked that he not tell her what she was thinking. Neal Admirari did not have to tell Knight that Liberati was getting off to a bad start.

"Look, borrow a car, drive to Bardstown, bring back supplies. Not that it would hurt you to abstain for an hour or two. After all, even journalists can use a stay in a monastery as an occasion to improve their spiritual lives."

During these preliminaries, Roger wandered in and, having arranged two chairs, lowered himself onto them. This caused sufficient distraction to change the mood slightly, and Liberati made the few announcements he had. The bishops would meet in the abbey church. This choice of venue had the advantage that the press could look down on them from the visitors' loft. Admirari mumbled that he had been looking down on them for years. The rye had induced a sardonic euphoria in him. He had smuggled a brimming glass back to his room and Knight had promised they would go to Bardstown the next day and get more. Liberati was straightforward on the point of the meeting.

"To see if there is a consensus among the bishops as to Cardinal Fergus's successor in New York."

"Who are the candidates, Monsignor?" Lulu van Ackeren from the *Register* always addressed Liberati formally and despite her youth exhibited a dated reverence toward the clergy. (Admirari: "It embarrasses some of them even to be called Father. Sometimes I think all that forelock tugging is Lulu's way of needling.") "I have heard Bishop Haley's name mentioned."

Hanratty spoke up. "I have heard the names of Toohy and Schmidt mentioned."

"Doubtless there will be others. The point, as I needn't tell you, is that something novel and important for the Church in America is taking place at this meeting. The bishops in conference and in full view of the press will attempt to be guided by the Holy Spirit as they undertake this important task."

"Did the pope ask them to do this, Monsignor?" Lulu asked sweetly.

Liberati's smile was indulgent. "That is a fascinating view of the Church, Lulu. A bishop in his diocese, and a conference of bishops in a nation, can initiate actions without being told to do so by the pope."

"I realize that, Monsignor, but hasn't this activity always been reserved to the apostolic delegate and the pope?"

"The apostolic delegate has always received nominations from individuals, among them bishops. What is new is that the bishops meeting here represent the NCCB and will collectively come up with a nominee."

One of the chairs he sat on tipped over with an attention-commanding bang when Roger stood up. "Wouldn't it be both a greater change and a return to tradition if the people of the archdiocese of New York had a say in the selection of their new bishop? I think of Anselm's election, and Saint Augustine's. The latter accepted more or less against his will. *Vox populi, vox Dei*. Why not go the whole way?"

Liberati peered over the others, a slight smile on his face. "I didn't catch your name."

"Roger Knight, Monsignor."

"This meeting is for reporters, Mr. Knight."

"That is my understanding. I am here as assistant to Philip Knight."

"Philip Knight. That is *obscurum per obscurius*, I'm afraid. Who is Philip Knight?"

"He is a private investigator employed by Harry Packard of the Free World Policy Committee. Mr. Knight has been rooting around in old stories of mine at the *Times'* morgue. May I suggest that this briefing be restricted to working members of the press?" Matthew Hanratty stood to say this. His body revolved as he spoke until he was facing Philip Knight. But it was Neal Admirari who answered.

"Knight is a correspondent for *Revelation*, a recognized periodical."

At the podium, a young priest came up and whispered in Liberati's ear. The monsignor then tapped on his podium with the side of his watch.

"Mr. Knight has been recognized by the Washington office as an authentic member of the press."

"Which Mr. Knight?" Hanratty sounded coldly angry.

"Philip Knight," Liberati said, after consulting with the young priest.

"But not Roger Knight, the gentleman who was just entertaining us with vignettes from church history?" It having been established that Roger did not have press credentials, Matthew lifted a hand as if he were hailing a cab. "Then I ask that Roger Knight leave this briefing for reporters. Apparently I must tolerate Philip Knight, who has been hired by Harry Packard to investigate me with an eye, I suppose, to smearing my good name."

Knight stood up. "As Roger said, he is here as my assistant. Could we forget this nonsense and get back to tomorrow's meeting? Is the procedure being followed here a first step toward the popular election of bishops?"

"I resent your characterization of my concern . . ." Hanratty began, but he was drowned out by the others. Agatha Kakia wanted to know if any women were likely to be nominated. This drew hoots and Agatha, who was dying for a martini, looked around with fire in her eye. Lulu's next question had to be repeated, but the second time it caught the attention of the others.

"Is it true that the conference suppressed a brief on the popular election of bishops based on the views of Serbati-Rosmini?"

Now Liberati was angry. He looked guilty as charged. The young priest came up to whisper in his ear.

"Lulu, I'm ashamed of you. Father Lewis tells me that such a brief arrived at the office but not in time for us to include it in the materials prepared for the bishops. May I say that all this talk of the popular election of bishops is getting us off on a tangent? Let's talk of what is being done, not of something else."

"You mean the unpopular election of bishops?" Admirari asked.

"Now, Neal, I know that you support the reason for this meeting. Let's not waste our time scoring points."

The briefing continued in this erratic and directionless way. It occurred to Knight that no one who ever attended a press conference could retain the idea that journalists are interested in finding out the truth. The point is to sting their victim into making an outrageous and quotable remark. By the rules of the game Liberati hadn't done badly, but he hadn't done particularly well either. When the meeting broke up, Knight's first concern was Roger, so he was not immediately aware that Hanratty was confronting him. "You don't frighten me, Knight. Tell Packard that. This kind of psychological intimidation is a new low, even for Harry. I shall go on writing as I like, without fear or favor."

"Who are you?" Knight asked ingenuously.

Obviously this was the last thing Hanratty had expected him to say. The idea! Pretending that he did not know Matthew Hanratty. The religion editor of the *Times* took one step backward, stared speechlessly up at Knight, then fled for the stairwell.

"Well done," Neal Admirari said, punching Knight's arm. "See you tomorrow."

Roger was rolling down the hall to his diminutive room. He had set his alarm for 2:45. He meant to get up for vigils. Knight meant to get up when he got up. The first session—called that to avoid the suggestion that Cardinal Carey would need only one to ram through what he wanted—did not start until nine. It was now not quite nine in the evening. It could have been midnight, it could have been two in the morning. Knight was sure it was half psychological but this seclusion and quiet made him very sleepy, so sleepy that his narrow cell-like room looked inviting. Soporific, as Neal Admirari might say.

4

THE CHURCH of the Abbey of Our Lady of Gethsemani was stark enough to satisfy a Quaker. As seen from the visitors' loft, it did not look as wide as it was because of the height of the sheer, white walls. The high, narrow windows contained glass stained with muted colors, gray, light blue, off-white, the uneven pieces modernistically arranged. The floor of the loft had a forward slant so that even sitting in a pew Matthew Hanratty had the sense that he was about to pitch forward and take his place once more with his erstwhile brethren. Except that the choir stalls below, their woodwork the result of craft and love, were now filling with bishops wearing red-piped cassocks with capelike shoulder covers. The pectoral cross and episcopal ring looked decadent in these austere surroundings. They came to the center of the church and, unlike the monks who bowed deeply out of respect to the Blessed Sacrament, doffed their birettas and genuflected. The little red beanie remained on the crown of the head when the biretta was removed and Hanratty resolved to get that into his story. It seemed somehow symbolic of a sleight of hand.

He was still seething from the press briefing of the previous evening. Liberati had let him down, there was no doubt of that. He deserved better of the executive secretary and Liberati knew it. It wrankled to think how easily Harry Packard could introduce his agent into the internal affairs of the Catholic Church. Not that Hanratty thought Packard was all that curious about a bishops' meeting. The real reason was the one he had publicly stated. Packard was making a crude attempt to intimidate a reporter, thinking mistakenly that it would be easier to work his will on Hanratty than on the bishops. The connection? Any fool could see that. Fergus and Packard had been friends, allies, as close as an agnostic and a believer could be. Matthew Hanratty had pulled few punches in reporting the intransigent and stonewalling tactics of Cardinal Fergus. Doubtless the two men had discussed what they would have regarded as his persecution. Since Fergus's unfortunate death Parkard had probably begun to associate Hanratty with the savages who had gunned him down in Rome. He would know this was irrational. But now with interest building in the way Fergus's successor would be chosen, Packard had decided to use this occasion to avenge himself on Hanratty for all past grievances.

Matthew Hanratty developed this script in his mind and as he did so he had not the least doubt that it represented the real world. There would have been little point in his vocation as religion editor if he did not prove a thorn in the flesh to people like Harry Packard. He *counted* on Packard's being a mortal enemy. Hanratty wrote with his enemies, not his friends, in mind. Progress is a fragile thing. There are always people and forces trying to stem it, stop it, turn it back. That is how Hanratty saw Harry Packard, that is how he had seen Cardinal Fergus. He would have been worse than naive if he accepted the fiction that Philip Knight was here as a bona fide member of the press. And that bloated brother of his!

Roger Knight sat in front of Hanratty now, taking up most of a pew. He sat in its exact center and it bowed beneath him. He was alone in the pew. He was asleep and audibly snoring. His dress was odd, very odd. Oriental? Or could he be wearing pajamas? A wicked thought occurred to Hanratty. Roger had risen for vigils at three, had fallen asleep, and spent the rest of the night in the visitor's loft. Hanratty's shoulder rose and fell in silent laughter.

His colleagues did not find it a joke that the whole of a first row pew had been commandeered so that they would have to look either over or around Roger or to stand in front of him at the railing if they wanted to follow the proceedings. Their discomfort did not diminish Hanratty's mirth. A lot of help they had been to him the night before. He was not worried about his own vantage point. After he had made certain his presence in the loft was noticed, he would slip away, using his familiarity with the monastery to get to a privileged position from which he could follow the proceedings up close. Neal Admirari suddenly slipped into the pew beside him. "When we're out together dancing cheek to cheek," he murmured as his thigh pressed against Hanratty's. Hanratty moved away from this disgusting, if feigned, intimacy while trying not to feel too judgmental. It helped that he knew Admirari was anything but queer. It was common knowledge that he was smitten by Lulu.

"I told her I'd turn Catholic, anything, but she spurns me."

Admirari was witty and amusing. Everyone said so. Hanratty was no judge. A sense of humor was a luxury he couldn't afford.

"I hope I'm not disturbing your prayers."

"I'm praying for you."

"Nymph in thy orisons be all my sins remembered. Have they started?"

"No." If was five after nine. "They're not all here yet."

"Hanratty Says Bishops Not All Here. Nice headline. A leader from our leader. Does Knight really bother you?"

Hanratty snorted in answer. In the front pew there were more stentorian snorts. Roger rolled back and forth; he seemed to be waking up.

"Buddha emerges from mystic state," Admirari whispered.

"I think he spent the night here."

"Such devotion. Where's Philip?"

Hanratty ignored that. To answer would have been tantamount to repudiating what he had said in the briefing. He would not treat Philip Knight as if he were a colleague.

"Excuse me a minute." He rose and tried to slip past Admirari but that annoying ass would not let him.

"You'll need permission to go to the lavatory."

"Neal, please!"

"I just stood up."

"Oh, for God's sake!"

"Well if you put it that way." Neal stepped into the aisle and collided with Philip Knight. Hanratty went around them and hurried up the aisle.

Below the loft was an abbreviated choir stall set at right angles with those that faced one another in the body of the church. Hanratty got comfortable on a folding chair. By half rising to his feet or tipping his body right or left he had a good view of the bishops. They were nearly all in their stalls. And Peregrine was in the place reserved for the abbot!

Hanratty stood up and stared. What on earth was the abbot doing? There seemed little doubt that he was there on invitation. Cardinal Carey, in a stall opposite the abbot, gave Peregrine a nod and the abbot gave the opening prayer.

"Almighty God, Father, Son, and Holy Spirit, we call down upon this gathering of successors of the apostles your blessing, your light, your love."

As the prayer continued, Hanratty sat marveling at how theatrical Peregrine's voice had become, not in the sense of being bombastic or fruity, but in the controlled solemnity of his tone, the modulations so minute as to be reminiscent of Gregorian chant. Hanratty had never seen Peregrine perform liturgically as abbot, but why should he be surprised that his old friend was so good? This place, this particular setting, having a Trappist abbot give the invocation, lent a dignity and impressiveness to the gathering of bishops that simply was not there when they met in the ballroom of a hotel. In suits, they looked like businessmen. Here they had the undeniable look of spiritual leaders. Peregrine's invocation seemed a genuine prayer, not the ritual bowing of heads and mouthing of trite phrases before the political infighting began. Abbot Peregrine created the impression that they had all just come into the presence of God and that this must alter their sense of what they were about. Finally, in his peroration—how irresistible—he quoted Hopkins. "The Holy Ghost over the bent world broods with warm breast and with, ah, bright wings."

Hanratty was thrilled. He was proud. He was moved. Peregrine's prayer had pierced the veneer of worldliness that always shocked Hanratty when he covered the gatherings of church leaders of any denomination. Religion, institutionalized, became a business, something to be run efficiently. Bishops had an annoying habit of feigned chumminess, just one of the boys, don't let all this religious patter put you off, we're just ordinary guys really. Try to imagine Peregrine slapping you on the back or pinching your elbow. But what was most palpable in the invocation was that this was the voice of one who believed. It almost seemed to Hanratty that Peregrine was acting as the agent of the religion editor of the *Times* and was up there socking it to the bishops in a way they had needed for a long time. But he rejected the thought as unworthy of the moment. He himself felt uplifted. Carey let a full minute elapse before speaking.

"Thank you, Father Abbot. The proceedings are now open. I will ask Monsignor Liberati, the executive secretary, to make some opening procedural remarks."

That quickly, it was business as usual. Except that it wasn't.

Liberati read blandly the proposal that, in keeping with the reforms of Vatican II, the mode of procedure of the synods held since the Council and the new code of canon law's definition of the nature and extent of the authority of national conferences of bishops, this meeting should take up the question of a fitting successor to the late Cardinal Fergus of New York.

Liberati read in a tentative way as if he expected at any moment to be interrupted. When he got through the statement there was a pause of a different sort than had followed Peregrine's prayer. Now was the moment when Archbishop Deegen would erupt. For starters, he might have a go at the invocation of the new code. Hanratty could have made the objection for him. He had read the relevant canons on his way down from New York. He would not have wanted the job of arguing that that section of the code provided even the suggestion of an authorization for what the bishops proposed to do here. The best that could be said was that it did not explicitly forbid it. But Deegen sat silent. Hanratty got to his feet, to make certain that the archbishop of New Orleans was indeed there. He was. He sat, staring straight ahead, his expression unreadable. Did he seriously mean to forego an opportunity to tie up the meeting with procedural wrangles? Carey cleared his throat.

"Are there any comments on the proposal?"

Bishop Crystal of Salt Lake asked how they would proceed. Carey fell upon the question as if it were a life raft and he afloat on fifty fathoms. Prepared for a procedural squabble, he wallowed in a detailed description of nominating and voting procedures.

"Do you have anything to add, Monsignor Liberati?"

Liberati had nothing to add. Carey declared the floor open to nominations. Archbishop Deegen rose in his choir stall.

"I withhold any judgment on the validity of these proceedings and put in nomination Bishop Toohy."

The nomination was seconded. One of Carey's minions nominated Haley. Now the scene was set. There were two candidates, there were two sides, a two-thirds vote was necessary for a nomination to carry. Father Lewis announced that there were exactly ninety-nine bishops in attendance. Sixty-six votes were thus required for a nomination. Voting would be by secret ballot.

If voting is the ritual of the modern republic, it seemed a literal ritual in the abbey chapel. On a table, placed where during choir the lector's podium stood, was a huge ciborium. The bishops approached this golden cup in measured lines, descending from the two choirs and advancing by twos up the aisle, each holding a slip of the stiff paper Father Lewis had distributed, folded once. Into the ciborium went the ballots. Hanratty did not time it, but he would have said that first ballot took half an hour. Father Lewis and Monsignor

Liberati counted the ballots while in the choir stalls the bishops whispered or talked aloud. Only Peregrine sat immobile, apparently deep in prayer.

"Monsignor Liberati, will you give the result of the balloting."

The result was inconclusive. Haley had received fifty-three votes, Toohy forty. The rest of the ballots were blank. Cardinal Carey rose.

"I would like to say a few words on behalf of Bishop Haley and on behalf of the majority who voted for him. Unfortunately that majority is not yet sufficient. Before going to a second ballot. I should like to indicate why Bishop Haley's majority should increase to the requisite two-thirds."

Carey was so boring and predictable in what he had to say that Hanratty thought his candidate might lose votes as a result of it. How shallow all the platitudes of liberal Catholicism sounded in this abbey church. Again Hanratty's eyes were drawn to Peregrine. Was he even listening to the cardinal archbishop of San Francisco? The thought came then that Peregrine could not in his role of abbot have had much to do with bishops. His travels would take him to other Trappist monasteries where his interlocutors would be abbots like himself. Hanratty was not sure of the ecclesiastical status of an abbot. He was a prelate, was he not? His liturgical garb was all but indistinguishable from a bishop's: miter, crosier, pectoral cross. But he was not a bishop. He could not ordain men to the priesthood, for instance. Had Peregrine ever seen so many bishops at any one time? It was unlikely. Cardinal Fergus had apparently come to the abbey, but Carey was a more standard sort of prince of the church. Peregrine should be intimidated. He should be definitely upstaged. Carey must have been condescending, however unwittingly, when he asked

Peregrine to sit in on the proceedings. Had he imagined a timid monk, hidden in his cowl, overwhelmed by all the high churchmen? Yet Peregrine sat with silent authority.

Carey's speech did not lose Haley votes; the second balloting brought the result of sixty-two for Haley and thirty-two for Toohy, with five blanks. When they adjourned for lunch it was with the thought that one more ballot or at most one more session would assure Haley's nomination.

The dining room of the guesthouse being inadequate for ninety-nine bishops, they were fed in the monastery refectory at a different time from the monks. Most of the bishops, Hanratty was informed, took the relative austerity of the surroundings much as retreatants did. Not that Peregrine apologized for the simple fare. Meat was served in the guesthouse, but it would have been too complicated to do that in the refectory and for so many. The vegetarian meal too was welcomed as if the bishops had been dying to take on ascetic practices.

"Father Abbot ate with them," Hyacinth told Hanratty, and Idelfonse the shoemaker elaborated.

"Such a young man, Matthew, yet they speak to him as an equal or more. And him as humble as the day he was born. God was good to us the day he gave us Peregrine for abbot. Do you remember him from your time here, Matthew?"

"We entered on almost the same day. We were novices together."

"And has God been good to you since you left us?"

Idelfonse was not someone with whom Hanratty cared to discuss his success in the world. It would seem worse than bragging. It would seem like pride.

Well, he was proud. He went for a solitary walk over by the bull pen and admitted to himself that it was no small thing to be religion editor of *The New York Times*. He wouldn't trade that for being abbot of Gethsemani any day of the week. He stopped walking. What an odd thought. Did Peregrine consider being abbot a form of success, as eminence? Certainly not. If he had authority it was the authority of a servant, a parent of sorts. Father Abbot.

A sign on a gate said "The Bull is in the Pasture." Warnings can be expressed in a variety of ways, a simple sentence like that, or a descriptive phrase. Wet cement. Or as a command. Keep off the grass. Hanratty took heed and started back toward the monastery.

No flood of sweet, sad memories assailed him as he walked here. No more did he look back on his married life, wringing the memories for whatever emotion they might produce. He had a way of moving out of the past definitively. He was no sentimentalist. He resolved to visit Merton's old hermitage but not to recall the days that were no more. He wanted to state with truth in his story that he had gone there again. On paper he would create a sense of nostalgia. Wasn't he better able to describe emotions because he seldom felt them? Peregrine too seemed immune to sentimentality just as he was free of ruthlessness. But when Matthew got back to the guesthouse and found Neal Admirari singing the praises of the abbot's performance, he registered a mild demur.

"It seems small praise, saying that a monk can pray."

"Pray?" Neal turned to him with a delighted smile. "Is that what he was doing? I couldn't hear very well up in the loft. Apparently you couldn't either. Where did you go?"

"Neal, as you know, I lived in this place for three years."

"Are you reenlisting?"

"Don't be absurd."

"I agree. I was worried. I thought maybe the Knight brothers had hired thugs to kidnap you and blunt your pen."

Hanratty smiled, being a good sport, wanting to wring Admirari's neck. Why did he have to be such a shit? Doubtless writing for the *NCR* was a pretty modest spot but it was surely better than working for a living. If only he had been able to voice such barbs and then handle adroitly the responses they would evoke.

Admirari was singing "In a Monastery Garden" when Hanratty left the group to go up to his room for forty winks. Honestly, Neal acted as if he was drunk.

The first afternoon ballot produced a sixty-five to thirty-two vote with two abstentions. Carey was at once happy and annoyed.

"Would someone care to change his vote?" he asked with forced sweetness.

"Point of order." It was Deegen. He wanted to know how it could be known that a vote was being changed since the ballots were not signed. Carey moved that the next ballot be signed but the motion was rejected. Once more the ritual of voting began. It was losing its power to impress, and Hanratty thought the bishops took less time about it than they had before.

This time there were no abstentions. The vote for Haley remained at sixty-five, one tantalizing vote short of the needed majority. Toohy received thirty-four votes. A motion was made to adjourn, but no one seconded it.

What happened next did not happen swiftly, but it was such a surprise that Hanratty was never sure of his memory of how it had happened. When he reconstructed it for his readers he had the distinct sense that he was writing fiction. Yet it happened and it happened like this.

Someone, it might have been Deegen, said "I wish Abbot Peregrine could vote. He might break the tie." But it couldn't have been Deegen, could it? No matter. Someone asked if further nominations could be made.

"I would like to nominate Bishop Schmidt."

And then another voice was heard, that of Athanasius against the Arians, as Hanratty inaptly put it. "I nominate Abbot Peregrine."

Total silence. Peregrine sat immobile in his abbot's stall. All eyes turned to him. He seemed an almost palpable alternative to this political wrangling.

"I second the motion," cried a more excited voice, and then cries of "Vote, vote, vote," were heard, and Father Lewis moved swiftly among them, distributing slips of paper.

A more than Trappist silence had fallen over the church when the bishops filed forward, two by two, and the procession regained the solemnity of the first ballot. Hanratty searched Cardinal Carey's face for a reaction to this surprising turn of events, but the archbishop of San Francisco looked neither elated nor depressed. Deegen's expression too seemed to take him beyond the pettiness of the previous sessions. Eventually the bishops were once more seated in their stalls. The ballots were counted but there was no longer any tension in the church. Hanratty thought again of the words of Hopkins that Peregrine had quoted that morning. *The Holy Ghost over the bent world broods with warm breast and with, ah, bright wings.*

"Do you have the results, Monsignor?" Carey asked Liberati.

Liberati read them. Haley ten, Toohy seventeen, Peregrine seventy-two.

Again they all looked at the abbot. He sat in silence for a moment and then he spoke. *"Non nobis, Domine, non nobis, sed nomini tuo da gloriam."*

Then he stood, rising in one flowing motion, and intoned the "Te Deum."

So it was with that ancient hymn of praise and thanksgiving that the representatives of the National Conference of Catholic Bishops solemnized their nomination of Abbot Peregrine of Our Lady of Gethsemani Abbey, Kentucky, to be the next archbishop of New York.

Book Two

Part 1

L I B E R A T I W A S N O T S U R P R I S E D when Cardinal
Carey emerged from the abbey church looking momentarily stunned by what had happened. Almost immediately other prelates crowded around to congratulate
him and Carey entered into the festivities with gusto.
Surely he had to feel a latent irony in the notion
that he had scored a triumph in the nomination of
Peregrine. Several days of careful planning had gone
up in smoke just before that final ballot. When Carey
freed himself and turned to Liberati his brow went up
and the corners of his mouth went down as he shrugged.

Liberati could think of nothing to say. By the time
it occurred to him that they could indeed claim to have

taken the initiative in choosing a successor to Fergus, Peregrine came out of the church and immediately there was a surge of bishops toward him. The others made way for Cardinal Carey and soon the archbishop of San Francisco was grasping the hand of Abbot Peregrine, his smile a mile wide. Peregrine might not have been his preferred candidate, but Carey was smart enough to go with the winner. Particularly a winner in need of the wise counsel of his elders.

Liberati thought of finding Lewis and going for a drink, but the company of the younger priest was always a mixed blessing. If anyone had a right to feel responsible for this outcome it was Lewis. The sight of Bishop Haley heading for the door decided Liberati and he hurried to catch up with him.

"Good choice, as far as I can see," Haley said. "I voted for him."

"A dark horse."

"In a white habit. Do you suppose Deegen knows something we don't?"

"About Peregrine? I doubt it. I'm still surprised he showed up."

"I could see him backing Toohy, but Peregrine? Maybe he would have switched to me if the meeting had dragged on." Haley laughed.

"You'll get a diocese," Liberati said.

"If I'm not careful." Haley dug Liberati in the ribs. "I'm going cross country. Want a good walk before dinner?"

"I better stick around."

"See you later."

Bishop Haley hitched up his cassock, went over a fence and set off rapidly across the field.

Liberati watched him go. He could believe Haley really did not give a damn. Go to New York? What a colossal headache a diocese that size would be, Haley had never been an Ordinary. (Winking, he would omit the article.) The little Maryknoller had dignity and pride but no vanity, if that made sense, and Liberati thought it did. He certainly seemed to be without ambition, as if he would be content to spend the rest of his days working with the USCC in Washington. Eventually, no doubt, Haley would be given some quiescent see and spend his last breath trying to raise it to what he considered responsible Catholicism.

He had come close to a totally different future in the abbey church in Gethsemani, close but no cigar. In the end, his fellow bishops had not been able to bring themselves to recommend him for the second largest see in the country. And Haley shrugged and went tramping off across the monastery fields. *I'm nobody. Who are you? Are you nobody too?* Emily Dickinson. Liberati stared out over the field but he no longer saw the diminishing figure of Bishop Haley.

Liberati's younger sister, Sylvia, had repeated that poem over and over when she was a girl, an incantation, a summing up of infinite sadness, worrying his parents, worrying Liberati too. Sylvia had been as wraithlike as the poet she loved. She was as dead as Emily now, dead for nearly fifteen years, her life snuffed out in an automobile accident one winter night when she was returning to Mount Holyoke. *I'm nobody. Who are you? Are you nobody too?* Sylvia's voice repeated itself with anguishing fidelity, as if she were there beside him in rural Kentucky, speaking softly in his ear the haunting words that seemed to presage her death at nineteen, the slight poem mocking ambition.

Well, if Haley did not see Peregrine's unexpected nomination as his own defeat, what of Toohy?

Liberati found him in the visitors' loft, seated, arms

folded, staring expressionlessly ahead. It would be back to Dubuque, no doubt for good, when, for a moment, New York had seemed a possible future. Liberati cleared his throat, and after a moment Toohy looked up at him. His brows lifted questioningly.

"Care to go for a walk, Bishop?"

Toohy would assume that Liberati wanted to talk official business—there was always some nonsense he could bring to the archbishop's attention—but he hoped that fresh air and a discussion of the day's unprecedented voting would make Toohy forget he had been called away from the chapel. Had he been praying or licking his wounds?

They had not walked far before they were discussing the vote.

"We speak loosely of the inspiration of the Holy Spirit, Monsignor. I believe the Holy Spirit does guide us. Alas, it is like the belief in providence. One hesitates to identify the inspired moments, just as one is loath to single out an event as providential."

Toohy was his own primary addressee. He cocked his head as he talked, as if fearful of missing a word, and he nodded in agreement with what he heard. They had come down the stairs from the loft and gone out to the parking lot by the guesthouse. Toohy stopped, interrupting himself with a raised hand. "Do I scandalize you, Monsignor Liberati?"

"Because you doubt Abbot Peregrine's selection was inspired and providential?"

Toohy shook his head vigorously and started to walk. "No, no, no. It was providential. What event is not? But inspired? I don't know. Now, if *I* had been selected . . ." He stopped and wheeled, pushing his face close to Liberati's. His smile was delayed and it was a relief when it came. If Toohy was being philosophical, it did not come as easily to him as it did to Haley.

They reached the road and turned to start back. Almost immediately Toohy drew to a stop. Coming toward them was the unmistakable figure of Roger Knight. The general effect of rotundity did not translate itself into easy movement. Roger looked like some great sea animal unjustly beached as he waved both arms in greeting and then let them come to him. Liberati made the introduction and Roger, taking the archbishop's hand, attempted to genuflect and kiss his ring. In stopping him, Toohy put his hand under Roger's elbow and was pulled off balance. Liberati rescued Toohy from a fall. Roger gazed at the archbishop of Dubuque with open-faced interest.

"I was struck by the description of your reading interests in a recent interview, Archbishop. Conservative Catholics in the wake of the French Revolution, fascinating."

Toohy ducked his head but smiled. "I came upon Chateaubriand early in life and he made a lasting impression. I don't know why. Other men are interested in baseball."

"Was it the *Memoirs*?"

"No. *The Genius of Christianity*. A big wonderful bogus book. I think of Chateaubriand as a *professional* Christian. There seems reason to doubt his religious beliefs penetrated his morals."

"Can one who writes so well produce a bogus book?"

"Do you read P. G. Wodehouse? He is an excellent writer with nothing to say."

When Liberati excused himself they were speaking of Barbey D'Aurevilly, his womanizing, his novels, his love of English literature. They sounded like sports buffs, exchanging arcane information, gusts of enthusiasm prompted by a remembered fact.

If it had been Monsignor Liberati's intention to take Bishop Toohy's mind off his troubles he had succeeded. He wished he could be similarly distracted from the growing resentment he felt for Father Lewis. The young man provided an uncomfortable reminder of Liberati himself at an earlier, more ambitious stage of his life. It did no good to deny that it had been Lewis, not himself, who had orchestrated this special meeting of the bishops. Nor could he imagine now that Lewis would have to shoulder the burden of defeat. Carey had already accepted Peregrine's victory. By now, buoyed by congratulations, he probably thought he had engineered it, no matter that the nomination had been made by someone else.

The only real question was, could Abbot Peregrine be brought within the Carey wing of the hierarchy. That there had been a meeting at all, that any vote had been taken, was thanks to Cardinal Carey. This was a truth that would doubtless be driven deep into the abbot's mind.

As he mounted the steps to his room, Liberati had a whimsical thought. What would Cardinal Fergus have made of this meeting and of its result? The obvious answer brought another thought. As inheritor of the Fergus wing of the hierarchy, Deegen was a far cry from the late cardinal archbishop of New York.

2

TALKING IT OVER with Roger, discussing it on the phone with Laura and Harry Packard, it seemed to Philip that he should run up to Superior, Wisconsin, and do a background check on Abbot Peregrine. The unexpected emergence of the abbot as the candidate of the American bishops delighted Laura, made Harry suspicious, and prodded Roger's curiosity.

Who had put the Trappist's name in nomination?

This had been much discussed in the bar in Bardstown to which the involuntarily sober press corps had fled when the conference came to an end. Even Matthew Hanratty was there, observing a sort of truce with the Knight brothers. So far as the others were concerned, both Philip and Roger were members in good standing of the fourth estate. But, then, Knight had put the first two rounds of drinks on his FWPC expense account. The gesture touched Lulu and Neal but Dolan from *Commonweal* was almost obsequious.

Neal Admirari said he would write that it was Haley who had first mentioned Peregrine's name.

"No, Deegen mentioned him first," Lulu said.

"He said he wished the abbot could vote so they could finish up."

"But Haley put his name in nomination."

Hanratty spoke apodictically. "It was Bishop Toohy. I was in the body of the church, below the loft where the rest of you were. I saw everything."

"Look," Lulu said. "I taped the sessions. Let's find out."

On the evidence of the tape, Toohy seemed to be the one who had put Peregrine's name forward. *Seemed.* Admirari was not convinced by the tape. Neither was

Lulu, oddly enough. There was a lot of echo and ir-relevant noise and more than one person had been speaking. Lulu was willing to say that Toohy had been talking when Peregrine's name was heard. But even if he *had* named him, you could not say he was the first.

Roger had no doubt that it had been Archbishop Deegen who was responsible for Peregrine's nomination. Knight wasn't sure. The question might be important and then again it might not. It all depended on what he learned in Superior.

In any case, if Lulu's recorder had picked up extrane-ous noise in the visitors' loft of the abbey church, it was difficult to hear it well in the racket of the Bardstown bar.

Despite a conversation with Dolan, Roger had been following the discussion of Peregrine's nomination. It was on their way back to the monastery that he said, "It was Archbishop Deegen who nominated him, though at that point it could have been anyone, I suppose. They were all swept up in the idea as soon as it was broached."

"By Haley?"

"By Bishop Haley, yes. But Deegen nominated him."

Over the phone Packard grew impatient when Knight recounted the discussion among the members of the press in Bardstown. "It figures," he growled. "They're all right there and they can't agree what they saw or heard."

"Surely the tape should have settled the matter," Laura said.

"Get a copy of it," Packard ordered.

It was decided to leave Roger at the monastery while Philip made the flying trip to Superior. The prospect delighted Roger, the more so because Archbishop Toohy was staying on at least for another day.

It was after dark when Knight got to Superior. He rented a car at the airport and stopped at a motel south of the city where he washed and ate before driving into town. It was a raw, rough-looking place, tipped toward the water as toward its reason for being. Knight had the sense of being on the edge of the world, though to the north there was the whole of Canada and beyond the Northwest Territories. He could imagine how it had been a century and more ago. Not much different from today, except perhaps more prosperous then.

The favored drink in the bar he stopped at was a glass of beer and a shot. Blended whiskey was what you got if you asked for whiskey. Not seeing any behind the bar, Knight decided against asking for rye. It might sound like an affectation and he did not want to draw attention to himself. Did he find it difficult to imagine Peregrine coming from such a town? The difficulty lay in imagining anyone staying.

He asked the bartender for a paper.

"I've got a *St. Paul Pioneer Press.*"

"How about the local paper?"

It was called the *Sentinel.* Knight would have liked to ask if there had been coverage of Abbot Peregrine's nomination as archbishop of New York. Local monk makes good. It was another topic not wisely pursued in that bar.

His motel, when he returned to it, was asparkle in the night as if it were noonday, but actually it was sound asleep. The empty swimming pool glittered blue-green under artificial light, the great sign beckoned late travelers into this plastic haven; it crackled and buzzed and there was a cloud of insects visible as Knight passed beneath it, following the taxi that had turned in ahead of him.

The bald-headed man in the back seat of the cab had the look of one of the monks he had left behind in Kentucky.

3

AFTER VIGILS the monks could either go back to their cells or have coffee. The library was a favored place, second only to the little sitting room beyond it where on chill mornings a fire crackled and the sense of camaraderie was almost palpable. Before his election as abbot, Peregrine had spent that time in the library reading. How the fare there had changed over the years. When he entered it would have been unthinkable to find news magazines available for perusing. That was the world they had left. Now that world came into the monastery in a dozen slick forms, with text and photographs and an outlook diametrically opposed to that which had led twentieth-century Americans to choose to live out their days in this austere place. Work and pray. *Ora et labora.* The old Benedictine motto. For his early morning reading Peregrine had preferred journals of theology and the spiritual life to those packaged perspectives on what was considered the news of the world. He did not need them.

After his election as abbot he sensed that the others were uncomfortable to have him there with them. His predecessor, Blaise, had been seldom seen save in his authoritative role. Peregrine had thought the others resented that and would like a change. Apparently not. He took up jogging.

He would change in the carpenter's shop, which was

some distance from the main buildings. When he set off he might have been, except for his close-cropped hair, any urban runner off to do his morning miles. Others ran to preserve or regain their health, to prolong life. But it was the contemplative aspect of jogging that appealed to Peregrine.

This had come as a surprise, but of course it had not come at once. At first the pain and weariness made the practice penitential, and he would come stumbling back to the carpenter's shop with leaden legs, pumping heart, sweat streaming down his face and obscuring his vision. It took ten or fifteen minutes of puffing collapse before he felt capable of a cold shower, possible thanks to his own makeshift plumbing. Once more in his habit, he returned to the main building with some semblance of the dignity of office.

But as he continued to run, the strain on his body lessened and he resisted the impulse to increase the distance and the time devoted to running. More and ever more would have insured the continuance of pain but by then he had found in the boring repetitive act a freeing of the mind, a soaring of the spirit, that turned a quondam penance into one of the most joyous deeds of his day. Some monks would have stopped running when they reached this point. The old school looked askance at any sought-after pleasure, or pain for that matter. Pains and pleasures come willy-nilly in the life of man. It is the monk's task to let neither become the guide of life. Both must be subjected to a higher telos.

Telos. Peregrine smiled. That had been a word favored by Richard his novice master. Later Peregrine learned that Richard had been a devotee of Kierkegaard. It had been the Dane and not the Greeks who bequeathed the word to him. Richard had been a great one for subjecting one's will to the will of one's superiors.

To his own, of course, but only because he was a stand-in for the abbot. The abbot was the supreme authority. Would Richard have been so insistent on that if he had dreamed that one day the gawky, awkward, and spiritually illiterate Peregrine would become abbot of Our Lady of Gethsemani? Perhaps Richard considered it a sign of divine mercy that he had been sent to the monastery in Utah before Peregrine's election. Peregrine, on his first visitation to the house in Utah, had spoken briefly with Richard.

"You are content here, Brother?"

"Yes, Father Abbot."

"You can return to Gethsemani whenever you wish."

"It is not what I wish, Father Abbot." Richard spoke the sentence without emphasis, leaving it amphibolous. Was he saying he did not want to go back or that what he wanted did not matter? Peregrine let the matter drop. Richard's bowed head had the look of a pomegranate. Ridged, imperfectly round, stubbled with spikes of hair. He kept his eyes downcast in an attitude of humility before his superior. Peregrine told Richard that monks now applied to use Father Louis's hermitage, wanting to spend a week or two of solitude there. He knew Richard had been one of Thomas Merton's admirers. Had he shared the artist monk's penchant for the hermetic life?

"There is no hermitage here," Richard said.

"Do you wish there were?"

Richard shook his head slowly. "That is not our life, Father Abbot."

So it wasn't. But becoming abbot turned one into a kind of hermit. Peregrine's main contact during the day was with Joachim, his secretary, a recent replacement for Walter who had been secretary to two previous abbots as well as to Peregrine. Walter had trouble con-

1 6 0

trolling his weight even on a monastery diet. Some months ago he had been felled by a stroke and now lay wasting in the infirmary. Joachim admitted to the ability to type, had none of the usual pious demurs when confronted with what might be considered a promotion, and Peregrine appointed him as Walter's replacement, though not without a sense of disloyalty that took him often to the infirmary. Yesterday, after the meeting in the abbey church, Peregrine had gone to the infirmary. Walter was ecstatic about the result of the bishops' conference.

"Have I been such a bad abbot, Walter?"

Never kid a kidder. Walter was notorious for the innocent pranks he played on his brother monks. But Peregrine's question threw him into consternation. He avowed that Peregrine was an excellent abbot.

"Then you want me to stay?"

For someone as simple and good as Walter, the question posed a difficulty of Solomonian proportions. He rose to the occasion.

"With God's grace you will make the right choice."

The beautiful thing about Walter was that coming from him such an expression was neither obsequious nor merely pious. Peregrine felt, not for the first time, what a chasm there was between these monks and their spiritual father.

The morning after the bishops' meeting, in shorts and hooded sweatshirt, Peregrine set off on his run as if he were escaping all the dignitaries who had stayed on as guests. But soon he was jogging in satisfying solitude along the path that skirted one of their fields, then led into a woods, and, beyond, to a vast uncultivated tract of land. He was master of all he surveyed on these morning runs, legal master, spiritual master. An abbot, even in the more genial post-Vatican II Church, retained most of the characteristics of an autocrat. Within reason, he could do whatever he liked. Travel, for example. The demands made on him in exchange for such autonomy were minimal. A monastery all but runs itself. He had not been abbot long before he realized what a temptation to pride, to laxity, to worldliness, his position was. Had he even wondered about this when Blaise was abbot? No. His predecessor had been a man of total rectitude, a monk to the soles of his feet. To be a religious superior was for him to be the servant of the community. There was little doubt that Blaise would have been as content in the humblest station in the house as he was with the eminence of being abbot.

Eminence. That was how one addressed a cardinal. It was easier to see the fittingness of the title as it applied to a Cardinal Fergus or a Cardinal Carey. From the months of his novitiate Peregrine had been trained to see the abbot as a figure of authority, but it was impossible to think of an abbot in terms of worldly rank. He occupied a special place in choir. He dressed only slightly differently from the other monks. At Mass he wore a miter and carried a crosier, the staff which had become bejeweled and stylized for bishops, but was unadorned wood, chastely carved, for a Trappist abbot. How many men would regard being first in a house like this as success?

The strange truth was that Peregrine had been more surprised by his election as abbot than he had been by the result of the bishops' meeting in his abbey church. He had tried to turn down the post of abbot, but this was taken as ritualistic humility, almost a sign that the choice had been a good one. After he was installed, Peregrine felt marked, set aside as a sacrificial animal is set aside. The early pains of jogging were welcome as recompense for his unworthiness. As the weeks passed and the pain receded he welcomed the early morning opportunity for solitary thought. It came to seem almost his principal act of worship. Almost. Mass, the Divine Office, these liturgical activities were the center of the monastic life. Work too was prayer, and in its way jogging was as well.

It was a crisp morning, there was a film of frost on the ground and his breath puffed visibly before his face like a reminder of mortality. The steady thump of his sneakered feet, the sound of his breathing, the sweat flowing down the sides of his body, sound and motion measured by time. A jay squawked shrilly, a rabbit, all but one with its environment, regarded him with unblinking eye, one ear angled, poised.

So in a way had Peregrine been poised for over twenty years, waiting, waiting for he knew not what.

Over the years the description of the monk's life as one of leaving the world had come to seem right to him. He had gradually lost touch with the man he had been before entering. He could no longer recapture his original motive for becoming a monk. It had been lost in being one. The realization came almost as a surprise. I am a Trappist monk.

Election as abbot shook his hope that he had been forgotten, that the distant incredible past had never been and he was only what he seemed. He had waited, thinking now it will begin. And nothing happened. Apparently this was not it. It was too fanciful to imagine that they could arrange the outcome of an abbatial election.

His nomination by the bishops' conference was another thing entirely. It was unmistakable now. They had not forgotten him. His choice could be attributed to the Holy Spirit, the hand of God. But Peregrine was convinced another power had been at work, a power that would reveal itself when he returned to his monastery, where Cardinal Carey and Archbishop Deegen and others awaited him.

4

THE SURPRISES BEGAN when Knight discovered at the newspaper's office that the *Superior Sentinel* had carried no local color story on the surprise nomination of its native son to become the next archbishop of New York. There were only wire service stories and they had not been featured. Clearly this was an item of national news the editors felt had no particular significance for the city beside the lake.

He had just returned the paper to the custodian when a short, red-faced man followed his belly into the room.

"Avalonic. Editor of the *Sentinel*. I don't know you."

"No reason why you should. Philip Knight."

Avalonic tucked in his chin and looked at Knight over the top of his glasses. "Never met before, did we?"

"I'm from out of town."

"Ah. Getting all the help you need here?"

"No complaints."

"Good. Good." He started out of the room and stopped. "If we had met, I would have remembered."

Knight was tempted to deflate Avalonic's balloon by telling him of the goof on the Peregrine story but at that moment the clerk dropped the bound volume Knight had just returned and the sound seemed to shoot the editor into the hallway. It was just as well. Before he chided Avalonic he wanted to see what the *Sentinel* had on the Green family prior to their son's departure for the Trappists. The girl who had dropped the book let it lie and looked abjectly at Knight.

"The little twit. He just loves to pop in like that and then I have to drop a darned book."

Knight adopted a sympathetic expression but he could think of nothing to say.

"He really means that. He never forgets a face. I wish he would forget mine."

"Have you worked here long?"

"He's my uncle."

"I see."

"Do you want anything else?"

He wanted microfilms of every issue of the *Sentinel* containing news about the Greens.

"What Greens?"

"Every Greens. I don't know. Are there many in town?"

"My uncle would know."

"I don't want to bother him if I can help it."

"I wouldn't let you. That's my job."

She did it thoroughly and he spent the rest of the day at the reader, running columns of photographed type past his aching eyes. Perry Green had won a spelling bee when he was in seventh grade. His address was given and that narrowed the field. Perry Green became an Eagle Scout at fifteen, which seemed young to Knight. It was. The story went on about the record-setting time it had taken Scout Green to rise to the pinnacle. Perry's mother was a member of the American Association of University Women and appeared on the society page with some regularity. She smiled confidently into the camera, dominating any group she was a part of. Mr. Green made the paper only once, when he was elected an alternate to the state convention of the Republican Party.

The last mention of any of the family was twenty-three years ago. They had been out on the lake when suddenly a small-craft warning went up. They did not make it back to the harbor before the weather hit and their boat capsized. Three days passed before the bodies were found. Perry Green, aged nineteen, was dead.

Knight sat back and rubbed his eyes. The human eye was not made to read microfilm for any length of time. He could almost believe it was weariness that accounted for the incredible story. He read it again, carefully. The context made it clear that all three bodies had been found, but a case could be made that this was an inference. There had been a service in Saint Benedict's Catholic Church, the parents and their son handled in one funeral Mass. Burial had been at Holy Angels Cemetery.

The caution that had made him hesitate to tease Avalonic about his failure to pick up the local significance of the Peregrine story now made him go back to the Greens he had set aside earlier. But none of the others provided any connection with Peregrine. There had been only one Perry Green and he had been drowned in Lake Superior along with his parents.

There remained the outside possibility that the boy's body had not been found and that he had been memorialized in absentia at the funeral Mass. Knight returned the microfilm to the girl.

"All finished?"

"I guess so."

"Where are you from anyway?"

"Out East."

"Find what you were looking for?" She glanced with mild interest at the reels of film.

Knight sighed. "It's not the first wild goose chase I've been on."

"Relatives?"

"How do you mean?"

"Genealogy. That's the big thing now. Half the people who come here are tracing their families."

"I try to forget mine."

"You and me both." She seemed to be referring to her uncle.

"Well, so long, Miss Avalonic."

"Hey, my name's not Avalonic. He's my uncle by marriage. My name is Bright, not too, as he says."

"What does he know?"

Holy Angels Cemetery was appropriately bleak. The entrance featured local stone, two great pillars of it between which hung a massive wrought-iron gate. A sign he had to get out of the car to read directed him to a secondary entrance. Before following the instructions, he let himself in and went to the cemetery office. This was housed in a building that must have been designed for the purpose but that nonetheless had the look of a redesigned residence. Knight crossed a large, empty hallway and entered a room whose main feature was a great curved window that distorted the out-of-doors. A man was seated very stiffly behind a desk in front of the window and was at first only a silhouette. He moved, so he was not a display. Knight approached and mentioned the plot whose location he sought.

"Recent?"

"Twenty-three years ago."

The slightest of pauses before the man pushed back from the desk and scooted in his wheeled chair to the filing cabinet. "Twenty-three years ago," he repeated the words dreamily, as if he were trying to remember the music. He pulled open a drawer. "Name?"

"Green."

"The family that drowned?"

"How do you happen to remember a thing like that?"

"I just do."

"After tweny-three years?"

"Memory is strange."

"Yours is. The parents and a son."

"Their boat tipped over in a storm."

"Surely you can't remember everyone buried here that well."

"Not everyone buried here is related to me."

His name was not Green but Sutter and he had been a cousin of Mr. Green. He had not worked at the cemetery then, that came later, after his accident. He rapped on one leg and produced a sharp sound. He had lost his leg in a fire.

"In a fire?" Dear God. Knight had an image of Sutter's limb burning away like a candle.

"I jumped through a window and all but tore my leg off. Accidents run in the family. So do noses." He snickered.

"Are all three bodies buried here?"

Sutter frowned in incomprehension.

"I mean, the boy and the two parents."

Sutter pulled a sheet halfway from the file. "All three. Not that I have to check. Plot H67d. Do you want to take a look at it?"

Knight said he did and Sutter wheeled back to his desk and produced a map of the grounds and began to mark it. When he handed it over, he said, "May I ask what your interest in the grave is?"

"I'm sorry but I can't divulge that information." He

had tried in vain to think of a plausible lie. Perhaps if Sutter had not been related to the Greens he would have come up with something. Sutter seemed undisturbed by his reply. He nodded as if acknowledging that he had stepped—or rolled—across some line.

"You did say that three bodies are buried there, Mr. and Mrs. Green and their son Perry?"

"All three of them in the one plot. Yes. Is there some doubt . . ." Sutter stopped himself. "I'm sorry."

"That's all right." He felt that he should be apologizing to Sutter for resurrecting, as it were, painful memories.

The grave was in a depression overlooked by a mountain ash. A quite large stone with Green engraved on it and then three names. Mildred and Basil and Perry. A ground squirrel scampered across the grass as Knight stood by the grave. It was still possible that there was some mistake, but the possibility was remote in the extreme. The Perry Green Abbot Peregrine claimed to be had lain buried here for decades.

He thought of returning to the *Sentinel* and asking Avalonic about the Green family. But first he would go back to the cemetery office and see if Sutter could cast some light. He drove his rented car over the crackling gravel drive and pulled up in front of the building. He crossed the porch, entered the house and was almost to Sutter's desk before he saw him.

He had tipped forward out of his wheelchair and apparently had not put out his hands to break his fall. His arms were tucked in close to his body, the palms of his hands exposed. The ugly gash in the back of his head suggested that Sutter had been in the next world before his body hit the floor.

5

H A R R Y P A C K A R D had taken the afternoon off and it was not until Laura got back from lunch that she learned that Cecily, a new file clerk, was also gone. For anyone other than Harry it would have been an odd way to celebrate the nomination of Abbot Peregrine to succeed Cardinal Fergus, but the director of the FWPC was no ordinary man. Poor little Cecily. They were going to have to be more explicit in warning the new girls. The call from Superior and the sudden and welcome sound of Philip Knight's voice dispelled Laura's pique.

Until she learned the point of his call.

"How can he be dead and buried and Abbot of Gethsemani? There has to be some mistake."

"Then there are two. The man in the cemetery office has been murdered. I am calling from the airport. My plane leaves in twenty minutes. I hope to be back in Kentucky before the body is discovered."

Even after she got the story straight, it seemed twisted. Peregrine had drowned in Lake Superior twenty-three years ago and his cousin was murdered while Philip was visiting the grave.

"Why would anyone want to kill him?"

"To remove the record of the burial. The book where Sutter looked up the location of the grave is missing. Someone is trying to destroy Peregrine's past. Which is crazy because it isn't possible. For one thing, there are all kinds of newspaper accounts. Oh my God."

"What's the matter?"

"Laura, maybe I better stay here. Let me talk to Harry Packard."

"He's not in."

"Where the hell is he?"

"Can I help?"

"I wish Roger were home rather than down in that damned monastery." He made an impatient sound and she realized he was worried about his brother. "Will you see Packard later today?"

"Probably not until tomorrow."

"Damn. Look, this is the problem. I have spent the day asking in various places about Perry Green. That is going to make me an object of interest when Sutter's body is found."

"But you're leaving town."

"I don't know." He told her about the girl in the newspaper office who had helped him trace Perry Green. And of Avalonic.

"Call him, Philip. If anything has happened to her he will know. Then get on that plane."

It's what Harry would have told him, Laura was sure of it, but as she said it, it sounded a good deal less noble than his concern for Miss Bright. He thanked her and hung up, and Laura was left sitting at her desk, stunned by his revelation. She felt foolish when she remembered how indignantly she had countered Harry's suspicions.

"Harry, he has been buried in a Trappist monastery for twenty years. Of course you haven't heard of him."

"I don't mean me."

"All right. No one has heard of him. That's the good thing about it. Twenty years of silence. What greater recommendation could there be?"

What pleased Laura about the nomination, apart from the unexpectedness of it, was the thought that someone holy had been selected for a high ecclesiastical post. It seemed time that there be bishops who were distinguishable from bankers or salesmen. Imagine a saint as archbishop of New York. Besides, Archbishop Deegen was for Peregrine, and that was all the endorsement he needed. Laura was pleased that all the plotting and troublemaking of Cardinal Carey and his friends had come to naught.

"They voted for Peregrine," Harry groused.

"What else could they do? Their own candidate couldn't make it. The place was taken by storm."

"Wendell Willkie."

She looked blank.

"You wouldn't remember Willkie. He was nominated in 1940 and it was a big surprise. A carefully orchestrated surprise. The galleries of the Republican National Convention had been packed with supporters."

"In this case, the only people in the gallery were the press."

"Tell me one thing," Harry said. "Who is disappointed that Peregrine was nominated? What kind of reversal or failure is it when nobody complains, nobody is disappointed, everybody is happy as a lark?"

Laura had been happy as a lark and now it turned out that Harry had been right to be dubious. She had been naive. How could a meeting engineered as that one had been bring a good result? Nonetheless, she sat there trying to imagine an innocuous explanation for Philip Knight's discovery. Peregrine was not Perry Green. Very well. Perhaps he had assumed the dead boy's identity to cover up some impediment in his own past to a monastic vocation. Years had passed, he had proved himself, he had been elected abbot. The whole thing could be made right.

How she wished she could believe that. How she wished she could think about that special meeting of the bishops and the nomination of Peregrine without thinking of Cardinal Fergus and his disturbing microcassette.

She reached for the phone and dialed the number of Myrtle's office.

"Myrtle Tillman, please," she said, surprised to hear a male voice when the phone was answered.

"Could I take a message?"

"I'd like to talk with Myrtle, isn't she there?"

"Not at the moment. Who's calling?"

Laura hung up the phone, surprising herself with her rudeness, but she had not liked the tone of the man's voice. He must be the supercilious monsignor Myrtle could not abide.

The phone in Myrtle's Village apartment rang and rang unanswered. Her inability to get hold of Myrtle made Laura uneasy. She should have persisted with that monsignor and found out where Myrtle was. She was tempted to call back but did not. She could not suppress the thought that Cardinal Fergus's tape might have put Myrtle in danger. Finally Laura did ring the chancery again, but by then the office was closed. In Myrtle's apartment the phone continued to ring unanswered.

Philip Knight telephoned again when he got back to Kentucky, reaching her at home.

"The girl's all right. But someone got at the microfilm collection and stole some spools. The girl told her uncle it must have been me. I was the last one to use them."

"Could someone actually remove every trace of Perry Green?"

"It looks like someone is trying."

"But that's crazy. *You* know about him."

"I know, sure. But how do I prove it?"

"Oh."

"Abbot Peregrine knows too."

"Philip, we can't permit him to become archbishop of New York. Who *is* he anyway?"

How eerie it was, the man she had so recently idealized turned suddenly into a sinister figure. She told Philip she was unable to reach Myrtle.

"The tape. Roger had the same thought."

"I wish you were home so you could check on her."

6

PHILIP KNIGHT came out of the phone booth in the Louisville airport. The terminal, all but deserted, was filled with odd echoing sounds. His flight had not been the last one of the night, however. Scattered throughout the waiting room were small clusters of people waiting for the flight due in from Chicago at one o'clock. Amplified voices issued from hidden speakers, and Knight felt pursued by bodiless spirits as he crossed to the revolving doors.

Outside the night was cool. He stepped from the curb and started toward the parking lot just as a voice announced as if from on high that cars parked in front of the terminal building would be towed away at the owner's expense. As far as Knight could see, there were no illegally parked cars. Perhaps the announcement was a recording. He imagined it going on and on with no one to hear it, like the telegraph key in *On the Beach*. Discovering that Perry Green had been dead for twenty-three years did odd things to his imagination.

In the van, following the faint cones of his headlights over the country road, he wondered what to do next. He had no obligation to confront Abbot Peregrine with the fact that he was an impostor. If the abbot's falsely assumed identity—or, more accurately, abandoned false identity—had any connection to the job he had taken on for Harry Packard, Knight did not see it. He was glad now that he had been unable to talk with Packard. Somehow he was sure his employer would have suggested a disquieting confrontation based on the discovery Knight had made in Superior. This was a problem Philip much preferred to discuss with Roger. He hoped his brother would see the wisdom of their piling into the van and heading back to Rye.

Roger was still awake, door ajar, light on, sprawled on the cot he had pulled to the center of the room so that he could spill equally over its sides. He listened impassively to Philip's story, which sounded incredible whispered in the wee hours in a guest room of a Trappist monastery. Roger began to pull at his ear lobes.

"So who is Abbot Peregrine?"

"That I didn't find out."

"I think we should."

"Why? More importantly, how?"

"We'll ask him." And Roger maneuvered a leg over the side of the bed, his toes twitching like feelers as his foot neared the floor.

"Roger, it's nearly one thirty in the morning."

"The monks will be up for vigils."

"Well, I won't. I am exhausted. I am going to get some sleep and I suggest that in the morning we get the hell out of here."

Roger shook his head, causing his jowls to sway importantly. "You can't. It looks as if Abbot Peregrine is his candidate."

"Whose candidate?"

"The bishop you've been hired to identify."

It was the obvious explanation, certainly, but Philip said nothing. This prompted Roger into an elaboration of the thought, and it was all Philip could do to keep his brother's voice low enough so that he did not waken everyone in the guesthouse. Fortunately, since the departure of the bishops, he and Roger had their end of the first floor corridor all to themselves.

The conspiracy Roger sketched was worthy of the fears of Cardinal Fergus, Philip had to grant him that.

"Start at the beginning," Roger said, as much to himself as to Philip. "Fergus is murdered in Rome. Along with others, but they are victims only because they happen to be with him when the assassin strikes. Cardinal Fergus is killed in order to quiet a voice of warning *and* to open up the see of New York. The next step is to fill the post with their own man. To that end, an unprecedented meeting of the bishops is called, and called here, and out of the blue, as it seems, the abbot, hitherto unknown, is chosen by the bishops as their candidate to succeed Cardinal Fergus. Philip, those who do not know what you discovered in Superior assume that the plans of the uppity liberal bishops went awry and a saintly Trappist, hidden away in obscurity these many years, was selected as a result of the all but palpable intervention of the Holy Ghost. And Peregrine is a mole."

"You don't know that."

"Like the bishop Fergus spoke of, he is a mole, planted here to wait for just this opportunity." Roger paused. "But others will discover that Perry Green is dead."

Philip finished his story, telling Roger about Sutter and the microfilm missing from the *Sentinel* morgue. Roger nodded, smiling, setting his jowls aquiver.

"Of course! That is just what they would have the audacity to try. They destroy the record so no one can prove . . ." He stopped and looked at Philip, suddenly serious. "You're in danger. They must know you found out about Perry Green."

Philip shook his head. "I don't think so."

"Why?"

"Because I'm here."

"Ah."

Roger might welcome it as Q.E.D. but Philip's relief was more than intellectual. He only hoped he wasn't whistling in the dark. On the flight from Chicago to Louisville he had told himself that if Sutter's killer had known of Philip Knight's inquiries he would have done unto him what he had already done to Sutter. It did not make sense that his investigation in Superior could be known and he be allowed to live. The concern he felt for the Bright girl had concealed a deeper concern for himself.

"Maybe you were simply too elusive for them," Roger said. Did he view this remark as praise?

"It's the Superior police I'm worried about. They'll trace me to my motel and conclude that I'm the murderer they're looking for."

Through the window Roger had left open despite the chill came the sound of a car on the road that ran some fifty yards from the guesthouse. The two brothers listened to the motor as if they could not continue their discussion until it passed. But it did not pass. It slowed and then shifted gears. Philip went to the window and looked out.

It was a pickup truck, one Knight had noticed before. Presumably it belonged to the monastery. After turning into the abbey road, the driver shut off his lights and seemed to coast down the slight incline toward the entrance of the cloistered yard. Then the truck went out of sight. There was no further noise from the motor. But the sound of a door opening and then shutting, not with a slam but carefully, was clearly audible.

"One of the monks?" Philip asked.

Roger shrugged. "What time is it?"

It was after two. Nearly two fifteen. Knight realized he was exhausted.

"I'm going to bed. We can talk in the morning."

"We can't leave, Philip. We have to find out who Peregrine is."

"What difference does it make?"

"He can lead us to the bishop."

Philip only nodded at the thought that he might so easily accomplish what he had been hired by Harry Packard to do. It had been a long day. He pulled the door shut and went down the hall to his own room. He got ready for bed in the dark and was asleep mere minutes after his head touched the pillow.

He did not sleep long. The sound of Roger crashing into wakefulness woke him. The alarm in the next room rang on until finally its sound was nipped, a bed and then Roger complained, and water began to run into the sink. Philip tried to will himself back to sleep, cleansing his mind as if it were a blackboard, seeking to fill it with nothingness and sink once more into oblivion. Who has ever fallen asleep by trying? Five minutes after Roger went audibly down the hall toward the chapel, Philip followed him.

There were no lights on in the visitors' loft and few in the church below. Knight went to the railing and looked down at the monks in their stalls. Their thin plaintive chant rose in supplication to God, presumably hovering over Kentucky and receptive to their prayer. Knight fixed his eyes on the abbot's stall. Peregrine was there, shadowy, a silhouette, scarcely visible. Who was he?

He turned and moved slowly up the inclined loft, past the massive figure of Roger. There were two or three others scattered about in the pews, doubtless praying along with the monks or joining them in spirit. Knight left the loft and in the hall outside wondered where he could wait in order to intercept Peregrine after the office was done. Roger was right. He must confront the abbot with what he had learned in Superior. He could not go back to Washington and let Laura know he had failed to put the question to Peregrine.

Philip went down the stone steps to ground level and entered the chapel beneath the loft. The voices of the monks were louder here but they were separated from him by the back wall of the chapel. There were doors to his left and right. He went to the right and pushed open the door. An arctic chill embraced him from the deeper darkness of the corridor. He stepped back and looked at the legend above the open door. Cloister. He went through and let the door close slowly behind him. He was in the enclosed part of the monastery where only the monks were permitted.

Good God, it was cold. It seemed to emanate from the walls, the floor, the low ceiling of the corridor and wrap him round. It was obvious here that the long habits of the monks, their cloaks and hoods, impressive as they were, had been designed for more than aesthetic considerations.

He moved slowly along the corridor, guided by the flickering flames of votive lights, which together with vases of flowers surrounded a Pietà. Knight was nearly upon the shrine before he saw the kneeling figure. One of the monks, unaccountably not in choir, almost prostrate before a rough-hewn image of Mary holding her slain son. It seemed indecent to come upon someone so rapt in prayer, and instinctively Knight began to back away in the direction from which he had come.

A hand closed on his arm.

He swung to face another monk, tall, his grip strong,

his hood pulled far forward over the head, the ghost of Christmas past. "Are you lost, Mr. Knight?"

The monk spoke softly and immediately began moving Knight more and more rapidly away from the shrine and his praying confrere. Knight had violated the sanctum sanctorum. Would this monk now punish him in some terrible way? He hadn't felt so scared since being mugged in Central Park.

"I want to speak to the abbot," Knight said and his voice sounded like that of a boy caught stealing. But he had to give some reason for having entered the cloister.

"Father Abbot is in choir, Mr. Knight."

"I thought I could catch him afterward."

The monk seemed to think. They were no longer moving. He lifted a hand and swept back his hood, and in the semidarkness Knight could make out the thin face, the shaved head, the oddly luminous eyes.

"We will go to the abbot's office."

The monk's grip tightened as they began again to walk. Knight felt that he was being led by a Seeing Eye dog. He did not want to go to the abbot's office. He wanted to get the hell back to his room. He felt like a fool. He had snuck into the cloister and been apprehended and now he was being taken to the principal for a scolding.

"I'll see him later," Knight said. He tried to stop but a struggle would have been necessary to halt his escort.

"After choir is a good time."

Everywhere else in the world this was the dead of night, the predawn hours. Here it was coming on visiting hours. They came to a door, which the monk opened. He then stepped aside so that Knight could enter.

"I am Joachim," he said, crossing the austere room to the desk. "I am Father Abbot's secretary. Do sit down." He indicated a chair next to the desk.

Knight sank slowly into the chair.

"You wish to interview Father Abbot, Mr. Knight?"

Knight could have cheered this reminder of the cover Harry Packard had provided him. Of course. He was a journalist, creeping about in the dark where he didn't belong in quest of a scoop. He nodded, affecting a world-weary air. Joachim put a long-fingered hand on a manila folder, the only item on the desk.

"Father Abbot understands that there will be curiosity about him because of his nomination. This folder contains the essential facts."

Joachim's voice was unmodulated, like the voices of the monks in choir as they intoned the line of a psalm *recto tono*. Knight's arm still felt Joachim's grip. It seemed even colder in the office than in the corridor outside. The essential facts about Peregrine's life? But he already knew what lies would be there.

Joachim opened the folder and began to read and as he did so he seemed to emphasize just the facts Knight knew to be false. The thin voice turned into audible sound the data from the file and, listening, Knight was assailed by memories of Superior, the Bright girl and, worse, Sutter. The monk had finished and was staring at him.

"Does this information match your own, Mr. Knight?"

Suddenly he realized that his fear was not merely a manifestation of the eerie strangeness of the monastic cloister. He got to his feet and to the door, but Joachim was no less agile. He was at Knight's side in an instant. Once more that powerful hand closed on Knight's arm. In the corridor hooded monks were streaming from the chapel. Knight wrenched free and joined them, lost in the sea of the community, safe for the moment.

He had to get out of there.

He had to get Roger and leave.

He thought of the shaved head in the car ahead of his own when he pulled into the motel in Superior. The sound of the truck returning, heard from Roger's window in the guesthouse, also seemed part of the puzzle.

If Joachim knew he had been to Superior and what he had discovered there, his life and Roger's were both in danger.

Part 2

I

WHEN ARCHBISHOP DEEGEN showed up in his office and said he wanted Liberati to come with him while he paid a visit to the apostolic delegate, there was little the monsignor could do but go along. He didn't have time to tell Father Lewis where he was going. He did not have time to ask the archbishop of New Orleans about the purpose of his call on the delegate.

Deegen had a car outside and there at the wheel was Lewis. The priest glanced swiftly at Liberati, lifted his eyes a trifle, then looked away. A double kidnapping?

At the delegate's, Lewis was left in the car and Deegen took Liberati by the elbow as they went toward the door.

"I want a witness, Monsignor. That's your role."

Liberati was not reassured.

"Do you mind if I smoke, Archbishop?" Deegen asked as soon as they were settled in Rossi's study.

The apostolic delegate shrugged, a martyr's look on his face, and Deegen struck a match. With a series of deep, steady puffs he began to fill Rossi's office with pungent cigar smoke. Liberati could not recall ever having seen Deegen smoke before. The cigar seemed a way of establishing parity. You would have thought that Deegen did not want his reputation for being ultramontane to suggest he had much patience with Vatican diplomats. His loyalty was to the pope, not to such enigmatic professionals as Rossi.

"I want to talk about New York," Deegen said, launching a gray-blue smoke ring.

Rossi nodded. "It is an important archdiocese." His eyes slid to Liberati, then back to Deegen.

"What did you think of our meeting in Kentucky, Archbishop Rossi?"

"I was aware of it, certainly. I reported its outcome to the Holy See."

Deegen said, "You were rightly outraged that we had been convened for such a purpose. So was I. It was grandstanding, pure and simple. I went to the meeting with the express intention of blocking efforts to get a majority vote in favor of any proposed replacement for Fergus."

"I believe you yourself nominated a candidate," Rossi said softly.

"A ploy to prevent a sufficient majority for Cardinal Carey's candidate." Deegen turned to Liberati, smoke escaping from the corners of his mouth. "The official candidate."

"Your plan did not succeed," Rossi observed.

"No. But neither did his. That isn't the point. Archbishop Rossi, I think we came up with an excellent

184

candidate and I don't think it should count against Abbot Peregrine that his name was put forward in so unorthodox a fashion. That was an extraordinary meeting, Archbishop. First of all, the setting was right. A monastery. The atmosphere was appropriate for serious consideration of important matters. Tell me, have you ever met Abbot Peregrine?"

"I regret to say I haven't."

"Let me urge you to do so. Ask him to come see you."

Rossi's training made it unlikely that he would respond directly to so abrupt a suggestion.

"Archbishop Rossi, let me sketch the situation as it is now."

Liberati sat blinking through Deegen's unflattering recital of the circumstances created by publicity-hungry people in the USCC and NCCB. But the damage had been done. The current problem was to control it.

"No, not just control it. The whole thing can be put to good purpose. Look, what if we had nominated Toohy or Schmidt? If that had happened, I would be offering totally different advice."

"What would your advice have been then?"

"That a statement be issued clarifying how bishops are actually appointed in the Roman Catholic Church. The straw vote taken in Kentucky could of course have been described as interesting to the Holy See. Nonetheless, the Holy Father would proceed according to time honored practice."

"That would have amounted to a public slap in the face to your national conference."

"A return slap."

"Not a very Christian reaction, Archbishop Deegen."

"The alternative would have been to collude in the usurpation of power. To give aid and comfort to Americanism."

1 8 5

Liberati felt he should say something, he wasn't sure what.

Rossi said, "But you would advise otherwise now?"

"Yes! The problem with following that advice is that the American press would interpret it as heavy-handed and autocratic, a willful ignoring of American desires concerning an important appointment in this country. We could have ridden that out, of course, but it would have been stormy weather."

"What has changed?"

"With respect to the deed done, nothing. What changes it all is the man named, Abbot Peregrine. I do not think a better man could be found."

"What are his characteristics?"

Deegen puffed on his cigar. "After the election, after the dust settled, some of us sat down with Abbot Peregrine. Monsignor Liberati was there too. Part of the stupidity of the proceedings was that few bishops knew anything about the man we had just recommended for New York. I don't think Peregrine would mind my telling you about that session."

"Did he accept the nomination?"

"On that I can quote him exactly. 'You must be clear that I am completely at the disposal of the Holy Father. I have no desire or ambition to become archbishop of New York. I came to this monastery with the expectation of living and dying here.' "

Rossi nodded noncommittally.

"He was asked about his vocation to the Trappists. You would have been impressed, Archbishop Rossi. We were all impressed."

"What attracted him to so austere a life?"

Liberati remembered that when Peregrine was asked the question, he fell silent as if he had never before had to describe the odyssey that had brought him to the

1 8 6

Trappists. What he then said was obvious, of course. But it did not seem so when he spoke.

"The sense of mortality," Peregrine said. What had turned him into a Trappist was the sense of mortality.

In Rossi's office, Archbishop Deegen put down his cigar, leaned back in his chair and stared at the ceiling, as if recapturing that session with the abbot of Our Lady of Gethsemani.

At the time, Deegen had taken Peregrine to mean that, having narrowly escaped death, he regarded his life as a gift from God, one that he would offer back to his creator. Peregrine considered the suggestion, then shook his head.

"Archbishop, have you ever watched a spider descend on its thread? Unless it is caught by sunlight the thread is invisible but we know it is there. It is the insect's lifeline, his way back whence he has come. How easily that thread can be snapped. What is our thread? An improbable mixture of gases that makes this planet hospitable to life. I have often read that the modern mind is unreceptive to the idea of God. Surely that cannot be true. The modern mind has a vivid sense of the precariousness of human existence. Nuclear war, the destruction of the ozone layer and the polar ice cap. A few years ago, it was the population explosion. Chemical wastes, upsetting the ecological balance. . . . I do not read the secular press very often, Archbishop, but when I do I am struck by the apocalyptic tone of so many articles. Man is mortal. That is an old truth; it is a modern one as well. What sense is there in a creature like ourselves, coming into existence and going out of existence, conscious of the process as it takes place? That is the great difference, setting off the human species from all the others. Humans reflect on their trajectory through time and that ability enables them to project beyond its ostensible term. In thought, and because of thought, we do not think our death is our end. A creature capable of thought cannot entirely cease to be."

Listening to Peregrine, Liberati had remembered the thoughts he had had in the Kentucky night before he was surprised by Abbot Peregrine—youthful thoughts, seminary thoughts. It had always seemed silly to think that a couple of sentences arranged in a certain way could produce a claim that could not be refuted. What Peregrine was saying sounded like the old proof for the immortality of the soul.

"Death," Peregrine had said, pronouncing the word in such a way that those listening to him had the sensation of hearing it for the first time. "Death."

"Our lives consist largely in distracting ourselves from the incredible fact that we must one day die. I did not want to lead a life of distraction. Here, in the monastery, our way of living is a dying. We spend our lives learning how to die."

Deegen's voice trailed away, leaving silence. After a moment, the delegate said, "You were impressed, obviously."

"Places like that monastery, men like Peregrine, keep the Church afloat."

Rossi nodded as at a pious remark.

"You will be impressed too, Archbishop Rossi, when you meet him."

Rossi stirred in his chair, as if disturbed by the suggestion that he do something. "Monsignor Liberati, you were at the meeting. What were your impressions of the abbot?"

It was at moments like this that Liberati knew he had acquired the soul of a bureaucrat. Without hesitation he said that Archbishop Deegen had put the matter most impressively. He indicated by his manner that he had no thoughts of his own, sharing so completely in those of Deegen. Obsequiousness, thy name is Liberati.

Deegen was impatient with the idea that Liberati's impressions were either here or there.

"Archbishop Rossi, I think it was providential that our bishops' conference was held in that monastery. I had never been there before. Chances are I might never have met Abbot Peregrine. When our meeting was convened there, we all were pursuing our own ends, good ends, I hope, but only superficially grasped. Our means were political and there was much vanity and ambition involved. We deadlocked and suddenly the thought of putting forward Abbot Peregrine came and an overwhelming majority immediately saw the wisdom of it.

Rossi rolled forward in his chair. "That is something that intrigues me, Archbishop. Is it so certain that the naming of Abbot Peregrine happened just because you could not find another candidate to attract a majority vote?"

"What do you mean?"

"Was it an accident?"

Deegen picked up his cigar. "No one planned the nomination of Peregrine."

"Who put forward his name?"

"Formally? I think I can claim that honor."

"Why formally?"

"I had heard the suggestion. Was it yours, Monsignor?"

"Father Lewis."

"Perhaps. There had already been a facetious remark about how good it would be if the abbot had a vote. One more vote and Haley would have been our nominee. That Peregrine might vote and that we might vote for Peregrine seemed two sides to one thought. Where do ideas come from?" Deegen seemed unwilling to give Father Lewis credit for the suggestion.

Rossi seemed undecided about whether to rise to the philosophical bait. Various nonanswers competed for possession of his dewlapped, ruddy face. And then came his Sibylline response. "I like your idea that I should meet with Abbot Peregrine."

"Good! May I ask if his name had ever been brought to your attention prior to our meeting in Kentucky?" As he asked this question Deegen slowly rotated his cigar in the ashtray, freeing a long, gray cylinder of ash.

"His name had been mentioned, yes. But not as a possible bishop, if that is the point of your question. Cardinal Fergus spoke to me of Abbot Peregrine on several occasions."

"He did!"

"He had made retreats at Gethsemani and was very impressed with the man."

"Ah. He is a saintly monk, Archbishop. I am not at all surprised that Cardinal Fergus spoke of him."

"He recommended him to me as a confessor."

"I can believe it."

"But not as an archbishop," Rossi added hastily. "Being archbishop of New York is very different from being abbot of a Trappist monastery. How many monks are there at Gethsemani?"

"Perhaps a hundred."

"A hundred." The way Rossi repeated the word invited reflection on the vast responsibilities that fell to the archbishop of New York.

"Abbot Peregrine is a man who could make the transition. I have no doubt of it."

"I will meet with him, Archbishop Deegen, but not here. I want to see him in his native setting."

"Good idea. Excellent idea." Deegen, his mission accomplished, definitively put out the offensive cigar.

Rossi rose with his guests. "I know you will tell no one of my plan to make a short retreat with the Trappists of Kentucky."

Deegen assured the apostolic delegate that he would consider their entire conversation as having taken place under the seal of the confessional. He was so delighted by the success he had had that he tried for loftiness in his final remark. If Rossi conveyed to the Holy Father the true caliber of Peregrine and the pope made the appointment, this would not be a victory for Deegen's adversaries. If anything, he conveyed to Rossi, Peregrine's appointment would be a setback for Carey and the whole Washington crowd as well.

Deegen awaited no response. It would have been unrealistic in the extreme to expect the apostolic delegate to acknowledge that there were factions in the American hierarchy and that he regarded himself as allied with one of them. Did it ever occur to the archbishop of New Orleans that his remarks put Liberati in an impossible position?

On the way out to the car, Deegen put his arm about Liberati's shoulder, and when they had piled in he said to Lewis, "Mission accomplished! Gentlemen, let's eat. I will treat you to dinner in any restaurant you name."

Liberati begged off. He would have lied just to get away from the triumphant Archbishop Deegen, but he had to let Cardinal Carey know that the candidate of the bishops' conference now commanded from Deegen a support so enthusiastic it must give pause to the archbishop of San Francisco.

A U S T I N C A R D I N A L C A R E Y had come away from Gethsemani with the thought that he had engineered a new departure in the American Church. Whatever initial befuddlement he had felt in the immediate aftermath of the election had been swept away when his fellow bishops crowded round to congratulate him. It was a coup. There was no doubt of that.

The beneficiary of the special meeting Carey had called at the monastery was apparently not so aware, however, who the fitting object of his gratitude should be. Carey told himself that Abbot Peregrine was stunned by this unexpected turn of events. With time he would realize who his patron was and act accordingly. For the good of the Church.

In the meeting with the abbot that had left so indelible an impression on Archbishop Deegen—as Monsignor Liberati's phone call would soon alert him —Carey had known the beginnings of doubt. Peregrine came through as a relic of the preconciliar Church.

Questions about the many pressing issues faced by the Church in America either drew a blank or were answered by an enigmatic smile. Carey had been around long enough to know the meaning of that smile. Peregrine did not agree but he was not going to say so. Now.

The flight home, archdiocesan affairs, and, above all, the almost universal hosannas occasioned by the bishops' decision at Gethsemani, drove doubt from Carey's mind. True enough, from time to time he would remember the candidate he had intended to emerge from the special meeting and wonder helplessly just what had gone wrong, but those were late night thoughts. Carey did not believe in endless reflection on what could not be changed.

Besides, even if he had been deeply dissatisfied with the choice of Peregrine, there wasn't much he could do about it. Imagine, in the face of all the favorable publicity the election had drawn, imagine Cardinal Carey, of all people, announcing that he begged to disagree with his fellow bishops and was withdrawing his support of Peregrine. In favor of whom? Did he want to put the matter directly back in the hands of the pope? Not on your life. Peregrine was his candidate, his creature, really, and everything would turn out all right.

And then Monsignor Liberati called to tell him of the weird visit he had just paid the apostolic delegate in the company of Archbishop Deegen.

It took a while to get clear what had happened. Had Lewis gone in too? Why not? Liberati wanted Carey to understand that he himself had had no choice in the matter.

"Of course I didn't want to go with him, but what was I to do?"

"He made that strong a case for Peregrine?"

"You remember the interview with Peregrine at Gethsemani, after the nomination. The sense of mortality, the spider on its thread? Deegen was obviously swept off his feet."

Carey put the best possible face on it. "Monsignor, what else can he do? Peregrine is our candidate. As Deegen can't lick us, he might as well join."

After several minutes Liberati sounded soothed, but Carey himself grew increasingly skeptical of the explanation he was giving. Had he walked into a trap? What stuck in his mind was Liberati's saying Deegen had taken credit with Rossi for Peregrine's nomination.

The sonofagun *had* put his name in nomination. Carey reassured Liberati, brought the conversation to an end, and put down the phone.

The spider and its thread! Listening to Peregrine, he himself had thought: that old time religion. Tears here below but a harp in heaven later. Was that the best Peregrine could offer the poor and oppressed? Cardinal Carey put seven ice cubes and three ounces of bourbon in a glass and settled back in his chair. Sipping, he told himself that the monastic life was really self-indulgent, though in a disguised way. Absolute absorption in the self. What in the name of God could a Trappist monk say to the people of New York?

Liberati had telephoned at five o'clock Pacific time. Carey remained in his office for the next four hours, skipping dinner, replenishing his glass, thinking the thing through. Step one was to accept the fact that he had been led up the garden path and had made a major mistake. Peregrine was not his candidate, he was Deegen's. If Deegen was that enthusiastically for him, he likely knew things about Peregrine Carey did not. He certainly must think Peregrine was his kind of guy. If that was true, he could not be Carey's candidate.

Step two was harder. That consisted in trying to figure out a way to rectify the mistake admitted in step one. Calling another meeting was out. Even letting his own supporters know he had changed his mind would be fatal. Whatever doubts he had about him, Peregrine was his tar baby; they were publicly linked. If he were going to stop the abbot, it would have to be privately, obliquely, subtly.

In the midst of this reverie, his phone buzzed, and he was told Hanratty wanted to talk to him. Carey did not take the call. He told Horvath he would take no more calls until further notice.

Carey had been home less than three days and already Hanratty was nagging him to demand a response from Rome to the action taken at Gethsemani. How could he handle a reiteration of that demand when his aim now was to remove Peregrine from the running? For the nonce, he would have to avoid Matthew Hanratty.

That was too bad, in a way. Hanratty would have been someone he could talk to about indirect ways of achieving his goal. The religion editor of *The New York Times* was a born intriguer. To whom else could he turn?

No easy question. But the answer came eventually. It came when he told himself that what he wanted was a Jesuitical solution to his dilemma.

Jesuitical. Of course.

He picked up his phone and put through a call to New York.

3

FOUR DAYS AFTER RETURNING from Kentucky, Hanratty took to referring to it as the phony war. The invasion had begun, the first city was captured, and then nothing. Was it possible the Vatican meant to take this lying down? Back in New York, he assumed initially that they were preparing a response, a counterattack. But there were only minor Vatican officials quoted as saying things that on a scale of blandness rated ten. They were awaiting official word of the meeting. When it was no longer plausible to pretend that the results of the Gethsemani meeting were unknown, it was said that the relevant congregation would weigh carefully the views of the bishops of the United States. Cardinal Carey did not return his calls; Liberati, when he finally called Hanratty, affected an insouciance only an idiot could feel, and Liberati was no idiot.

"These things take time, Matthew."

"It is not a matter of time. What is going on?" Liberati did not know or would not say. Hanratty could not believe the executive secretary would keep mum if anything was being done to prod the Vatican. Liberati did not receive gracefully the suggestion that he get off his ass and make a few phone calls. Starting with Rossi.

"Look, Monsignor, let me spell it out. If the bishops of the United States say on public record that they want Abbot Peregrine to be named archbishop of New York and their wishes are ignored, do I have to tell you what this does to the USCC and NCCB?"

"Matthew, the bishops never claimed they could themselves name the next archbishop of New York. We —that is, the bishops—simply made known . . ."

"You're giving up."

He could hear Liberati trying to master his impatience. Well, it was about time someone told him how inept he was.

"I think I understand your point of view, Matthew."

"My point of view? For the love of God, the bishops are going to be a laughing stock."

"That is your view."

"Liberati, I guarantee it. I will plaster that simple fact all over *The New York Times*. Look, I am going to call Rossi myself."

That was an empty threat. Hanratty had no wish to be given the runaround by some flunky in the residence of the apostolic delegate to the United States. Rossi himself was an artful dodger who had never yet given an exclusive interview to the religion editor of *The New York Times*.

Hanratty's disposition was not helped when he called San Francisco and was told the cardinal was on retreat. He was willing to believe Carey took a day off from time to time, but the man had just returned from several days in a Trappist monastery where he had had plenty of chances to pray as well as to conduct the bishops' meeting. Was it possible Carey was resting on his laurels somewhere, unaware that the silence from Rome was sapping the Kentucky meeting of any force it might have?

Hanratty was surprised when Father Lewis telephoned. "Did Monsignor Liberati return your call?"

"We talked."

"Good. I left word for him at America House."

"America House? He's here in New York?"

"Obviously he didn't tell you where he was calling from."

"What's he doing with the Jesuits?" And then a light dawned. "Is Cardinal Carey there too?"

"Mr. Hanratty, if Monsignor Liberati didn't tell you of the meeting . . ."

"Thank you, Father Lewis."

He slammed down the phone. Clearly something was afoot, something that involved journalists—America House was where the Jesuits published their prestigious magazine *America*—and Hanratty had not been invited. He seethed. After all he had done for Carey! For the first time in years Matthew Hanratty felt excluded. He reminded himself that he was religion editor of *The New York Times* but this failed to restore his sense of importance. It did no good to pretend that Carey's presence in New York, attending a meeting with the

Jesuits, had nothing to do with the naming of the next archbishop of New York. And it was stupid. Didn't Carey know what the pope thought of the Jesuits?

Within five minutes he was on his way to America House.

The little lady who answered the door was deaf. She got it into her head that he wanted to go to confession and gave him directions to the church.

"Cardinal Carey," he said, very distinctly, so she could read his lips. "I am Matthew Hanratty."

She narrowed her eyes and concentrated on his lips, which felt like Silly Putty as he mouthed his message. She shook her head slowly.

"You'll have to go to the church."

"Oh for God's sake."

She closed her eyes and nodded. She took him to have emitted what in his youth had been called an ejaculation. A fleeting memory of spiritual bouquets teased his mind but he shook it off, pushing past the woman into the hallway. In the distance a black-robed figure was walking away.

"Father!" Hanratty called. "Father, wait a minute."

The man stopped and looked over his shoulder. The light from the door would have made Hanratty's face invisible. In any case the priest had an impatient look.

"Confessions are heard in the church, sir. Not here." He turned and resumed his departure. Hanratty grabbed the cleric by the elbow. When they faced one another Hanratty realized how large the Jesuit was. His expression was one he might wear reading Pascal's *Provincial Letters*. Did he think Hanratty was one of those screwballs who show up at rectories and religious houses and attempt to parlay pretended penitence into enough money for a bottle of cheap wine? The expression did not alter when Hanratty said, in a strained voice suggestive of twisted shorts and emphysema, that he was the religion editor of *The New York Times.*

"Is that right?" The priest's eyes darted toward the woman who had answered the street door. It might have been a signal.

"Yes, that's right! I am Matthew Hanratty. My sources tell me that Cardinal Carey of San Francisco is here."

"Hanratty . . ." It was coming to him. Then he had it. "Sure, sure." Incredulity was gone. "Of course! I read you all the time. My name's Fairley."

"Don't you write for *America?*"

The man was flattered. A lucky guess. Perhaps he reviewed books. It turned out that he wrote little homilies for the magazine. Hanratty had never read them so he could deal with the man in an unprejudiced way.

"What can I do for you, Mr. Hanratty?"

"It is important that I see Cardinal Carey."

"He is in a meeting now."

"Yes, I know. But if you could get word to him that I am here and must see him . . ."

"Oh, that shouldn't be too difficult. Would you mind taking a seat in the parlor?"

Hanratty did mind, a lot, but what the hell could he do? He started back down the hall and the crone made as if to open the street door, to let him out or perhaps to hurry him on his way to a confessional in the church. Hanratty dove into the claustrophobic parlor as into a haven.

The chairs in the room had aqua-colored plastic cushions that had not worn well. He lowered himself gingerly into one whose seat had preserved some convexity. A large, low table more or less in the center of the room was piled high with reading matter. Magazines mostly, Jesuit publications, *America, The Month,* several mission magazines. It was easy to forget that the Jesuits had missions. Hanratty thought of the role they had played Christianizing this continent. Isaac Jogues, Marquette. The *Jesuit Relations*. Once, in high school, Hanratty had taken a volume of *Jesuit Relations* from a library shelf and soon he was hooked. He very nearly read himself into a vocation to the priesthood. To the Jesuits, to be exact, until he found out they would not ordain him until he was thirty-three and had put in time teaching high school. Not Matthew Hanratty. His relations with Jesuits had been only so-so over the years. There was something condescending in their attitude toward non-Jesuit priests, and, as for laymen, forget it. The pope's shock troops. They had become shocking and were no longer his troops. The adjective Jesuitical came to mind as he brooded over the meeting going on elsewhere in this building. He snatched up a magazine, and began to leaf through it until he realized what he was doing, and flung it back on the pile. The goddamn place was like a dentist's office.

Less than five minutes had passed before he suspected he had been abandoned. He should have asked for the homilist's name, Or remembered it: the man had said who he was. Why should he trust him anymore than the wacky witch who answered the door? This place had an air of craziness he had not noticed on his last visit, but then he had never before been asked to cool his heels in a waiting room. He had been whisked right through to the inner sancta with the other dignitaries. This was worse than humiliating.

He got to his feet and looked at his watch. 2:07. All right, at 2:10 he would . . . what? Explode. He should have accompanied that priest rather than permit himself to be shunted off to this ungodly waiting room.

Hanratty went to the door and stuck his head out. The crone seemed to inhabit the area just inside the front door. She turned and saw him. Did she have a hunched back? He had not noticed that before. Her hand groped for the doorknob and Hanratty darted back to the comparative sanity of the parlor.

It was demeaning to be kept waiting like this. It was an insult to him and showed contempt for *The New York Times*. Who the hell did that nameless Jebbie think he was dealing with? But his real gripe, and he knew it, was with Cardinal Carey. Carey had pulled a fast one on him, but when he received the message that Matthew Hanratty was waiting for him he would be sorry he had even tried.

At a sound in the hallway, Hanratty burst from the waiting room, nearly colliding with the homilist for *America*.

"Ah, there you are. The cardinal sent this note."

"Thank you, Father. Thank you."

"Brother."

"I beg your pardon?"

"I'm not a priest. I'm a brother."

Hanratty had torn open the message. It had come in an envelope, a sealed envelope! America House stationery. Inside was Carey's scrawl. "Matthew: I will call your office before 5. ac"

The self he wished he was would have retraced the Jesuit brother's steps, yanked open the door and gone in search of the meeting where Cardinal Carey and Liberati and God knew who else were discussing God knew what. The self he was decided not to give the messenger the satisfaction of witnessing his disappointment. Hanratty nodded, put the note in his pocket and headed for the street door. The little old lady had it open before he was halfway there. Hanratty gave her scrub bucket a kick, soccer style, one that could have been interpreted as accidental, and stepped out into the jungle.

4

R U N N I N G , he felt as the fox must feel, behind him a baying of dogs, the thunder of hooves, the haunting sound of the hunter's horn. Enemies he had feared as nameless and unknown now converged on his monastery and on himself with identities, credentials, and every right to put to him questions he could never answer to their satisfaction.

It was four thirty in the morning and Abbot Peregrine was out for his regular run on the grounds of the monastery of Our Lady of Gethsemani. The predawn world was milky, as if it sought to be the objective correlative of a blind man's effort to see. The year was dying, sap receded, leaves clacked dryly before their fall. The sound of the world was his own breathing and the earth asserting itself against the soles of his running shoes, sending tremors up his legs to his aching knees, alternating, on and on, the rhythm of running.

His breath was visible before his face and the sweat felt cold on his body though his face was flushed and if anything he was hot. Once he would have caught cold from far less a chill. Now he felt immunized by the strenuousness of this regular running. Speed and effort, without destination. Running seemed a metaphor of life.

He remembered the disbelief with which he had looked around him when he first came to the monastery and realized there were monks who had been here a quarter of a century, half a century, more. How to avoid the thought that their lives had been wasted, all those years spent in exactly the same spot? The years had stretched before him in his mind's eye and he was filled with despair. But Father Richard had told him, "Now is all you have. Today. 'What if this were the world's last night?' Do you know the line? No? John Donne, a lovely poet. Get through today, son. That is all you have to do. Yesterday is gone and tomorrow does not yet exist."

This proved to be excellent advice. Perhaps he had only a month here, a year, who knew? In the meantime, he would think only in terms of hours, of the day he was in.

But his thought that a monk's life was pointless because he was going nowhere, led him to search for a contrast. Was it travel that made the difference? From point *A*, one went to point *B*. But travelers envy the steady, solid lives of those in the countries through which they pass, romantically imagining themselves Greek peasants, residents of a small town in France, or living in an English village. Life without routine is pointless, but routine makes any life seem absurd.

Death. Dear God, the first burial he had witnessed here. Hanratty had still been here, they had both been novices. Old Father Methodius died, that very night they waked him in the church, and next morning after Mass they carried him out to the graveyard, the stiff old body in an open coffin, beak of a nose not smelling the morning air, the cowl pulled for the last time over his shaven skull. Methodius was lowered into the ground and covered with dirt and a blessing, and they went away. To work. To prayer. To the routine from which Methodius had been freed. Peregrine could have cried out at the hideousness of it, as if the monks had invented death. But what was the alternative to their practice? Dressing up the corpse to make it look alive, waking it in a room with false decor and professional undertakers simulating sorrow? The body laid in a make-believe bed in a steel box would be discreetly covered, lowered into a concrete receptacle and covered with flowers only until the mourners or heirs were out of sight. The difference was one between realism and pretense. Out of his horror at that funeral, Peregrine had found the beginning of a real attraction to the monastic life, to this place, to Gethsemani. He felt that he had been rescued from a world of make-believe and allowed to see life in its stark reality, its simplicity, its beauty.

Men sleep and rise and eat and work and sleep again and in the end they die and are put away in the ground to rot. That is the basic script. Birth, copulation, and death. T. S. Eliot. Richard's reference to Donne had set Peregrine to reading poetry. The monk substituted prayer for copulation, that was all. And how could he fail to fall in love with the psalms that daily he sang with his fellow monks in the choir of the abbey church? Prayer is a kind of protest against the capital punishment that is life.

> He will overshadow thee with his shoulders:
>   and under his wings thou shalt trust.
> His truth shall compass thee with a shield:
>   thou shalt not be afraid of the terror of
>   the night.

2 0 4

Of the arrow that flieth in the day, of the business that walketh about in the dark: of
invasion or of the noonday devil.

The noonday devil. What did the phrase mean? The
liturgy was piled high with thoughts that Peregrine
could not comprehend. It seemed important to probe
them for meaning. He read Saint Augustine's lengthy
comments on those verses of Psalm ninety. He was never
sure he knew who the noonday devil was but he sensed
the approach of this daylight enemy.

The regular round of his day had made a monk of
him. He had entered wary and frightened and all but
totally ignorant of the life. He had ended by seeing
that there was nothing extraordinary about it at all. It
was at most a heightened version of what every mortal
faced: the extinction that retrospectively mocked man's
hopes and dreams and fears. The more central death
became for him, occupying the core of his conception of
life, the less credible he found it.

Immortality. God. The bread he received each morning at Mass became a living bread, and Peregrine one
day realized that not only had he become a monk, he
had become a Christian as well. After that metamor-
phosis his election as abbot was a mild punch line. It was
more fearsome when the bishops had turned to him as
their nominee for the archdiocese of New York. Must
he accept it as the will of God? Like death? He suspected that there were other wills at work, wills riddled
with convictions he himself had shed as the monastic
life worked its transformation on him.

Today Archbishop Rossi, the apostolic delegate,
would come to interview him. This time he could
not expect Joachim to assume the burden for him, as

he had with the journalists, acquainting them with the alleged facts of the abbot's life before he entered the monastery.

Peregrine had never before imagined that his assumption of the identity of Perry Green would ever become a matter of interest. And in fact, it did not seem to interest anyone now. Only Matthew Hanratty had alluded to it in print.

When he showed up at Gethsemani the first time he had known almost as much of the life of Perry Green as of his own; indeed his own early years had become increasingly remote and unreal during the training he had received for the role he would play. He was actually several years older than Perry Green. The boy had been chosen because of their physical resemblance, his out-of-the-way minor city, and his exemplary life, a commendation to the novice master. When faith had come, Peregrine had prayed daily for Perry Green, gone so young into eternity in order to provide him with an identity.

Did he have an obligation to confess publicly that his religious life had begun as a charade? Perhaps Archbishop Rossi already knew. How Peregrine wanted to believe it did not matter. He was no longer Anatoly Vojdya. It even seemed to him that if it was God's will he could accept the appointment to New York in good conscience.

Did he himself want it? No. Did he not want it? Again, no. He wanted God's will and his nomination had come about in so surprising a way that he could see God's hand in it. It was difficult to not regret, however, that he had allowed the bishops to meet here in the first place. One way or the other, his life would never be the same again.

He left the path that, having taken him through a wood, ran along its edge for half a mile, and struck out across a pasture, its terrain rough and rising toward another stand of trees beyond. He seldom returned to the monastery this way and soon regretted his decision. The clayey soil was wet from recent rains and clung to his shoes as if the earth were trying to get a grip on him, slow him down, and stop him. He was more than usually exhausted when he came within sight of the monastery buildings. However objectively ugly they might be, they never failed to stir in him a feeling of tenderness and love. The prisoner ends by loving his prison. Who said that? he imagined Father Richard asking. Is a loved prison still a prison? Anonymity suddenly seemed the most desirable blessing God confers. To be nobody was particularly attractive now as he neared a confrontation with a visitor whose mission could well be devastating for the abbot of Our Lady of Gethsemani.

Rossi had arrived and been put in a guest room within the cloister. Father Joachim reported this with no visible sign that the presence of the apostolic delegate in the house disturbed him.

"When will Archbishop Rossi see me?"

"I thought you might want to show him the cloister garden. It seemed to me you could converse there as well as in this office."

"Why do you suppose he has come, Joachim?"

"To interview you about New York."

"Did he say that?"

"Why else would he have come all this way?"

How reasonable Joachim was, how untroubled. Did he imagine that soon he would be secretary to a new abbot? Did he perhaps see himself behind this desk?

The election of a new abbot always followed the death of the old abbot. Would the election this time be occasioned by his appointment as archbishop of New York? The monks would take this in stride, he knew. And they would feel sorry for him, having to go back into the world he had left.

And so Abbot Peregrine went down the dim, cool hall to the guest room for his interview with the apostolic delegate to the United States of America.

5

CARDINAL CAREY DID NOT CALL at five. He did not call at five thirty. Hanratty sat glowering at his phone, his mind teeming with imaginary scenarios that might have been played out at America House. The memory of himself sitting in that dismal waiting room, all but in the custody of the Grimm Brothers' hag who looked after the door, squeezed an anguished groan from his constricted chest. It was bad enough to have something going on involving Carey and the Jesuits without his knowledge, but to be frozen out after he had discovered it, well, that was too much.

The Jesuits. God, was Pascal right about the Jesuits. It served them right that they had been bumped by the pope, replaced by Opus Dei, people who could be trusted.

At 6:01 his telephone rang.

Heroism can show forth in small matters as well as great. His poised hand waited into the third ring before he allowed it to descend upon the phone. Like a batter at the plate, he inhaled and spoke as a calm man might.

"Matthew, forgive the delay but you will understand when I explain. Are you free?"

Hanratty hated himself for the way the anger drained from his heart at the sound of the cardinal's voice. A smile stretched involuntarily across his face. If he had had a tail he would have wagged it. He told Carey he was free.

"For dinner?"

Hanratty looked at his watch as if it would remind him of appetites felt by the rest of men. He had not really enjoyed a meal since before his days as a Trappist. Was that the reason for his indifference to food, that failed try at asceticism? Perhaps. He preferred to think of it as anorexia journalistica.

"What did you have in mind?"

"I'm sitting here thinking of a steak. A nice big steak. Interested?"

Hanratty mimicked the enthusiasm of the average starving male. They made arrangements to meet at Gallagher's.

On the way to the restaurant, he began to think of the occasion as Cardinal Carey Reports to Matthew Hanratty. He should never have indulged the unworthy emotions of the afternoon. It was absurd to think that Carey would try to ignore the religion editor of *The New York Times*.

Carey was there when he arrived and it struck Hanratty that the cardinal in street clothes could be any one of a thousand men of the cloth. They shook hands and were swept away to their table in an alcove where Carey ordered a Manhattan. He himself asked for Perrier water. Until the drinks arrived, little was said. Carey rearranged his silverware, fussed with his napkin, wore a determined look. After a healthy pull on his drink he looked at Hanratty right in the eye.

209

"Peregrine is out, Matthew. I am withdrawing my support."

Hanratty began to choke. On water, making a remedy difficult. His eyes filled with tears, he held his napkin to his mouth, painfully aware that Carey looked as pleased at the effect of his remark as he looked concerned for his choking table companion's welfare.

"He just won't do," Carey said when Hanratty subsided.

Hanratty shook his head. Carey was crazy if he thought he could go on public record as supporting Peregrine, reap all sorts of favorable publicity for the deed, and then just drop him. He told the cardinal these simple truths. Carey smiled.

"I mean it. You'll be eaten alive." Hanratty would be among the diners. Carey's smile was unnerving. "Did the Jesuits talk you into this?"

Carey frowned. "Now, Matthew. You know me better than that. I had made up my mind before coming east. Peregrine's great champion is Archbishop Deegen. He nominated him. He has gone to Rossi to urge his acceptance. The more I thought about it the clearer it became that Deegen had manipulated that meeting . . ."

"That's not true."

". . . manipulated that meeting into accepting a conservative throwback."

The cardinal had another Manhattan but Hanratty switched to table water. The difficulties of the discussion that followed were two: Matthew found it hard to maintain that Peregrine was really a liberal, that he could be counted on to vote with the Carey block in conference meetings. That was the big difficulty. The other was Carey's maddening smile. So Hanratty returned to his first point.

"You will be made to look—because this is what you will be—a man who had a courageous idea and then backed off at the first whiff of disapproval from Rome."

"I know. That is why I will not back off."

"I don't get it."

"I owe the solution to Lollard. I knew what I ought to do but what you warn of stopped me. I spoke to Lollard on the phone and he urged me to come to America House and talk about it."

Kenyon Lollard, S.J., had joined the Society after a decade and a half on Wall Street. He managed provincial finances, a fact that had enabled many a radical Jesuit to live in carefree ease while protesting American capitalism. He had a great reputation for shrewdness and holiness but still he seemed an odd one for Carey to turn to.

"The solution is not to do what you decided you ought to do? That is not just Jesuitical. It is nonsense."

Carey leaned forward and whispered in capital letters. "I let the Vatican do it for me."

"Aha!"

"So it isn't nonsense, is it?"

No, it wasn't. Carey could connive at his own failure and emerge the seeming victim of Roman intransigence. The Jesuits in Rome would do all they could to insure that the usual procedures were followed in naming a successor to Fergus. Vatican bureaucrats would have the satisfaction of thwarting the wishes of the NCCB and Carey would have the twin satisfactions of martyrdom and getting rid of Peregrine.

"I still think Peregrine is a good choice," Hanratty said, but his tone was wistful rather than convinced.

"So does Archbishop Deegen."

"What if Deegen convinced the delegate?"

"The decision will be made in Rome, not Washington."

It seemed an odd fact for Carey to take comfort in. Perhaps there had never been a chance that the Vatican would accept the bishops' choice. What had once seemed a threat to an inspired election now became the way for Carey to have his cake and eat it too.

When he put Carey into a cab outside Gallagher's, the prelate was feeling no pain, his euphoria due to elation rather than alcohol. Before the door closed on him, he asked Hanratty once again to share the cab.

"I have one more thing to do at the office, Your Eminence. Good night, sleep tight."

The cab swept away and Hanratty started back to the *Times*, avoiding the unsavory types who tried to press into his hand lurid ads for various massage palaces in the vicinity.

An idea circulated in his head. A story. Without revealing Carey's secret, Hanratty wanted to be on record so that an ex post facto claim not to have been fooled would be credible. He had half a mind to phone Lollard for help.

Part 3

_____

_____

THE WALK IN THE CLOISTER GARDEN was a
ritual dance, with Abbot Peregrine trying to anticipate
the direction in which Archbishop Rossi would take the
conversation.

"Are you receiving many new vocations here, Father
Abbot?"

"Yes, we are. Thank God."

"Severity attracts?"

"The severity of our life is often overstated, Archbishop."

"I doubt that. Surely not everyone who comes here
stays."

"That is true."

"Have you yourself ever regretted coming here?"

"Not since I fully understood why I am here."

The archbishop's shoes crunched slightly on the gravel walk. He wore cassock and zucchetto, and one fat hand played with the jeweled cross that hung on a thick gold chain around his neck. Peregrine sensed that the Italian prelate had turned to look at him, but he kept his own eyes on the fountain. He should have had the water turned on, nuisance though that would have been. Brother William had already shut off the water and drained the pipes for winter. What is so useless as a dry fountain? *As the hart panteth after the water brook, so does my heart pant for thee, O my God.*

"There are many stages in the understanding of a vocation."

"Yes."

"Do you know that I entered the seminary when I was eleven years old? I put on my first soutane at that age." Rossi smiled, a sad, indulgent smile. "In my country it was feared that a boy who was not taken out of the world before he became a man and felt the attraction of women would find it all but impossible to resist them and enter the seminary."

"Things have changed."

"Our practices, perhaps, but not human nature. There are fewer vocations now. Perhaps they are better ones," he added dubiously. "I am sorry that I do not know the status of your order in Italy."

"The monasteries there are prospering, Archbishop. In every sense of the term. That is the bane of the monastic life."

"What do you mean?"

"Monks leave the world, withdraw to some wilderness, build a monastery, work and pray. Too soon they prosper. Their success attracts others. Commerce begins. And there are internal consequences."

"Such as?"

"There grows up a distinction between choir monks and field monks, priests and lay brothers. A caste system. Work and prayer are subjected to a division of labor. It is difficult to remain poor."

"An interesting philosophy. But poverty of spirit . . ."

"That is the most difficult poverty of all. Its opposite, spiritual poverty, is more easily come by."

Rossi smiled at the paradox. They came to the end of the path and turned. Rossi stopped before the fountain, which he obviously found intriguing.

"Brother William designed it."

"I miss fountains most of all. Roman fountains. The fountains in this country, well. . . . But this one, it is magnificent."

"I could ask William to turn on the water."

"Oh, no, no, no. I am sure it has been shut down for the season. I would not dream of it. Besides, there is something melancholy but beautiful in a dry fountain. Dust gathers, a dead leaf here and there." There was indeed a fine silt in several of the scoops William had hewn from the rock to serve as basins in the staged flow of the water; they were so calibrated that the tempo of the flow altered as the water descended and returned to its source. There was a legend inscribed at the base. *Fons et origo.*

"Father Abbot, would you tell me about the bishops' meeting that was held here?"

"What could I tell you that you do not already know?"

"First of all, how did the meeting happen to be held here?"

"Cardinal Carey asked if they might come. He remembered a meeting held some years ago at the Benedictine Abbey of Saint John's in Minnesota. He thought it had gone particularly well. I understand too that journalists have been making adverse comments about the somewhat luxurious settings in which the bishops often meet."

"Hotels, yes. A ski resort, on one occasion." Rossi pulled at his lower lip. "Yes." It was difficult to say whether he was approving or disapproving. "Did Cardinal Carey say why they did not go back to Saint John's?"

"No."

"You see my point. If meeting there had been successful once, why not repeat the experience?"

"Perhaps he had read Kierkegaard."

"Aha!" Rossi stopped and his face was aglow with pleasure. "You know *Repetition*? A fascinating book, drenched with romanticism as well as criticism of it. What pseudonym did Kierkegaard use for that work?"

"Constantine Constantius."

Rossi was genuinely overjoyed. The diplomatic veneer that had marked his manner was suddenly gone. Did Peregrine know Cornelio Fabro? This learned priest had translated the Danish theologian into Italian. Rossi had studied with Fabro, privately. "He was a severe taskmaster. He made me learn Danish."

Peregrine protested that he was not a scholar, but he had read a good deal of the writings of Soren Kierkegaard.

Earlier Peregrine had imagined the conversation would founder for want of topics other than the one that had brought the apostolic delegate to Gethsemani. Now the danger was that they would bound from idea to idea, guided only by Rossi's enthusiasm.

"I am surprised you ended up in diplomacy, Archbishop."

"For my sins, for my sins. I speak generically. But

2 1 6

I am not a scholar either. Do not imagine that an academic career has been thwarted. No, no. I am a dilettante. With that, Father Fabro would emphatically agree." Rossi laughed but his expression remained sad. "Besides, Father Abbot, we must be willing to make sacrifices for the Church."

Peregrine nodded. "That is how I felt when I was elected abbot."

"And how did you feel when the bishops named you as their choice for New York?" Rossi's manner altered as he asked the question.

"The same."

"Yet you accepted their nomination?"

"I expressed my willingness to accept the will of God."

"Did the nomination come as a surprise to you?"

Peregrine looked at Rossi. Was it possible that, despite the exuberance of the scholarly tangent, Rossi was the contact he feared?

"I was completely surprised, Archbishop."

"Were you present at the meetings?"

"Yes."

"Exactly how was your name put before the conference?"

Peregrine thought. It was, after all, the important point. But the truth was he had been totally unprepared for the nomination. At the moment it occurred, he had been reflecting on the pettiness of the procedure. Nominations, speeches, votes. Yet somehow the Church survived this sort of thing. Besides, what was the alternative?

"Has it occurred to you that someone might have come to the meeting with the express purpose of nominating you?"

"Few of the bishops even knew I existed."

"It would take only one. What bishops had come here previously?"

"Since I became abbot, only three. The archbishop of Louisville, of course. Johnson, the auxiliary bishop of Fargo. Cardinal Fergus."

"Ah yes. Fergus."

"He made his annual retreat here."

"I know."

"That surprises me. He was very secretive about it. Once he actually came in lay clothes. I am sure none of the other guests had any idea who he was. Another time he wore a choir robe and joined us for office throughout his stay."

Rossi smiled. "Cardinal Fergus had a flair for the dramatic. He told me of coming here. He mentioned you. He was very close to the Holy Father. You made a great impression on him."

"He was intense, but I admired him very much."

"Did he discuss the state of the Church with you?"

"Hardly. He left such matters behind when he came here. For five days he simply stopped being the cardinal archbishop of New York and looked after the state of his soul. Prayer, meditation, reading."

"Father Abbot, if the Holy Father were to follow the advice of the bishops' conference, there are some questions I would have to ask you."

"Archbishop Rossi, I wish to withdraw my name."

Rossi had been holding his pectoral cross with the thumb and finger of one hand. He let it go. "You said you would accept the will of God."

"I think it is the will of God that I remain here. The penitent belongs in a monastery."

"We are all penitents, Father Abbot."

"I am unworthy of such consideration."

"Would you accept if it is the Holy Father's wish?"

Peregrine had half surprised himself when he withdrew his name, but the statement flooded him with relief and he knew it had been the right thing to do. If he did not accept, he did not have to tell Archbishop Rossi about himself. There seemed no danger that the pope would insist on his acceptance. Whatever pressures had been put on the Vatican by his nomination would be removed by his withdrawal. Archbishop Rossi should be elated. But the apostolic delegate might not have heard Peregrine.

"I will ask you the questions I always put to a candidate for the episcopacy."

"Archbishop, there is no need."

Rossi lifted a hand in mild protest. He had come to Gethsemani for a particular purpose and he would fulfill it.

Rossi began, and Peregrine was slightly surprised to find that it was a short catechism on the nature of the episcopal office that he went through, a discussion of the relation of bishop to pope and the function of national conferences of bishops. Rossi wanted to know if Peregrine accepted the magisterium in all its amplitude as defined in *Lumen Gentium*, the dogmatic constitution on the Church written by the conciliar fathers of Vatican II.

"I do."

"Do you know the credo of Paul VI, Father Abbot?"

"Yes."

"The Holy Father asks that I kneel with the candidate before the Blessed Sacrament while you recite that creed. Would you have any objections to that?"

"Certainly not."

"Ah, Father Abbot, we must be so careful nowadays. Some have likened our situation to that of the fourth century. Who is an Arian and who is not? There are bishops whose fidelity to the magisterium is, to be oblique, elastic. They seem far more interested in receiving a good press than in preaching the good news. The Holy Father demands the strictest orthodoxy of those he consecrates bishop."

"That is wise."

"And there are political infidelities as well as theological ones."

Rossi's voice had not changed, but Peregrine sensed that they had reached the crucial point. Was it possible that Rossi knew all there was to know about him? Suddenly it seemed imperative that he should. He drew the delegate to a ledge of the fountain that William had designed for sitting.

"Archbishop Rossi, what I now say to you, I make a confession."

"Under the seal?"

"For the moment I would like it to be a confession, penitent to priest."

"Very well."

They sat side by side on the ledge and Peregrine whispered to the Italian prelate the secret that had been buried in his heart for over twenty years. Rossi's expression was unreadable, but the thought that none of this was news to him did not seem incredible. How quickly Peregrine was able to describe the enormous sacrilege he had been sent to this monastery to accomplish.

"What specificially were you to do? What was your assignment?"

"I was to wait here until I was contacted."

"By whom?"

"I don't know."

"And you were willing to do that?"

"I came here," Peregrine said.

"Yes. I wonder how many there are who could be relied on to show such unquestioning devotion to a cause?"

"It was my training."

"Has no one contacted you during all these years?"

"No one, Archbishop."

"Not even after your election as abbot?"

"No."

"Extraordinary."

"This is why I withdraw my name. For a moment, longer than a moment, after it had happened, I thought . . ."

"Yes?"

"No matter. If I were named archbishop of New York, a contact would be made."

"There has been nothing since the conference here?"

"Nothing."

"I suppose it has occurred to you that you may not have been the only one to receive such an assignment. I suppose it has also occurred to you that your nomination was not an accident but that the stage was being set to put you into action."

"I have thought of those things." Peregrine felt beneath his fingers the fine dust that had gathered in one of the basins. "Nothing will be the same now. I cannot accept the nomination. Perhaps I cannot remain here."

"Why not?"

"If my name was put forward as you suggest, my refusal puts me in danger."

"Perhaps you would be safer here in the bastion of your monastery."

"I cannot endanger my brothers." The relief he had felt in saying he would withdraw his name was gone now. It was as he had said, nothing could ever be the same again. Whether it had been engineered or not, the nomination was an opportunity he would be expected to seize.

"You could resign. Go somewhere else. To another monastery. Become a hermit, perhaps."

He would have thought Rossi was baiting him if he had not been able to look into the apostolic delegate's eyes. Rossi bore a great responsibility and no matter what happened he was taking a risk himself. Peregrine did not want the Italian to doubt him. The apostolic delegate had to believe he was being told the truth, he had to believe Peregrine, an admitted member of the KGB, if any future other than the hermetic one he had just sketched was to lie ahead.

"First, I would like to finish my confession."

He explained to Rossi that he had long ago confessed to his unbelieving condition when he entered the monastery, and to his reception of the sacraments without faith.

"I did not mention the mission that I had by then rejected. I was given absolution. To go into all that detail seemed unnecessary and I feared it would make my confessor think I was mad. Once I nearly broached the subject with Cardinal Fergus, but I did not. I put it all before you now and ask God's forgiveness."

Rossi gave him absolution, slowly, deliberately, and Peregrine traced the cross described by the delegate's ringed hand, touching his shoulders, left then right. For some moments afterward they sat in silence.

"I will tell these things to the Holy Father, Peregrine. If you release me from the seal."

"Of course."

"I cannot predict his reaction."

"Tell the Holy Father that I will do whatever he wishes."

Rossi brought his hands together in an attitude of prayer and studied Peregrine for a moment. "Father Abbot, I am glad you told me all this."

"You do not seem surprised."

Rossi smiled. "You mentioned Cardinal Fergus. Such matters were much on his mind."

"I told him nothing of myself."

"I almost wish you had. It worried him greatly, the possibility that men and women would enter religious life, the priesthood, with alien ends in view. The Holy Father shares the cardinal's concern. Cardinal Fergus had reason to believe that there is a member of the hierarchy who is a member of the KGB."

Peregrine could not pretend to be surprised at that. He was moved by Rossi's suggestion that he might have discussed all this with Cardinal Fergus. Of course. The cardinal would have understood.

"Did he name him?"

Rossi shook his head slowly. "Simply knowing who the man is does not solve the problem, Father Abbot." The delegate rose.

Errant clerics were often sent to Trappist monasteries to do penance. Where could a Trappist be sent? It seemed certain to Peregrine that he would be removed from his post.

"Let us go to the church, Father Abbot. We can still recite the credo of Paul VI together."

He took Archbishop Rossi into the abbey church and together they knelt on the step of the sanctuary platform. The apostolic delegate had brought with him a yellow-covered pamphlet, a Saint Paul's Editions copy of *The Credo of the People of God*. Peregrine took it and with a steady, resonant voice read the lengthy affirmation of faith that the beleagured Paul VI had drawn up when he perceived what forces were trying to ally themselves with the Vatican Council and redefine its spirit. The paragraph headed "Temporal Concern" Peregrine read with special emphasis.

We confess that the Kingdom of God begun here below in the Church of Christ is not of this world whose form is passing, and that its proper growth cannot be confounded with the progress of civilization, of science or of human technology, but it consists in an ever more profound knowledge of the unfathomable riches of Christ, an ever stronger hope in eternal blessings, an ever more ardent response to the love of God, and an ever more generous bestowal of grace and holiness among men.

A clearer antithesis to his youthful convictions Peregrine could not have imagined.

When he was finished, he remained kneeling for half a minute more, then helped Rossi to his feet and accompanied him back to his room in the cloister. There the apostolic delegate took his hand.

"This has been a most fruitful morning, Father Abbot. I will be returning to Washington as soon as possible."

"Will you need help with your travel arrangements?"

"I should like transportation to the airport, if you would be so kind."

"Whenever you wish. Father Joachim will take you."

Rossi opened his door and turned on the light in order to see the face of his watch. "In an hour?"

Joachim was waiting for him in his office.

"Did everything go well, Father Abbot?"

"Yes."

"What is the news?"

The question was so uncharacteristic of Joachim that Peregrine stopped to stare at his secretary. But it was absurd to expect the monks to be unaffected by his imminent departure from the monastery. It seemed certain now that he would be going, though not where Joachim imagined. No doubt the other monks in various ways had been pestering the abbot's secretary for news. It was no small thing to the community if there was soon to be a new abbot.

"I think that I shall soon be leaving here, Joachim." It was like saying he was soon to die.

"Congratulations."

How tempting to tell Joachim the truth. His secretary, while a good monk, still retained a slight worldliness, a trace of sophistication. It seemed unlikely that Joachim would think it a great coup for the monastery if he had become archbishop. But would he be indifferent to the thought that his abbot might be asked to step down?

"You will be able to do more good in New York than here, Father Abbot."

"That sounds like a criticism."

"You know it is not."

"I know, Joachim. Thank you. I hope I will always do God's will." He looked at his secretary. "I think I am doing it now. Joachim, I withdrew my name. I will not be going to New York."

Joachim's eyes widened slightly but his expression did not change. "You said you would be leaving us."

"Not for New York."

"I don't understand."

"I cannot explain it now, Joachim. Archbishop Rossi needs a ride to the airport. He wants to leave in an hour. Can you take care of that?"

Joachim's eyes met his for a moment, then turned opaque. "Yes, Father Abbot."

After the door shut behind his secretary, Peregrine

sat at the desk and closed his eyes. Soon Joachim and all the others would know the bizarre truth about their abbot.

What if he had remained what he was when he came here and now had the chance to become archbishop of New York? Peregrine opened his eyes and looked across the room at the closed door. Dear God, what an opportunity. There were those who would never forgive him for turning it down. He sat back and tried to remember the man he had been.

He had been trained to represent the forces of history by subverting the organization that was the single greatest obstacle to human progress. To call it an opiate was inadequate to describe the way religious belief sapped the energies of mankind. Pie in the sky, the promise of a post mortem reward, made any injustice tolerable in what was called this valley of tears. More importantly, the concept of God was an alienation, the taking of human traits and projecting them into a great beyond, so that human beings became frightened of an imaginary apotheosis of their own powers. Creator. It was man who created God. All those attributes of the creator had to be brought back from heaven and restored to man. Feuerbach, Engels, those two as much as Marx, but they were right, Marx had seen that they were right, and taken it over. Convinced of this, Anatoly was willing to do whatever he was asked in order to weaken the institutionalization of this oppressive theft from man.

He had been prepared to accept the idea that his task would be a modest one, chipping away as opportunity presented itself, nothing much, perhaps, yet, allied with the efforts of others elsewhere, a contribution to the ultimate goal.

He was chosen because his grandfather had been a

hero of the Revolution and both his father and mother were in intelligence, serving in embassies and consulates throughout the western world, in Italy, in England, in the United States. Until he was seventeen, Anatoly had accompanied them on their assignments. At that age he returned to Russia for special training. He had lived so long in the West without adverse effects that his desire for work similar to that of his parents seemed certain to be accepted. He had never dreamt of the assignment he was offered. Dumbfounded, he nonetheless accepted without hesitation. It meant that he had already seen his parents for the last time. He ceased to be who he was and became Perry Green.

The identity was available. The distance between Superior and Gethsemani, Kentucky, was far more than geographic. He had known a moment of self-doubt when he was told he would become a Trappist monk.

"Do you know what that is?"

"Vaguely."

"Come back when you have a precise understanding."

He went away and read and was appalled. Dear God, he was being plunged into the Middle Ages. Yet, despite his initial horror, he felt the beginnings of a fascination. He was attracted as an actor is attracted by a difficult role. Perhaps in an historic sense he would accomplish little in the assignment that was being given him, but it would take genius to do it at all.

So he had entered the monastery and learned with growing skill to mimic the life of a monk. The time of his novitiate was difficult; more than once he had been tempted to compare reactions with Matthew Hanratty, but he had decided from the very beginning that, improbable as it was, he must assume that he could easily arouse suspicion. His best defense was to become an exemplary monk, guided at first by his own negative reactions. The more repulsion he felt, the greater was his effort to conform.

And then that funeral, the burial of Methodius. That had been a turning point. Not that there had been a dramatic change. There had not been. But the routine of the life slowly eroded his unbelief. Is it possible to pray that many hours a day without coming into contact with the addressee? One day Peregrine realized that he was a monk. He believed it all. This was his real life. What he had been before was unreal. He began to pray for his parents.

Sitting at his desk, Peregrine realized how shattered he had been by his conversation with Rossi. The bright prospect of New York that for a short time he had thought to be ahead of him was gone, but so was the life he had lived for over twenty years. He would have to steel himself for exile.

How silly to think that his past could be so simply put aside, a whispered sin absolved and then forgotten. Who you are and where you came from. Peregrine's eye fell on a manila folder lying on his desk. He opened it. His own dossier.

He glanced at the first paper, a birth certificate, and then he began paging rapidly through the contents of the folder. His first reaction was that a miracle had taken place. It was as if his unformulated prayer had been answered and God was delivering him from his past.

His name was now Francis McGough and, although he had still been born in Superior, Wisconsin, the date was no longer February 1942 but April 7, 1940. Someone had provided him with a new identity.

But who? And why?

It was too late to be useful now, too many already knew him as Perry Green.

His eyes went to the closed door. Joachim? Abbot Peregrine sat very still. He had thought the moment of truth would come later. Joachim.

Yes. The possible became probable, then more probable. Finally it was a hypothesis he had best assume was true. His secretary was not who he seemed. He remembered selecting Joachim and it seemed now that the monk had not only been willing to become his secretary but had subtly volunteered for the job.

There was a single knock on the door. Joachim.

"Come in."

"I am leaving with Archbishop Rossi."

"When you return, I want to talk to you."

Joachim nodded.

Peregrine rose and came around the desk but his eyes were on Joachim. The secretary bowed, withdrew, and pulled the door shut.

Peregrine had been unable to engage Joachim's eyes.

2
_____

HE HAD TALKED WITH HARRY PACKARD, he had talked with Laura, he had talked with Roger. He ended up talking to himself. Finally, in desperation he went down to New York and talked with Matthew Hanratty.

The cadaverous journalist occupied his office like an interloper and Knight thought he detected something that was less than respect for Hanratty in the woman who showed him in.

"Are you still masquerading as a newspaperman?" Hanratty asked. He was tipped back in his chair, one leg folded over the other, not at the knee, more like the crotch. He hugged himself as if he were his own last friend. His tone was more taunting than nasty.

"I'm a private investigator."

"I know that. What exactly is it Harry Packard hired you to do?" Hanratty's embrace of himself became more intense. "Does it have anything to do with Cardinal Fergus?"

"Nice guess. First, let me ask you some questions about Abbot Peregrine."

Hanratty unwound and sat forward. "You can forget about Peregrine, Knight. He's a dead letter."

"You think the Vatican will ignore the bishops' nomination?"

"Something like that."

"I thought you were for him. You don't seem too saddened by the prospect."

"It was a nice idea."

"Who writes your stuff, Hanratty? You were ecstatic when the bishops made their choice."

Hanratty bristled at the suggestion that his prose was the product of a pen other than his own. "I applauded the innovative move, yes. I still do. But I am now convinced it was a futile gesture. Noble but futile."

"Is Cardinal Carey as philosophical as you about this?"

"You'll have to ask him. I still don't see what interest Harry Packard has in all this. The man isn't even Catholic."

"Neither am I. You are. You knew Peregrine years ago, I understand."

"That's right."

"What was his name before he entered the monastery?"

"Perry Green."

"You're sure of that?"

"Of course I'm sure. Why, do you doubt it?"

Laura had imagined a young man entering a monastery under a false name, that of a dead friend. "There could be valid reasons for it. Perhaps there was something in his past that would have been an obstacle to entering."

"Wouldn't that be an odd way to enter the religious life?"

"Oh, I don't know. You get a different name when you enter anyway so what's the difference? Becoming a religious is a way of becoming sort of anonymous."

"But pseudonymous?"

She had put the idea forward halfheartedly—Laura could not easily give up the elation she felt at the news of Peregrine's appointment; she had taken it to be a thwarting of Cardinal Carey's connivings—and it did not withstand much scrutiny. One needed letters of recommendation to join a monastery, from one's pastor, from employers, others. Such a deception would involve quite a number of people. Besides there was the killing of Sutter to testify to the importance of the Perry Green name.

He was tempted to tell Hanratty about his trip to Superior, what he had learned there, about Sutter's death. It was not pleasant to be told he was inept. But the reporter's manner seemed to stem from his original reaction to the mention of Peregrine. He thought the nomination was dead.

From a phone in the lobby of the *Times* building Knight called Packard in Washington.

"Matthew Hanratty thinks that nothing is going to come of the nomination of Abbot Peregrine."

"Why?"

"He didn't say."

"It hasn't been withdrawn." Silence on the line as Packard thought. "Maybe they don't have the stomach for a fight. Maybe they know they can't win." He was trying ideas as one might turn over cards at solitaire. "Where are you calling from?"

"New York."

"Come to Washington. I think you and I ought to pay a call on the apostolic delegate and tell him what you've found out."

"What's the point if Peregrine is out of the picture?"

"I don't like loose ends."

"You're the boss."

He telephoned Roger to tell him he would be going on to Washington. He also told him of Hanratty's conviction that Peregrine would not be named to New York.

"They must have discovered what you did."

"I don't think that's it. Hanratty is sure Peregrine and Perry Green are the same person."

"He is a sly man."

"Not that sly."

"Tell me what you said to him." Roger hummed through the recital, then said, "It will pique his curiosity, depend upon it. We have to consider what we are going to do when your trip to Superior comes to light."

"I was thinking of pleading innocent."

"Ho ho. I hope it doesn't come to that."

"Thanks."

"Sutter was shot, wasn't he?"

"Could we talk about something else?"

That was a mistake. Roger got going on a lecture about Saint Bernard of Clairvaux. He was still fascinated by the Trappists. Philip suggested he take a vow of silence and hung up.

GLORY BE TO THE FATHER, and to the Son, and to the Holy Spirit, Amen.

Abbot Peregrine in his choir stall made the jackknife bow monks make as they sing the great doxology at the conclusion of a psalm. Father John leaned into the organ as they straightened and in peripheral vision the abbot could see his monks step forward to turn the pages of the huge books propped up before them.

How he loved this choir. The task of singing the office was one of which he would never tire although it was often what outsiders found most difficult to understand about the monastic life. It was not simply that it was prayer, already unintelligible to the worldly man, but that it was the repetition of the same prayers and that so much time was devoted to doing it. The problem was, it did not seem to be *doing* anything at all. What possible good could come from having perfectly able-bodied men trade the verses of the psalms across the choir? And not just occasionally but daily, not just once a day but again and again from before dawn until dusk. The hours. That is what the word had meant for centuries, those specified times of day when monks chanted psalms. Matins and lauds, the two now collapsed into vigils, then prime, tierce, sext and none, counting the movement of the sun across the sky to evening, to vespers, and then, before retiring, compline, the end. Why the repetition? Well, why does a lover repeat again and again I love you? What more important thing can one do than praise and glorify God? In this choir they were the church at prayer, the *ecclesia orans*, and they acted for everyone, not just themselves.

The economy of salvation, states of life, the body of

Christ of which all are members—Peregrine had long since ceased to find such concepts odd, though he never ceased to marvel that, entering as he did, he had nonetheless come to accept those things as true. When he was elected abbot he interpreted it as a punishment rather than an honor, not that he had put it that way to his fellow monks. Quite rightly he had recognized that his new duties would prevent him from living fully and without interruption the monastic life. He had to travel, nationally and internationally, to represent the monastery in various ways, yet he was the one man ultimately responsible, morally, spiritually, legally, for the various activities of the monastery, its farm, its cattle, its cheeses. On several occasions he had sent Joachim in his place to reduce the time of his own absence. Nonetheless, his burden was light when he considered that what he did enabled the community to go on without worry or concern. It had been a far different matter a week ago when he had stood in this very spot and heard himself nominated as the bishops' choice to become archbishop of New York.

His first impulse had been to cry No, remove my name. Here was punishment indeed, to be taken entirely from the monastery to perform tasks of which he had only an imperfect understanding. Twice before Archbishop Rossi's visit he had started to look up the archdiocese of New York in reference books and twice he had closed the volumes after reading a paragraph or two. The sheer dimensions of the task overwhelmed him. Nothing in his background had prepared him for such an enormous responsibility. Besides, he felt an almost physical pain at the thought of leaving the monastery. But it was that very pain that had prompted him to reply as he had, surprising himself if not Archbishop Rossi. He tried not to think of the future only in the negative, as not being here in Gethsemani. What he would miss more than anything else was the opportunity for prolonged prayer.

After discovering the alteration of his dossier, he had waited at his desk for Father Joachim to come in and explain what had happened. His secretary had obviously left the folder there so he would look at it. But the blank door remained closed and blank. There was no point in putting it off. Peregrine rose and went down the hall and tapped on Joachim's door.

No answer. After a moment he opened the door and looked in. The room was empty. And then he remembered that Joachim was taking Archbishop Rossi to the airport. The thought was unsettling. Filled with foreboding, Peregrine had gone off to choir.

The office ended, Peregrine remained in his place. He was still there when Hyacinth tugged at his sleeve. The expression on the guest master's face was enough to tell Peregrine something had happened. He stepped from his place, bowed profoundly toward the Blessed Sacrament, and left the church as slowly as he could manage. Hyacinth had scurried ahead of him. Outside the church he turned and looked up at Peregrine.

"There's been an accident!"

"Archbishop Rossi?"

Hyacinth's head bobbed up and down. "Joachim was not injured."

"How is the apostolic delegate?"

Hyacinth looked at the floor. "The police are in the guesthouse."

So was Father Joachim, a mug of coffee held in both hands. The bandage on his brow was the only sign of the accident, and it had the look of a prop. He gazed steadily at Peregrine but the abbot turned away in order to listen to the account of the sheriff. His name was

Hankey and he seemed to want to conceal the pistol strapped to his side. These monks made him ill-at-ease. He spoke to Peregrine but he could not meet his eyes. You would have thought it was his fault the pickup had gone off the road.

"Not too much damage to it, Father. Nor to your friend over there. The other fellow, now. He should have fastened his seat belt. He banged his head against the dashboard." The sheriff rubbed his nose with the back of his hand. "He's dead, Father."

"I gave him absolution," Joachim said.

Again Joachim looked steadily at the abbot. He might have been warning him to react properly to this grim occurrence. Joachim did not make the sheriff's task any easier. When Hankey mentioned the rain as a possible reason for the accident, the secretary said, "This happened just before the rain started." Only Peregrine would have thought Joachim did not want Rossi's death to seem an accident.

"Who's the next of kin?" the sheriff wanted to know.

Peregrine said, "I'll take care of that, sheriff. I'll see that the proper people are informed."

When the sheriff was gone and there were just the three of them—Hyacinth, Joachim, and Peregrine—the abbot said, "When you feel up to it, Father Joachim, come to my office."

He had made the difficult call to the delegation in Washington before Joachim came. He closed the door and stood in front of the abbot's desk. Peregrine laid his hand on the manila folder.

"My identity seems to have changed, Father Joachim."

"In what way, Father Abbot?"

"I think you know."

It seemed absurd to be discussing pieces of paper in a

manila folder now, but they had everything to do with what had happened to Archbishop Rossi.

Joachim's eyes had been fixed on a point slightly to the left of the abbot's head. His hand went to the bandage on his forehead and he allowed their eyes to meet. "When you were given the identity of Perry Green it could not have been predicted that things would turn out as they have. There was not sufficient time to remove materials in Superior and thus deflect any inquiries."

Peregrine looked at his secretary as if he had never laid eyes on the man before.

Joachim waited, mimicking the obedient monk, but what was he, really? Peregrine saw something of the fraud he himself had been before faith came. Joachim was outwardly indistinguishable from the other monks. He was exemplary, there was no other word. Was it possible that he went daily through the motions while retaining a purpose like that his abbot had when he first came? Of course it was possible.

"Your opportunities have increased," Joachim said.

Peregrine nodded.

"Is there anything else, Father Abbot?"

"Why did you kill him?"

Joachim did not answer. He would have found a question about his method more intelligible. Peregrine could imagine Joachim's strong hand slamming Rossi's head into the dashboard as he eased the car into a ditch.

He let him go.

Peregrine went to the file and removed Joachim's folder, knowing it would tell him nothing of who the monk really was. He had entered twelve years before. Twelve years. A decade shorter than his own stay here. How long had he himself imitated the life of a monk before he became one in truth? Less than five years? Yes, less than that, but even during those first years there had been a gradual erosion of his resolve to keep a shell closed tightly around his soul—not that he would have used the term then—to keep out light and warmth and preserve the ice-cold purpose. He had been assigned to wait until by command or the opportunity of circumstance he could do something to further the cause. The cause. Could he say now what that cause was supposed to be? Revolution, the overthrow of oppressors, obeying the laws of history. Had he ever heard those empty words and slogans and felt a stirring of the heart? Indeed he had. Did Joachim return to those cold certainties as protection against the view of life embedded in the daily routine of the monastery? That in itself would require something akin to monkish meditation.

When he came out of his office half an hour later, another door opened and Joachim appeared in the hallway.

"How do you feel, Father Abbot?"

"I should ask you that question. It is you who has been in an accident."

"I was in no danger."

Peregrine thought how those same words a week ago might have sounded edifying, the expression of Joachim's confidence in the divine mercy.

They stood in the corridor outside their offices. Beyond, a door opened and there was a glimpse of the cloister garden. "Come, Joachim. Let's walk in the garden."

A thin, pale sunlight slanted into the courtyard and it was bitter cold. Here he had walked and talked with Rossi, a saintly if sophisticated man. Now, with Joachim, he felt in the presence of evil. They put their hands in their sleeves and walked back and forth on the gravel as if establishing a rhythm for their words.

"You have been here a dozen years, Father Joachim."

"I do not keep track of time. There is no point."

"Have you found this life difficult?"

"There are far more hazardous tasks one might have been given."

"Hazardous?"

"I do not underestimate the difficulties here. The psychological assault never lessens. One's manner, the routine, all conspire to undermine one's sense of purpose."

"But you have never weakened?"

"No, Father Abbot. But you have. I assume you told Rossi everything."

"Is that why you killed him?" It was almost a relief that Joachim had seen that his abbot had indeed become a monk.

"You heard the sheriff, Father Abbot. His head struck the dashboard." Joachim lifted his hand and tore away the bandage from his forehead. Peregrine was almost surprised to see that it had concealed an ugly, quite real wound.

"Why do you think I have weakened?" I am talking with a murderer, Peregrine thought. This man killed Archbishop Rossi because of what I told him.

"I watch you. It is my assignment. They were right to elect you abbot. You've been one of them for years."

"I have been here for twenty-two years."

"That doesn't matter."

"It matters to me."

"I know. That is the problem. And now you are going to be archbishop of New York."

"I have refused."

Joachim shook his head. "I suggested that course. I

told them you would be no good to us. I was overruled. You will go to New York and do what is expected of you."

He would not debate the point. He would do what he would do and no one could force him to do what he had no wish to do. He lifted a hand in dismissal and Joachim started away, but then he stopped.

"You think you are free of the past. You are not. Your mother is still alive."

He turned and walked away, seemingly a monk like any other, his heavy shoes crunching on the gravel.

Your mother! Each day Peregrine prayed for his parents. Suddenly he was assailed by memories of them, particularly of his mother. But he had no way of knowing whether Joachim was telling the truth. Nonetheless, the threat was flattering. At least they gave him credit for human emotion.

Peregrine left the monastery two hours later. Old skills returned and he was certain no one followed him. His destination was the hermitage Thomas Merton had built far off in a secluded part of the vast monastery grounds. None of the monks was using the little house at present. Abbot Peregrine went to this refuge in a roundabout way. He drove an abbey car to Bardstown and left it parked in the main square of the town. Then, wearing khaki pants, a turtleneck sweater, and denim jacket, he walked back to where he could cut across the fields to the hermitage. How he wished he might just disappear, become no one, escape the past that had suddenly put in a reappearance. He thought of simply going away.

But first he needed solitude and prayer and, he hoped, light. Whatever he did, he did not want it to be the result of his own calculations of self-interest. It was difficult to know what he should take into account in his reflections. Only one thing was certain: he would not do what Joachim expected of him. He could not. Not even to save another's life. He would die first.

He realized now that he had thought of Archbishop Rossi as a protector. By telling him everything, he would put himself into the delegate's hands. What he had actually done was to put Rossi in mortal danger. May he rest in peace. May his soul and the souls of all the faithful departed through the mercy of God, rest in peace. Amen. Amen.

Through a fold of field he approached the hermitage, low, flat-roofed, white. On the porch a rocking chair moved slightly in the wind. Peregrine paused before crossing the clearing to the house. No smoke rose from the chimney and there was no sign of habitation. It was indeed empty.

He climbed the steps and crossed the porch to the front door and pushed it open. Inside, there was a musty smell. That could be cleared by touching a match to the fire already laid but he did not want to attract attention. Warmth, food, sleep—they would have to wait. He had more important things to think about.

A sitting room, a kitchen, a bedroom, a small chapel. That was the hermitage. In the chapel there was the suggestion of an altar, a picture of Our Lady of Guadalupe, a kneeler. Peregrine lowered himself onto the plain board of the kneeler, rested his elbows, closed his eyes. Let us put ourselves in the presence of God.

His senses dulled, the external world receded, he seemed to drop like a spider on a thread, down, down, down. In his mind the words of the "Ave" formed. Hail Mary, full of grace. . . . Each word ballooned singly before his mind's eye yet was linked to the others to form a thought. Pray for us sinners, now and at the hour of our death, amen.

Despite his effort to concentrate entirely on the prayer, he heard the footsteps outside, barely audible, stealthy. Danger was as real as air in the room and he breathed it in slowly as he might his last breath. And waited. The malevolent presence behind him seemed to exert pressure on his back and he readied himself, awaiting the blow he was certain would fall.

No! He would not offer himself up as a sacrifice. He rose from his knees in one movement and slipped into the kitchen where he eased open the door. He thought of removing his shoes but did not. He lay on his stomach at a corner of the house and warily looked around it.

Joachim had stopped ten yards from the hermitage and the light topcoat he wore over his habit tossed in the wind. He held a rifle loosely in one hand. His head was cocked, listening, but the wind was behind him. Peregrine eased back, got to his feet and dashed a few yards to an oak whose trunk was gnarled and massive. He got behind the tree and waited.

The wind brought the sound of Joachim's passage through fallen leaves and then Peregrine could hear him moving across the porch of the hermitage. Had the door squeaked like that when he himself entered? He had not then been worried about being followed.

Joachim meant to kill him. He would murder him as he had murdered Archbishop Rossi. His leaving the monastery as he had would remove all doubts. They would know now they could not trust him or make him do their bidding. So he would have to be removed.

The kitchen door opened, not stealthily but in a burst, and he could hear Joachim thunder into the area behind the hermitage. And then the game began, a boys' game, a game learned in schoolyards and parks.

Using the tree as his shield, Peregrine moved as the movements of Joachim suggested, now slowly, now fast, keeping out of sight. His heart was in his throat. If he moved too swiftly and came into Joachim's view, he would be killed.

He stood still now, his heart in his throat. Joachim was not six feet from the tree. Did he know his quarry was behind it? It is said the experienced hunter senses the presence of his prey before he sees it.

"Father Abbot. Father Abbot."

Peregrine could not believe his ears. Joachim's tone was almost sweet, wheedling. But it was desperate. Joachim did not know if he was there.

And then there were the sounds of his secretary going away and it was all Peregrine could do not to shout out his relief. He wanted to sink to his knees and pray, but he did not yet dare make a sound.

Book Three

Part 1

M YRTLE T ILLMAN was staying with her brother
Jimmy and his wife Delores in Chappaqua when the
call from the chancery came.

It was one of those October days when the turning
of the leaves had reached its height and she and Delores
and the younger kids who were not yet in school had
spent the afternoon just driving around the country
roads drinking in the beauty.

Delores was thirty-one but looked years younger, and
Myrtle sometimes imagined she was Delores's mother-
in-law rather than her sister-in-law; it made the difference in age and youthfulness more bearable. Delores
was not hard to get along with. Or immature. A woman

who could handle four kids the way Delores did had all Myrtle's admiration. She simply did not know how the girl did it. The twins ricocheted around in the back seat as they drove, never still, never quiet, yet Delores was calm as could be and kept up a running conversation with a somewhat rattled Myrtle and attended to her driving as well. And Myrtle had thought that keeping up with Cardinal Fergus was a job. She could not have done what Delores did for all the tea in China. Jimmy was far luckier than he deserved, luckier than he seemed to realize. She sometimes felt the impulse to take him aside and tell him that. Then she really would have sounded like a mother-in-law.

When they got back to Chappaqua and came down the hill past Horace Greeley's house, now a gift shop, Myrtle asked herself why she should live her life shut up in the city when this lovely countryside and small town life were so obviously more human and healthy and attractive. A job? With her secretarial skills and background, she had no doubt she could land a job locally. She could even use her chancery connections and get taken in at one of the larger parishes, one large enough to afford her.

The possibility invited fantasy. Maybe if the twins would shut up for half a second she could indulge it. If she did move up here she would live near Jimmy and Delores, but not too near, not in Chappaqua. Nieces and nephews are fine but a steady diet of them might be more than she could bear.

Jimmy was already home when they got back to the house. "You got a call from New York, Myrtle. The number is in there by the phone."

She glanced at her watch. It was after five.

"He said call back whenever you got home, it didn't matter how late it was."

Jimmy must have been impressed by the caller, going by the expression on his face. That was something she had missed on this visit, and Myrtle would admit it only to herself: deference. Maybe deference wasn't the exact word, but when she worked for Cardinal Fergus and came for a visit she was really someone special. This time, having heard Jimmy tell two or three people that she *used* to work for Cardinal Fergus, the one who was killed in Rome, Myrtle asked him to drop it, it made her feel like a widow. She could see now she had lost a lot more than an employer when Cardinal Fergus was shot. Jimmy worked in a nursery and could make plants grow better than anyone she had ever known, but he was a simple man. By contrast, she always felt the soul of sophistication, dropping little remarks about the cardinal, the chancery, this and that.

"Did he give his name, Jimmy?"

Jimmy shook his head. And he wouldn't have asked. Country boy. Well what was so bad about that? He had Delores and the kids and a steady job and a house in Chappaqua worth five times what he'd paid for it, not that he had any intention in the world of selling.

The number Jimmy had written on the back of an envelope was that of the chancery office. Myrtle dialed the familiar digits—she could have dialed this number in her sleep—and listened to a far off phone ring once, twice, three times. It was answered on the fourth ring.

"Chancery office. Monsignor Barrett speaking."

"Monsignor, this is Myrtle Tillman."

"Oh good. Myrtle, I'm sorry to bother you on vacation but this is important, as I think you'll agree. Abbot Peregrine called and wants to talk to you. I gave him your brother's number and he said he would telephone you there tomorrow. I thought you'd want to know." He sounded like one of Santa's helpers, which was fine;

his tone made it easier for Myrtle to control her excitement.

"Did he say what time tomorrow?"

"There you have me. I should think early in the day though. You know Trappists. He called here at the crack of dawn. Well, at ten."

"Thank you for telling me, Monsignor."

"Myrtle, he insisted on this: the call is to be completely private. He doesn't want anyone to know he's in New York. Understand? No one. He was most insistent on that. Curiously insistent, I might add."

"He's in New York?"

"I think he expected to see you in person."

"Have you seen him?"

"No." That single word spoke volumes. Was Monsignor Barrett being nice so she would let him know what Abbot Peregrine wanted? He should know her better than that. Abbot Peregrine could rely on her to keep confidential what he said. "I suppose he's exercising prudence, Myrtle. If he acts as if his nomination is in the bag, it might not be."

She wasn't going to get into that kind of speculation. The thought that the abbot might not be coming to New York was unwelcome. The thing to do was to hold her feelings in abeyance until she spoke with him on the phone.

After she'd hung up she sat for a moment in the hallway looking at herself in the mirror above the telephone table. She put her shoulders back and lifted her chin. It didn't help much. She looked her age. She was a real widow who scarcely remembered the days of her marriage, it had been so quickly over, Patrick Tillman dying of complications and pneumonia after a routine appendectomy. Sue, she had been counseled, take them to the cleaners. She had not been remotely tempted by the thought of becoming rich as the result of Patrick's death. She could support herself, she told her father, and she had. She had gone to work for Fergus and his each elevation had been better than a raise for her. Now, like Patrick, he was gone and while the archdiocese of New York would not just push her into the street, there was no job at the chancery that faintly resembled the one she had had. This visit to Jimmy and Delores had been intended as a time for quiet reflection on what she would do next. The phone call seemed the promise that she would get her old job back. She shut her eyes and prayed it was true.

"Myrtle?"

Delores stood beside her, looking concerned. "Is everything all right?"

"Everything is fine."

Delores's eyes dropped significantly to the phone. If Jimmy had been too diffident to ask Monsignor Barrett for his name, Delores would never ask directly what the phone call had been about.

"I will be receiving a call tomorrow from Abbot Peregrine."

"The new archbishop?"

"Designate. That's right." It didn't really matter, telling Delores and Jimmy about the call. How could she keep it secret? Now she felt as she always had here, the urban sophisticate bringing tidings of the great things going on in Manhattan.

Delores was ecstatic at Myrtle's news and this suggested to Myrtle that Jimmy and his wife must have been feeling sorry for her. That had not occurred to her before, and she wasn't sure she liked the idea of Delores and Jimmy whispering and wagging their heads and looking sad behind her back.

The sound of something falling sent Delores dashing

for the kitchen. Jimmy was in the living room drinking beer from a bottle and frowning over the sports page.

"Get through okay?"

She repeated the message to Jimmy, as if he hadn't already heard her tell Delores, and he was happy as a lark for her. Like Delores he just assumed that this call meant that the archbishop designate wanted her as his secretary. How she hoped they were right, but what did Delores and Jimmy know about the chancery office or Abbot Peregrine?

That night when they mentioned going to a movie, she persuaded them to go without her. She would stay with the kids. For heaven's sake, this was their chance to get away. Delores looked as if getting away from the house and the kids was the last thing in the world she wanted.

"We won't be long Myrtle."

"For heaven's sake, have fun."

When the doorbell sounded she had already put the kids to bed and was watching a silly show on television. The sound of the bell scared her to death and her first impulse was to ignore it. But she couldn't do that. It might be a friend of Jimmy and Delores. Besides, this was Chappaqua.

In the hallway, she turned on the porch light. A priest stood on the doorstep. Myrtle's fears disappeared and she opened the inside door.

"Are you Mrs. Tillman?"

He was a tall, thin man with a funny haircut and Myrtle was struck by the cut of his suit. It looked like something he'd picked up in a discount house. The Roman collar hung loose and unfamiliar on his neck; even his large eyes seemed filled with awkwardness.

"Yes, I am." And just as she was about to ask him

who he was she realized this must be Abbot Peregrine. "Are you Abbot Peregrine?"

He smiled. "The chancery called you?"

"Yes."

His expression suggested he had asked Monsignor Barrett not to. The screen door locked by twisting the handle and Myrtle had some trouble getting it unlocked.

When he came into the room and just stood there until she asked him to sit down, Myrtle had difficulty imagining this man filling Cardinal Fergus's shoes. But if he acted awkwardly, his manner was alert and keen.

"Monsignor Barrett tells me you worked for Cardinal Fergus."

"Yes, I did. For many years. I worked for him when he was just an auxiliary bishop."

"Just?" And then he smiled, a very pleasant smile. "I knew him. Not well, but I knew him. He sometimes made retreats with us."

"I know."

"Of course. I don't imagine he had any secrets from you."

"I was his confidential secretary."

"You must have been very reliable if Cardinal Fergus was satisfied with your work for so many years."

Myrtle felt her face flush. She wanted to tell him that she was a very good secretary, that she had never had a serious complaint from the cardinal, but how could she blow her own horn like that? She bowed her head in assent.

"Are we alone here?"

"The children are upstairs."

"Children. A Trappist doesn't see many children."

Myrtle hoped he wouldn't ask her to wake them up.

It had been a real relief when the fooling around had stopped and they had gone to bed.

"Mrs. Tillman, I want to speak confidentially. There is a very important question I want to ask you."

He fell silent but he was not expecting her to say anything. Myrtle liked him. He reminded her a bit of Jimmy, not in looks but in manner. Country boys, simple Simons, good as gold.

"Cardinal Fergus had pronounced political views, did he not?"

"Oh, yes."

"He was a firm opponent of communism."

"Yes, he was."

"When he was at the monastery, we would talk, he and I, but he was not with us to discuss politics. He was a wise and holy man. Because I know that, it is difficult for me to think of coming here to succeed him. I do not have the cardinal's gifts. But I do have the same outlook on the world."

Was he saying he would not be coming to New York? Doubt diminished the pleasure she had felt on learning that he was not among those who thought Cardinal Fergus was crazy for being fearful of communism. If Abbot Peregrine was wavering about succeeding Cardinal Fergus, she could help him by telling him something about the job.

She assured Abbott Peregrine that he could do the job, she had no doubt of it. It was difficult. She didn't mean to suggest otherwise, and it gave very little free time, but Cardinal Fergus throve on it. She was certain he would have been active for years if he had not been. . . .

She could not say it. She would never get used to the idea that someone had actually just walked into a room and shot Cardinal Fergus and all those other people. And then bragged about it afterward!

Abbot Peregrine said, "Cardinal Fergus was assassinated by the people he rightly feared and wanted others to fear."

"It's so hard to believe."

"The same people shot the pope."

"I don't think Cardinal Fergus ever feared for himself. But he and the pope talked about these things. Cardinal Fergus left a microcassette with me, summarizing what the Holy Father told him."

Something like a sigh escaped him. "The pope gave him an assignment."

"How did you know?"

"Archbishop Rossi, the apostolic delegate, told me." He waited, and when she said nothing he went on. "He also suggested that Cardinal Fergus had successfully accomplished that assignment."

Myrtle wasn't sure what he meant, but she assured Abbot Peregrine that the pope had been right to rely on Cardinal Fergus.

"You know what the assignment was?"

It would have been disloyal to Cardinal Fergus to misrepresent what he had said, but she didn't want to make Abbot Peregrine think he was, well, odd. Still, the abbot had said he shared the cardinal's view of the world. So she gave Abbot Peregrine a summary of the tape.

"He said there is a disloyal bishop?"

She nodded.

"Where is that tape now?"

"In my safety deposit box. Cardinal Fergus told me to put it there."

"In New York?"

"Yes."

"That sounds like a tape I should hear. Don't you agree?"

"I think Cardinal Fergus would have wanted you to."

He asked if she could come to the city the following day and she said, yes, of course. She felt that she was already working for him. Besides, it really made sense to give him what Cardinal Fergus had left with her.

"Would you like a transcript of the tape as well?"

"That would be helpful."

"I'll get it."

They arranged that he come by her apartment the following afternoon. She would pick up the tape and he could listen to it there. At the door, emboldened, she asked what had happened to his forehead. He had a nasty bump and there was a large, unhealed cut. He smiled. A nice smile, she thought. "I bumped it."

"You should put a bandage on it."

"It will heal more quickly this way."

When he left, she stood in the doorway, having turned off the outside light, and watched him walk up the street. Walk. He was headed in the direction of the station, doubtless going back to New York tonight. Perhaps she should have asked him to stay. But that would have been too much of a burden on Jimmy and Delores.

She didn't mention the visit to them when they came home, full of some silly science-fiction movie they had seen. There was a special and probably mildly sinful pleasure to be had from listening to them talk while she was keeping such exciting news from them.

Delores said, "The kids would have loved that movie."

"We'll take them," Jimmy said vaguely.

"I'm going back to New York tomorrow, in the morning," Myrtle announced.

They stared at her. "What about your phone call?"

She could not keep to her resolution to tell them nothing.

"I talked to him tonight," she said. "That's why I have to go to town."

After that it would have been impossible not to let them get all excited for her. Delores made hot chocolate and they sat up until midnight, Myrtle talking about her work at the chancery but swearing them to secrecy about the fact that Abbot Peregrine had contacted her.

"Of course we wouldn't tell," Delores cried.

"You can count on us," Jimmy said. But he sounded as he had when he said they would take the kids to see that movie.

2

H E S E T O F F for San Francisco by bus. From Denver he telephoned Cardinal Carey and it was several minutes before he was put through. Peregrine began to suspect that he had made a mistake. He had wavered between going to New Orleans and Archbishop Deegen and coming to Cardinal Carey. Carey had represented the more difficult path so, good monk that he was, that is the path he chose.

"I tried to reach you when I heard of Archbishop Rossi's death." It might have been a question.

"I must talk with you."

"Yes?"

"I am coming to San Francisco."

For a moment he thought Cardinal Carey would refuse to see him, but suddenly the phony voice on the line became affable. When would Peregrine arrive? The cardinal would have him met at the bus depot. They could talk at Saint Mary's College in Moraga.

Perhaps the driver had never picked up a visitor at the bus depot before. Once they got out of the city, he seemed to take every opportunity to study his passenger in the rearview mirror. The silence between them grew uncomfortable but Peregrine could think of nothing to say. Making the effort seemed insincere.

"Are you married?"

He could not say how old the driver was. He wore a checked hat, its brim turned up all around, and hair grew luxuriantly in his ears. The car smelled of smoke but when Peregrine suggested that the man smoke he was given a reproving look.

"I was."

"I see."

"I'm not divorced, it isn't that. My wife's dead."

"I'm sorry. Are there children?"

"No."

Silence again. Peregrine found it impossible to construct a life out of the few facts the driver gave him. They suggested tragedy. But tragedy called for a disconsolate figure and the driver was laconic, somewhere between fifty and sixty, the toothpick he chewed more suggestive of comedy.

"How long has it been?"

The driver looked at his watch. "I picked you up at ten ten."

Peregrine let it drop. Was the driver relieved? He continued to dart glances at Peregrine via the mirror.

Maybe he would be asked for a report on his passenger's demeanor.

He discovered that Cardinal Carey had not yet arrived but he was welcomed by a Brother Benignus. He met several other Christian Brothers as he settled in, and he found it hard to think of these pudgy, well-groomed men as religious. It wasn't that he judged them adversely, but they were so different from the monks at Gethsemani. The religious life was clearly a variegated thing, but isn't that as it should be? Nevertheless, as he had with the driver, he felt in alien surroundings. And the Christian Brothers found him odd in turn.

Always before when he traveled as abbot, he had kept to himself so that the interval in the world, between abbeys, made little or no impression on him. The world he passed through was the one he had put behind him as a monk. The world had now become the place in which he must hide from Joachim, but this only made it stranger to him. It seemed unbelievable that the world was taken to represent temptation; he would cheerfully give up anything he saw if he could return safely to his monastery. And not as abbot. To be the least in the community would be infinitely preferable to being chased into the world like this. But he could not offer Joachim another opportunity to murder.

The world, the flesh, and the devil. Women had always been strangers to him: they simply had not fit into the plan of his life, before or after his conversion. All the chatter about celibacy had made itself heard even in the monastery. Was it fair to demand of priests an unmarried life? His masters in the Soviet Union had not hesitated to demand celibacy of him, nor had he seen it as a major sacrifice. It is not difficult to say no to the unknown. After he had truly become a monk the thought of placing another person between himself and God was intolerable.

The brothers at Saint Mary's seemed at ease in their celibate life although they were not contemplatives. They were teachers for the most part. He spoke with an apple-cheeked professor of philosophy who wore a gray coat sweater and a blue dress shirt open at the collar. He had studied in Rome as a young man and had returned to the college thirty years before. He had been there ever since.

"What is your subject?"

"Metaphysics."

Peregrine nodded. He could not even imagine a life spent teaching such a subject. Brother Felix looked as if he might answer at length if asked what it involved.

Felix said, "You've been given a room in the same corridor where the cardinal stays."

"That's very kind."

"If you like cardinals."

It seemed to be a joke. Peregrine felt somewhat as he had when he first learned English, the nuances of the language eluding him.

Later he visited the college church, a cool, high-ceilinged building whose white walls, dark wainscoting, and tile floors made it seem older than it was. The architecture of the college was Spanish mission, the buildings linked by covered walkways. The sun was as much an enemy as a friend here. The softly molded hills in which the college sat were green now, but in summer they baked brown.

Peregrine knelt and fixed his eyes on the sanctuary where his Lord was sacramentally present, body, blood, soul, and divinity, under the appearance of bread. He remembered how as a novice he had watched the monks bow profoundly whenever they passed the tabernacle and it had slowly dawned on him that they really believed Jesus was hidden away under lock and key, a presence as real as that of the other monks. The belief was no more odd than the belief that there is a hidden God on whose will the entire universe perpetually depends, a hidden God, far off yet near at hand, nearer to me than I am to myself. Hopkins.

> Thou mastering me
> God! giver of breath and bread;
> World's strand, sway of the sea;
> Lord of living and dead;
> Thou hast bound bones and veins in me, fastened
> me flesh,
> And after it almost unmade, what with dread,
> Thy doing: and dost thou touch me afresh?
> Over again I feel thy finger and find thee.

It was difficult not to resent the change that had taken place in his life in a matter of weeks. But he owed it to the president of the Bishops' Conference to tell him about himself, about Joachim, about Archbishop Rossi's death.

Cardinal Carey in old clothes was a nondescript fellow, reminiscent of the all but illiterate monk who ran the carpentry shop at Gethsemani. He suggested a walk up into the hills behind the school but when they set off, he said, "Whoa, not so fast. I want a stroll, not a march. We can hurry coming down."

The incline was seldom steep, yet in half an hour they were able to look down on the campus as if from an airplane. Carey sat on a boulder and squinted at Peregrine.

"Father Abbot, I'll be frank. I no longer favor you as the next archbishop of New York."

The horizon suggested the knuckles of a hand and Peregrine let his eyes drift along the profile of hills. Was it possible that Joachim had communicated with Cardinal Carey during the day-and-a-half bus ride?

"What have you heard, Your Eminence?"

"Nothing, nothing. There's nothing personal in this, Father Abbot. For that matter, my change of mind need not be made public. I tell you as a matter of frankness. My considered feeling is that we were too hasty in our choice and too influenced by the locale in which we met. I mean it as no offense when I say that I don't think you are the man for New York."

"I agree."

"You do?"

"I came here to tell you that I wish to withdraw my name. You and the other bishops knew nothing about me then, and you don't know much about me now."

"Yet the apostolic delegate went to see you. Perhaps nothing you said to him matters now, given that horrible accident, but I wonder what was said."

"It was no accident, Your Eminence."

"I beg your pardon."

"Archbishop Rossi's death was no accident. He was murdered."

Carey pressed both hands tight against the boulder on which he sat, as if fearful of falling off the mountain. Peregrine crouched beside him and took up a handful of reddish dirt. While he spoke, he let the dirt sift through his fingers and when his hand was empty he replenished it. He might have been measuring the time it took him to tell Cardinal Carey his history, Joachim's revelation of his similar mission and then the fact that he had killed Archbishop Rossi.

"But why?"

"Because I had told the archbishop that I could not

accept an appointment to New York and that I did not see how I could remain abbot of my monastery. Joachim's job was to make sure I went to New York. He would have killed me too if I had stayed."

Incredulity flickered across the cardinal's face but did not remain. "My God. And my fear was that you were too conservative."

There was no doubt that what he had told Carey came as a complete surprise. He stood up, tried to laugh, grew serious. Half turned away, he looked at Peregrine over his shoulder.

"How Kevin Fergus would have enjoyed this. His worst fears realized. Moles among the clergy."

"He was right."

"The question is, are you lying?"

"Why would I?"

"I don't know. None of these things would have happened, you would not be telling me of them, if we had not held our meeting at Gethsemani. Next you will be telling me that your nomination was engineered."

Peregrine said nothing.

"Did you tell Rossi who you are?"

"Yes."

"What was his reaction?"

"He was less surprised than you are, I think."

"Did he ask you to withdraw?"

"That wasn't necessary. I withdrew my name."

"How did he react to that?"

"He went on to do what he had come to do, questioning me, having me recite the creed; he said he would put it all before the Holy Father."

"And now he is dead."

They started down then, but neither of them seemed in a hurry to return to the campus. When they reached the bottom, Carey stopped and turned to Peregrine.

"About a bad bishop among us? I've heard that be-fore. Little more than a hint, but it was meant seriously. Paredi, one of those killed with Fergus, made the re-mark. Speaking of Fergus, have you heard anything of a statement he left? No? Well, why would you? A re-porter told me about it."

"What did it say?"

"I thought you might be able to guess, since you knew him." Carey made a face. "Abbot, what bothers me about your story is that it *does* sound like Fergus. And you knew Fergus."

"What I've told you is the truth, Your Eminence."

After a moment, Carey nodded. "All right." A bleak look appeared on his face. "My God."

He took Peregrine's elbow and they continued toward their residence building. "After supper we are going to put through a call to New York. To Matthew Han-ratty."

"Do you think this should be made public?"

The suggestion stopped Carey in his tracks. "Good God, no. I want to ask Hanratty if he can get his hands on the statement Fergus left."

3

NEIL ADMIRARI HOPPED OUT OF BED and padded naked across the room to the window. Outside, Manhattan sparkled in the setting sun, the whole island turned chiaroscuro at twilight. Twilight. Lovely word in any language *"Le crépuscule de la civilisation,"* he murmured aloud.

"What?"

Lulu's golden hair lay on the pillow, the sheet was tugged up under her chin giving her the look of an ear of corn, a corn-fed midwestern maid. He felt love for her and hatred for himself. He had promised himself it would be different with Lulu. He was courting her, not seducing her. But he had done so much of the latter and none of the former that it was hard to honor the distinction. And now they had gone to bed in the afternoon after a lovely lunch.

Lulu lay looking at him as other wenches had and he wanted to kneel beside the bed and beg her forgiveness. He must be in love with her. He welcomed the thought as extenuating, but it only increased his anguish.

He said, "I think we should get married in Saint Patrick's. All right? Will your parents mind?"

"I can't."

"Busy?"

"Neal, come here. This happened so quickly we never had a chance to talk, really talk. You don't know a thing about me." Holding the sheet between her teeth, she sat up and propped a pillow behind her. She patted the bed. "Come on."

There he was, naked as a jaybird while she was draped in a sheet. She kept her eyes intently locked with his as he walked back to the bed. "Custody of the eyes," he said. "Custody of the children too."

"There weren't any."

He laughed, but her look remained serious. When he sat on the bed he felt sandbagged. "Don't tell me all about it."

"Neal, I have not been *hiding* anything. When would I have told you? Why would I have told you?"

"What the hell are you talking about?"

"My marriage," she screamed. "My goddamn stupid mistake-of-the-half-century marriage."

"Oh."

"We didn't live together four months." She was calm again, deadly calm. "It was wrong and we both knew it from the start. He was about as ready to marry and settle down as he was to go to the moon. Neal, I am getting an annulment. I am assured that there is every reason to be optimistic."

He was actually shocked. The idea that she had been through a wedding ceremony, nuptial Mass, white gown and veil, three bridesmaids, both sets of parents all gussied up, with special music, and the readings chosen by the couple themselves—God, what a cliché! To do all that and weeks later say it was all a mistake and so long Charlie? He was shocked.

Oh, if his employers at the *National Catholic Reporter* only knew how conservative he really was in his bone's marrow, how he hated all those relentlessly smiling priests with their sprayed hair and cassette courses for sale and the flakey nuns and the weirdo peace bishops who seemed a little ashamed they had to live on such a screwed up place as planet earth! Their real beef was the human condition. Original sin. And the paper's staff. Ye gods. Try to find a Catholic journalist who isn't full of neuroses and resentments. The Grudge Pack. The Sick Pack. Marriages? Forget it. No wonder they all wrote feelingly of the pastorate to divorced Catholics, of single parents. Talk about special pleading.

He had just assumed that Lulu was another breed entirely. The paper she wrote for was conservative to moderate, unquestionably orthodox theologically. If someone had told him a week ago, in Gethsemani, in that bar in Bardstown, that he would be in bed with

Lulu van Ackeren before the month was out, he would have washed their imagination out with soap. He wanted to honor her, to put her on a pedestal. He would bay at the moon for her. He had wanted to marry her.

"I will be free, Neal," she said in a small voice.

He nodded. So she told him all about it and he sat through the recital of her marriage and the details of her annulment efforts as if this was exactly the kind of conversation he had expected to have after their first passion was spent and the drinks and the lunch had worn off. While she spoke, he slipped into his shorts and trousers. On his feet, he began to pace. He did not realize that what he was doing was rehearsing the response he must give.

Dear God, how bitter to think what thoughts had been his earlier when he strolled nude to the window, innocent as Adam before the fall, exulting in his guilt nonetheless. He would have told her that they must not sleep together again before they were married. Of course, they would marry. One did not go to bed with someone like Lulu van Ackeren except with the noblest intentions.

The memory brought him close to tears. He had thought she was a virgin, the condition in which he might have taken her to the altar. Her admission had made her a woman like all others. Emotionally scarred, carrying a history, soon to be unmarried thanks to the new-found compassion of marriage tribunals.

She stopped talking. He had returned to the bed. He looked down at her. From her hairline a few strands were brushed across her forehead though most of her hair was swept back from her face. He sat again on the edge of the bed and she put her hand on his bare back.

"I thank God I didn't get pregnant."

"Just now?"

She made a face. Suddenly he felt very tired. Why had he started to get dressed? He wondered if she would stay the night. The prospect was exciting and surprisingly plausible. He had not thought of Lulu in terms of sensual excitement. He had cast her for a madonna role, wife and mother, chaste, torrid in the dark but a little ashamed afterward. And above all, emotionally stable.

He said, "I am a very matriarchal person."

"I noticed." She tweaked his breasts.

Later, in the shower, he studied his chest. Old men developed breasts, but his seemed only the standard token tits men have. Why do males have nipples at all? He felt almost hemaphroditic and all because Lulu had tweaked him. He had not invited her to shower with him, wanting to regain the notion that she was unlike the rest of her sex.

Hanratty telephoned while Lulu was taking her shower. "Carey is belatedly taking seriously what I told him about Fergus's last statement."

"Good God, Matthew. Don't tell me you believed me?"

"Cut it out, Neal."

"If you say so."

"Fergus did leave some kind of document, didn't he?"

"Far be it from me to contradict the religion editor of *The New York Times*."

"Goddamn it, Neal, were you lying to me?"

In other circumstances, he might have gone on teasing Matthew, but the water in the bathroom had been turned off and the moment was not propitious. He assured Matthew that there was indeed a document. He had not seen it, but his sources were unimpeachable. (Lulu had a friend named Cecily at FWPC.)

"Where can I get hold of it?"

Admirari did not want to get Cecily into trouble. He made an arch reference to the late cardinal's amanuensis.

"Myrtle Tillman?"

"That's the woman."

Hanratty hung up the phone. Lulu emerged from the bathroom on a cloud of steam, head swathed in one towel, body in another. How lovely, lithe, and long her legs looked.

"Come here and let me unwrap you."

"Neal, I am starved. If I don't get something to eat I will faint from hunger."

They went out for pizza and beer, dressed like kids, Lulu somewhat comic in a pair of his jeans. They went to a place in the Village where they would be overlooked as tourists from New Jersey or some other outback. He wanted to know all about her. Not her marriage, to hell with that, but what kind of person she was.

"How did you become a conservative? What are your parents like?"

"Conservative?" Her nose wrinkled as she questioned the word. "Politically? I've never been able to figure out what it means so far as being a Catholic goes. I just want to be orthodox. I was raised on a ton of novelties, in grade school, high school, college. Religion was all touchy-feely stuff and we were always being told how wonderful it was now and how awful it used to be. I thought it was pretty awful now. I looked into the bad old days and found people like Chesterton and Merton and Maritain. Where are the people like that now? And there used to be dozens. This was progress? I got so I couldn't stand the sight of a nun, and I could spot them at a hundred yards even without the habit. Another thing I discovered was how nuns used to be. What an eye opener. I wanted to be a Carmelite."

"The Little Flower."

"And Teresa of Avila. Edith Stein. Strong women. Brilliant women. Saints. Try to imagine them at a meeting of nuns today. For that matter, try to think of Mother Teresa at a meeting with some of these nuns."

"So what happened?"

"First, it turned out that there are various kinds of Carmelite. Not all have escaped renewal. I shopped around, literally. There wasn't a Carmelite convent anywhere near where I grew up. Actually, I was relieved that I couldn't walk down the street and find the Carmel of Avila or the Carmel of Cologne. The upshot was that I kidded myself into thinking that Carmel had let me down. I still feel guilty about it. I should have entered." She looked over her shoulder as if distracted by other diners. "Maybe that had something to do with my marriage flopping."

"I was in the seminary for awhile."

"I know."

"Oh?"

"One made inquiries," she said obliquely.

Flattered? Of course, but, perversely, he was a trifle disappointed too. His interest in Lulu had been built on the assumption that she did not know he existed, that he would have to begin from less than zero and win her heart only after heroic efforts. The thought of her checking him out the way she had checked out Carmelite communities was a sad one.

"Have you ever read about acedia, Neal?" They had left the pizzeria and were walking back to his apartment. His arm was about her shoulders and hers was across his back, her hand in the rear pocket of his jeans.

"Tell me about it." Her hand on his buttock seemed an undreamt of intimacy.

"A deadly sin, sloth. The noonday devil. If you read

your *Summa* you will find Saint Thomas talking about it as a distaste for spiritual things. I used to think I had it." She looked up at him, her eyes in a squint. "I thought so because I hate religious news, the sort of thing we cover. USCC, NCCB, meetings, conferences, symposia, on and on and on. What do they have to do with religion? Mainly they're low-grade politics. Look at the Peregrine matter."

"What do you think of him?"

"Nothing. I don't know a single thing about him. Only that he let the bishops play games with him."

It was an interesting point. Lulu was unimpressed by what had impressed everyone else, the abbot's dignity and poise during the bishops' meeting.

"It couldn't have happened if Cardinal Fergus was still alive," Lulu said.

"I won't argue with that."

"I really admired that man."

"I know. That's why I called you a conservative."

"And you're a liberal?"

"Well, my paper is. What was the word for sloth again?"

"Acedia."

"I think I've got it too."

She pinched him. "Where?"

"You're close."

"That's Lust, another capital sin."

4

M Y R T L E S O U N D E D bright as a button on the telephone and no wonder. Laura was delighted that Abbot Peregrine had been to see her in Chappaqua, although she was as surprised to learn that Myrtle was there as she was that the abbot of Gethsemani had gone so far to see her. For the first few minutes of the conversation it was as if the man they talked of was not the same man Philip Knight had discovered was not Perry Green.

"I'm visiting my brother and his wife. That is, I have been. I wanted to call you before I catch the train to the city. You remember the transcript I gave you of the tape your uncle left with me?"

"Of course."

"I am going to let Abbot Peregrine hear the tape, Laura. I think I should, don't you?"

"Will you be working for him?"

"It looks that way." There was not a smidgin of doubt in Myrtle's voice. Laura felt uneasy at Myrtle's announcement that she was going to let Abbot Peregrine listen to Cardinal Fergus's microcassette, but it seemed to make sense if Myrtle was going back to work at the chancery. It seemed another sign that he was a good selection for archbishop. What would Harry Packard do if he had to find a replacement for her?

That was when Laura remembered the abbot was not who he claimed to be. "Myrtle, maybe you shouldn't show it to him just yet."

"I think he should hear that tape and I want to be with him when he does."

"What is he like, Myrtle? Is he what you expected?" How on earth could she tell Myrtle what they had learned about Abbot Peregrine? She tried to imagine herself saying he was not, or had not been, Perry Green, and it sounded silly. Had Myrtle even heard that was supposed to have been his name? And so what if it had not been? It was one thing to draw what seemed to be obvious conclusions from the revelation of Abbot Peregrine's murky past with Harry Packard or the Knights, but she sensed that Myrtle was not in a receptive mood for such doubts, not when she had the prospect of getting her old job back, returning to the chancery as secretary to the new archbishop. If Peregrine did indeed become the next archbishop of New York.

Myrtle said, "Laura, he is even better than I expected. He is simple, but shrewd. Wise. He has pretty much the same outlook as the cardinal did, on the Church, on politics."

"How on earth did he find you in Chappaqua?"

"Laura, I am speaking to you in the utmost confidence. He doesn't want anyone to know that he has come to New York."

"Why not?"

"I didn't *quiz* him about it, Laura," Myrtle said in a chilly voice. "Besides, it makes sense."

It almost sounded as if Myrtle had used the cassette as bait with Peregrine. Laura found it hard to blame her. Visiting her brother in Chappaqua as the maiden aunt must be depressing when there was no exciting job in Manhattan to return to.

"The reason I'm calling, I wonder if you could make a copy of the transcript and send it to me."

"But how can I get it to you, Myrtle. What did you have in mind?"

"Send it Federal Express. That way I should have it tomorrow."

"Well, I could."

"Good. I have to run now to catch my train."

"Keep in touch, Myrtle."

Laura did not call Federal Express. She would not have made a copy of the transcript without telling Harry Packard. For that matter she did not even want to tell him of Myrtle's phone call. He would have been furious at the suggestion that such a document be put into the hands of a man who had lied about his background and who was probably as bad as any of the people Cardinal Fergus had worried about. Harry Packard might be right. On the other hand, he might be wrong and Laura did not want to stand in the way of Myrtle's getting her old job back.

For the next hour she tried to decide whether it mattered that Myrtle did not know what Knight had found —or not found—in Superior, Wisconsin, about Abbot Peregrine's life before he entered the monastery. It seemed unfair to keep such information from her; on the other hand, she continued to feel, as she had on the phone, that such doubts would not be welcomed by Myrtle at the moment.

Laura added to her feelings of guilt by not telling Harry Packard of Myrtle's call. This would have been difficult in any case. He had called his secretary to say he would be working at home most of the day, and when Florence had come to tell Laura, she made certain their eyes did not meet. Florence had beautifully shaped hands, long fingers, enhanced by the length of her nails. Her hands worked oddly as she stood in front of Laura's desk, as if they were seeking an absent throat. Laura did not ask Florence if anyone else had also called to say they were taking the day off.

Matthew Hanratty phoned at 9:45 and got huffy when she told him Mr. Packard was not in.

"Where can I reach him?"

"Can I take a message?"

"Who is this?" He paused, as if wondering whether he should repeat he was religion editor of the *Times*. Laura gave him her title. "Look, what do you know of a message left by the late Cardinal Fergus?"

"I think you know my response to that, Mr. Haggerty."

"Hanratty!"

"Mr. Hanratty. If Mr. Packard wishes to return your call, you can talk with him . . ."

"Listen, I just talked with Cardinal Carey of San Francisco and Abbot Peregrine . . ."

Her laughter stopped him.

"What's wrong?" he demanded.

"Abbot Peregrine called you?"

"In company with Cardinal Carey, yes."

"May I ask when that was?"

"They called late last night from California."

"Did they?" Laura smiled, grateful to have proof that the reporter was deliberately lying in order to get past her defenses.

"Do you doubt me?"

"Where was Abbot Peregrine when they called?"

"With Cardinal Carey."

"In San Francisco?"

"In California, yes."

"Mr. Hanratty, I happen to know that Abbot Peregrine was not in California yesterday. He could not have been. Good-bye."

She put the phone down gently but that did not diminish the satisfaction she felt in doing it. How easily, if she had not spoken with Myrtle, she might have been moved by his lies to tell the reporter things he had no right to know.

Less than ten minutes later, Laura was told she had a call from San Francisco.

"Miss Ramey, this is Cardinal Carey." There was no doubt that this was the voice of the cardinal archbishop of San Francisco. Laura said hello in a small voice. "I have just received a telephone call from Matthew Hanratty."

"So did I."

"That's what he said. He said something else, something curious. About Abbot Peregrine."

"He claimed that Abbot Peregrine was with you in California."

"Yes."

"Is Abbot Peregrine with you?"

"We have been together for two days, Miss Ramey." Cardinal Carey paused. "Would you like to speak with him!"

Before she could say yes or no there was the distinctive silence that results from a hand being put over the phone, and then another voice spoke.

"This is Abbot Peregrine speaking."

Laura's confusion was now complete. The disdain she had felt for Matthew Hanratty's attempt to get information from her by means of a lie had been about to transfer itself to Cardinal Carey when she was suddenly confronted by the fact that there was one Abbot Peregrine too many. If the real abbot of Gethsemani was with Cardinal Carey in California—and Laura found it impossible to think that a cardinal archbishop would deliberately lie to her—then who had gone to visit Myrtle in Chappaqua? It seemed the simplest thing to put the question to Abbot Peregrine.

"Myrtle Tillman was Cardinal Fergus's secretary?"

"For thirty years."

"And she told you that I had come to see her? I didn't, you know. Did she describe the man who came to her?"

Laura sorted through her thoughts. "She said he was thin and tall. And that he looked like a monk."

"Can you contact Myrtle Tillman? You must tell her she should not confide anything Cardinal Fergus might have left with her to that man. She should have nothing to do with him at all."

"You know who he is?"

"Can you reach her?"

"I think so."

"That must come before anything else. Myrtle Tillman may be in grave danger."

The phone went dead. Immediately Laura began to dial the number of Philip Knight.

5

MONSIGNOR BARRETT WAS RELUCTANT to give Matthew Hanratty any information about Cardinal Fergus's former secretary, so reluctant in fact that Hanratty was suddenly sure he was on to something. His hunches had been only intermittently reliable in the past but this time he was sure there must be a connection between the call from California and Barrett's unwillingness to tell an old friend like Matthew Hanratty a simple thing like where he could get in touch with Myrtle Tillman.

"Could you give me some hint of your interest, Matthew? I gave my word not to say where she is."

"Who is she hiding from?"

Barrett's hearty laugh was perhaps 45 percent genuine. "Do you ever take a vacation, Matthew?"

"Have other people been trying to reach her?"

Barrett frowned. "Who on earth would be pursuing the secretary of a former archbishop?"

"I for one."

"Give me a hint why you want to see her."

"Isn't this a bit odd, the head honcho of the chancery running interference for a little old lady? Look, Monsignor, everyone but me seems to know of some last statement Fergus made. I want to talk with Myrtle Tillman about it."

Barrett's smile was thin-lipped. "Don't waste your time, Matthew."

"You're the one wasting my time. Where is she?"

He was given a phone number in Chappaqua and when he dialed it he was told that Myrtle Tillman was on her way back to the city. The train she had taken was due at Grand Central in ten minutes. Hanratty met the train and, impressed by the determination with which his quarry moved through the crowd, decided to follow her. She went directly to the chancery, and Hanratty took up his station across the street.

At first he felt odd standing across from the archdiocesen building. Tourists came and went, pedestrians continued to flow past on the sidewalk, street traffic was unrelenting. He himself might have been invisible. Wasn't that the old cliché about the city, anonymity, nobody noticing anybody else, a dropping of inhibitions because if anyone did notice you he was a stranger you were unlikely to see again? How many people in New York did he know? An infinitesimal fraction of the population. More people knew him than vice versa, but he was still a raindrop in a lake. Such thoughts did not bolster his sense of significance.

Seen from Madison Avenue, St. Patrick's was in some ways more impressive than from other vantage points, more proportional to its surroundings. There was even a little greenery to relieve the granite and asphalt aspect of the avenue. On the corner of the building a bronze plate commemorated the two days John Paul II had stayed there. Myrtle would emerge from the same door she had entered. That was the assumption of his vigil and he did not want to subject it to critical scrutiny.

He felt a strange excitement, lurking there unnoticed. Stake-out. No, better to think of it in terms of the apprentice reporting he had never had to do, investigative journalism, Jack Anderson, digging out the story. Most of the things he wrote came to him ready-made, more or less. He had missed a rung or two on the ladder of success and he felt a bogus nostalgia for an experience he had never had.

His presence made sense only if he believed Carey, discounted Admirari's too typical dust-throwing the night before, and relied on his own hunch that something was afoot. He had time now to let his thoughts form. The key was the interest Harry Packard and FWPC showed in the Fergus statement, hiring Philip Knight and his fat brother to investigate God knows what. He had little difficulty thinking what use Packard and his ilk might make of a Fergus statement bewailing the leftward drift of the Church and even suggesting that this could only be explained by infiltration. Everything depended on who made such fears public and how they were interpreted. And when. Packard would want to manipulate Fergus's successor. Hanratty wanted the statement so he could use it to show that Cardinal Fergus had been off his rocker in the last months of his life, filled with paranoid fears. The Cold War Cardinal had ended up with a frostbitten mind.

Incredible and irrelevant—that was the double note he would strike when he blew the posthumous whistle on Cardinal Fergus. It did surpass belief that a leader of the most powerful sect in Christianity should think his Church vulnerable to takeover by a few well-placed Marxists.

The irrelevance aspect was one he might not write up, but it summed up his own views. Imagine that Russia or China or Cuba—why not Poland?—had put people in seminaries, convents, monasteries. Concede it was possible. Grant that it had been done. What did that have to do with the real problems facing the West? Why should our attention be diverted from oppressed people to the fate of the bureaucracy of the Catholic Church?

Not to mention the fact that there were all kinds of people, missionaries and theologians among them, who no longer saw the big opposition between Christianity and Marxism that Fergus had made a career out of emphasizing. What if alleged subversives were really Christians in the deepest sense of the term, recapturing the revolutionary teaching of Jesus that the official Church had been downplaying for centuries?

Across the street, Myrtle emerged from the doorway and began to walk rapidly uptown. My God, how easily he might have missed her. He stepped out onto the sidewalk and began to walk, keeping on the opposite side of the street and some twenty yards behind her.

At the corner he crossed the street and continued to follow her up Madison Avenue. She walked purposefully, obviously with no thought that someone might be following her. But then he himself did not walk as if he in turn were being tailed. When she entered a bank he came to a halt. The thought of waiting in the street again did not appeal. Besides, for all he knew, she was simply cutting through the bank.

He pushed through the revolving doors and came into the oddly churchlike vastness of the bank. Where had Myrtle gone? He moved circumspectly around the great rotunda of a room until he saw her. She stood at a counter, filling out a form. Safety deposit boxes. Ah. He stood at a table in the center of the vast room and laid a deposit slip before him on the glass top. His own account was in another bank. Money was one of the things he genuinely did not want to think about. He had more, much more, than he had ever wanted and his hoard induced feelings of shame. He should give it all away but he could not bring himself to do it and that made him feel worse. He had become unwillingly dependent on those savings, a series of numbers in a book that made him feel secure. God!

Myrtle was admitted behind the counter and led away by the woman who had taken the slip from her. Hanratty moved up to the counter where Myrtle had stood and, tempting fate, he picked up the pad from which she had torn the slip after filling it out. Her writing had made an impression on the next sheet. He tore it off, folded it and put it into his pocket. More fantasy.

After several minutes he retreated to the center of the room. The hum he heard was that of commerce, speculation, greed. Wall Street, the Big Board, Dow Jones. He could not even think of such things without a mental sneer. His thoughts about economics were rudimentary. If he had not spent time in the monastery, he might have been an advocate of such small, self-contained communities. But even the Trappists had been unable to resist the lure of the market; they went into trade with cheese or beer or honey. The excuse was that they needed cash for farm machinery. His monastic experience had made him wary of socialism as a panacea. He did not hate an economic system. He hated the necessity for any system at all.

Thirty yards away, still behind the counter, Myrtle was coming toward him, and she was looking straight at him. He flushed with embarrassment while his face searched for an appropriate expression. But her lack of reaction to seeing him made him realize that she could not. Given her age, he must be less than a blur. He sighed aloud. He had been holding his breath.

Myrtle came out from behind the counter through a

swinging brasswork gate and the way she clutched her purse against her side told him what he wanted to know. She was carrying something she had not been carrying when she entered the bank. After casting a near-sighted glance about her, she headed for the revolving door. Emboldened by her weak eyesight, Hanratty went through the door while it still moved with the push she had given it.

Myrtle was already at the curb where a cab swooped in at the signal of her lifted arm. She leaned in the window to give the driver her destination. In she got and off she went. The address she had given was downtown. Matthew was committed now. He would follow her there and see if she had made a rendezvous.

6

ONCE SHE HAD THE MICROCASSETE in her purse, Myrtle felt as jumpy as she had before turning the transcript over to Laura Ramey. The little plastic box also brought back the moment when Cardinal Fergus had handed it to her and solemnly referred to it as his last will and testament.

She was glad she didn't have the transcript as well as the tape with her now. She half regretted having offered to provide a transcript as well as the tape. Laura hadn't been all that enthusiastic about Myrtle's willingness to let Abbot Peregrine know the worst. Well, Myrtle trusted her own judgment on that. She could already imagine herself working for Abbot Peregrine.

It was nearly noon when she left the bank, but she caught a cab immediately and was on her way to her apartment. Abbot Peregrine had said he would meet her there at twelve o'clock, so she would be a little late.

This was a bad time to make good time but she quelled the desire to tell the driver to hurry. A glance at the cabbie's license informed her that he was Iranian or Turkish or some such thing. Honest to pete, New York was becoming more and more of a foreign city all the time. You would have expected Cardinal Fergus to be annoyed by something like that, but he hadn't been. He had a special fondness for Puerto Ricans. Of course he spoke their language. As far as Myrtle was concerned they all ought to learn English or go back where they belonged. Once she had given a driver the Algonquin as her destination and found him looking it up under *g* when they were stopped by a light. Cardinal Fergus explained to her that the man had taken El to be an article. Honestly.

She held her purse on her lap and gripped it with both hands. What would Abbot Peregrine think of the microcassette? He could listen to it in her apartment, using the unit the cardinal had purchased for her so she could take care of the overload of work without spending all her time at the office. The more she thought about it, the surer she was that giving the tape to Abbot Peregrine was the proper thing to do. Let Laura advise caution if she wanted, she had not met the man.

She should have noticed Abbot Peregrine as she approached her door, but there was no sign of him at all until suddenly he appeared beside her as if he had dropped out of the sky.

"Oh my, you frightened me."

His smile was apologetic. "I'm sorry. You must understand that it is not comfortable for me to be out in the world like this. I am the one who feels frightened."

"You better get used to it."

"Yes."

She clamped the purse tightly under her arm again as she unlocked the door. He stood beside her, head down, arms just hanging at his sides. How tall he was. And—she could not stop the thought—what an odd choice to succeed Cardinal Fergus. She broke a rule by riding up in the elevator with him; she always insisted on riding alone, she didn't care who the other passenger might be, man or woman. She felt vulnerable enough in that slowly rising cage alone, but the thought of being cooped up with a thief or mugger or pervert was too much. She made exceptions for close friends, of course, but wasn't Abbot Peregrine more a stranger still than a friend?

"That cut doesn't look much better than it did last night."

His hand went to his face. "It will heal soon."

"I'll give you a bandage."

"Thank you."

He couldn't keep his eyes from her purse but he didn't ask if she had picked up the microcassette. She didn't tell him either, not until they were in her apartment. Before she took off her coat, she snapped open her purse and brought out the tape.

"Here it is."

His fingers quickly closed around it, making it disappear. It might have been a magician's trick. She showed him the machine on which to play it and went into the kitchen to make tea. She cocked her ear, waiting to hear Cardinal Fergus's recorded voice, but there was only silence. After she had the water on, she looked into the living room. He had clamped his hands over the headset and was listening with his eyes closed. Myrtle felt a little cheated. She realized she had been looking forward to hearing that tape again, to hearing Cardinal Fergus's voice.

The phone rang as she turned back to the kitchen and she snatched it up as if she were afraid the noise would disturb Abbot Peregrine. Small chance, the way he was concentrating on that tape.

"Myrtle? Oh, thank God. I've been trying to reach you all morning." Laura's sigh of relief came fluttering over the phone.

"I just this minute got in."

"Myrtle, you said you met Abbot Peregrine yesterday. In Chappaqua. Is that right?"

"That's right."

"Myrtle," Laura said urgently, then stopped. When she spoke again she seemed deliberately to be keeping her voice calm. "Myrtle, you couldn't have. Abbot Peregrine was in California yesterday. All day. He is still there."

"That's nonsense."

"It's true. What did the man you saw look like."

The derisive laugh that formed in Myrtle's throat would not come out. If this call were from Monsignor Barrett she could dismiss it as a bad joke, but Laura wouldn't do such a thing. She looked into the living room and her eyes met Abbot Peregrine's. His hands went to the earphones as if to press them more closely to his head. Still clutching the phone, Myrtle backed into the kitchen.

"I can't say now." Her words sounded like a plea. Who was the man in the living room if he was not Abbot Peregrine? Her dead-bolt lock and double chain no longer protected her from the unknown. She had admitted it into her apartment and locked it in with her.

"Is he there with you now?"

"Yes."

Laura inhaled audibly. "Myrtle, listen. And be calm." Laura might have been addressing herself. "You have to get out of there immediately. Use any excuse, but get out of there. As soon as you have, call me."

"Who . . ."

"Is there a cut on his forehead?"

"Yes."

"It's another of the monks. Now everything is going to be all right. But you must leave immediately, just get away, and then telephone. Do you understand?"

When Myrtle hung up the phone she felt that she was cutting herself off from the outside world, from safety and friends. Who in the name of God was the man in her living room?

She came out of the kitchen and crossed the room, ignoring her guest. As she began to unlock the door, he looked up.

"What's wrong?" He stood beside her. It alarmed her, that he should move with such speed. His smile was the same as before but it no longer seemed that of a country-bumpkin monk.

"I'm out of tea." Her voice was thin and strained.

"Don't bother. I don't want tea."

"But I do!" Her voice was an octave too high. His smile faded.

"Who was on the phone?"

She ignored him and turned again to the door. His hand closed over hers when she gripped the bolt.

"I want to talk to you about Cardinal Fergus's tape."

"Ah." The question completely clarified the situation. He took her hand and led her away from the door. His smile had returned, and it had a mesmerizing effect.

"Who are you?"

2 8 6

"My name is Brother Joachim. I am Abbot Peregrine's secretary. I regret deceiving you, but I am acting
for Father Abbot. It was you who took me for Abbot
Peregrine last night and I did not correct you."

"You lied?" The feeling of moral superiority was
exhilarating, and swiftly gone.

"I lied, yes. Who was that on the phone?"

"A woman from the Free World Policy Committee . . ."

"Laura Ramey."

"Do you know her?" Oh dear God, let him be harm-
less, just someone who knew people she knew. But it
had been Laura who warned her about him.

"I want to talk to you about the tape."

It was a distraction from her fear. She nodded.

"Who is the bishop he refers to on the tape? The
KGB agent."

"He didn't say."

"On the tape, no. But he must have told you his
suspicions."

She shook her head. "He didn't tell me."

"I find that hard to believe."

"Well, it's true."

He looked at her expressionlessly. "Very well. But
you must have guessed who it was." He was still holding
her hand and his grip tightened. She tried to tug it free
and found she couldn't.

"Oh, I wish I hadn't given you that tape."

"Why?"

"Why are you so curious about it?"

He led them to the couch. They sat. Why was she
doing what he wanted? She felt like screaming. She
wanted to run. But her mind was quickly rid of such
nonsense. Laura's advice returned. The point was to
get out of there. But how! Damn that locked door.

He said, "Who wouldn't be curious to learn the name of a bishop who is a KGB agent? I want you to think, Myrtle. Think of occasions when Cardinal Fergus spoke of such things. You must have had some suspicion of the man he had in mind."

"If I did, why should I tell you?"

For answer, he twisted her arm, bending the elbow away from her body, causing an intense pain. He relaxed the pressure and the pain went away.

"Think, Myrtle. Think. What bishop did Cardinal Fergus have in mind?"

"I don't know!"

His powerful hand began to turn but he did not twist her arm. How evil his smile now seemed. "You may think you don't know, but you do. I know how proud you were to work for the cardinal. You worked for him a great many years. No one would have been closer to his way of looking at things than you. I think we can assume that buried away in your mind is the name of that bishop."

"Why is it so important to you?"

Her question hung in the room like a frozen example of stupidity. She saw her grasp of the situation reflected in his eyes. He nodded, as if to encourage her.

"I must know, Myrtle, and you are going to help me."

He did not believe her. He was convinced that she knew the name of the traitorous bishop. And then she realized something else. Her presumed knowledge doomed her. Whether or not she gave him a name, he would not leave her alive, thinking she could identify someone as treacherous as himself.

Again an eerie calm came upon her. If she was going to get out of this, it would have to be on her own. No one could help her. Laura was in Washington, and no one else knew she was here with this impostor.

She lifted her foot and stamped down as hard as she could on the toe of his shoe. Surprise and pain loosened his grip and she got her hand free. She fled from the room, down the hall to the bathroom. Inside, she pushed the door shut, but before she could lock it, she felt him grab the outer knob. He began to push. Myrtle leaned against the door, braced one foot against the bathtub behind her, and held fast. She could not shut the door completely but it stayed where it was, open perhaps three inches.

And then his hand appeared, snaking around the opened door, trying to find her. She rolled her weight to her right shoulder, to keep out of his grasp, and the door began to give. Myrtle quickly distributed her weight more evenly and then bent down toward that flexing, menacing hand.

Her teeth closed on his index finger and she bit as hard as she could, feeling the flesh give way, and then the knuckle.

He yanked his hand away with an outraged shout. Myrtle slammed the door and turned the lock.

Her breathing had all but stopped, but now she began to gasp for air. She sat on the toilet and looked around the little room. Sink, tub, linen closet. There was a small, frosted window, its steel frame heavy with paint that had been put on lavishly to cover the rust. Outside was an airshaft.

She had nowhere to go. But for the moment she was safe.

He had stormed away after getting his hand free. There was only silence on the other side of the door. Then she heard him returning. The door shuddered as he struck it. With his hand? His shoulder? The closed door no longer seemed safe.

Myrtle stood in the tub, turned the window handle

and pushed it open. She stood on her toes and put her head through the window and for a moment had the exhilarating illusion that she was free. Blank walls relieved only by windows like her own, all of them closed, a sheer drop to a tar-covered area below.

Behind her the door shuddered under his repeated blows. The panel cracked.

Myrtle pulled open the linen closet door. It was two feet deep, with four shelves, all piled high with linen. The shelves were sustained by inch-square strips of wood but the shelves themselves were loose.

Myrtle emptied the bottom two shelves, shoving their contents onto the upper shelves, then took out the lower shelves and propped them against the back wall of the closet. She got in, crouching, and pulled the door shut. She closed herself into the dark and listened to the bathroom door start to give way.

She opened the closet door a crack. There was a great splintering sound and then he crashed into the bathroom. Myrtle pushed open the closet door and stepped through the destroyed door into the hallway.

In her bedroom she looked wildly around. There was nothing there with which she could protect herself. The crucifix on the wall? No! She couldn't use that as a weapon. She picked up a can of hairspray from her dresser and turned. He was standing in the doorway.

She shook the can and sprayed him, directing it at his eyes. He put up his arm, but too late. He backed into the hall. She had her hand on the door, but stopped. She did not want to go through that again.

He had taken out a handkerchief and brought it to his eyes. Sensing her presence in the hall, he took it away. She gave him another blast and he lunged at her blindly. She sidestepped him and ran into the living room.

If she had been able to unbolt the front door silently she might have gotten away. But the noise brought him on the run. She darted away from the door and he went to it, feeling about for her. Myrtle turned away and her eyes fell on the bronze bust of Our Lady the cardinal had brought from Rome.

There was a prayer of apology on her lips when she brought it crashing down on his skull.

Once. Twice.

Then again and again. Long after he had slumped to the floor and stopped twitching she continued to strike at him with the bronze madonna.

Then she went down the hall and through the shattered door of her bathroom and threw up.

7

WHEN PHILIP KNIGHT ARRIVED on Twelfth Street the meat wagon was at the curb and three patrol cars blocked crosstown traffic, setting off a symphony of horns. He wended his way among the cars and reached the door of Myrtle's building just as Matthew Hanratty was hustled out in the custody of two cops, an expression of furious indignation on his narrow face. Belief in his own star, if not in God, returned when he noticed Knight.

"Thank God!" he cried, digging in his heels and succeeding in slowing his escort. "Will you please tell these idiots who I am?"

The cop closest to Knight had a face reminiscent of a map of central Europe and was otherwise familiar. Senski? That was it. And he remembered Knight.

"Who does he claim to be, a reporter for the *Times?*"

Senski nodded and his companion snorted. Knight stopped them before they carried Hanratty away. "How is she?"

Already he was wondering how he would tell Laura. If there had been hope for Myrtle, they would have brought her down before bothering with Hanratty. The reporter sputtered between the cops. To hell with him. But it was Hanratty who answered his question.

"Myrtle Tillman is perfectly all right. Physically. She *is* in a state of semishock, far too distraught to identify me."

"Is she really okay?"

Senski nodded and Knight brushed past him to the door. An outraged shout came from Hanratty.

"Do you know this guy?" Senski yelled before Knight went through the door.

Knight turned and looked down into the impassive face of Senski and the pleading face of Hanratty. If the news about Myrtle had been bad he would have left the sonofabitch to his fate. It seemed what Roger would have called a thanksgiving offering to assure Senski that Hanratty was what he claimed to be.

"But he told us he lives here and he don't."

Knight shrugged and pushed through the door. He wasn't going to waste more time unraveling Hanratty's inept lies.

He got upstairs in time to see the dead, distorted face of Joachim before they zipped up the rubber bag. Dead? Lipscomb from homicide told him what had happened. My God! Knight could not believe it. Beyond Lipscomb, he saw Myrtle seated in the middle of the couch, on the edge of the cushion, staring straight ahead. The bronze madonna was already wrapped in plastic.

She looked at Knight with wide, unblinking eyes when he came to sit beside her.

"Laura asked me to come."

And Myrtle burst into tears. In the hall, someone dropped one end of the rubber bag and there was an eerie thud. Knight put his arm around the weeping Myrtle, as much to hide the gruesome goings-on in the corridor as to comfort her. Looking around, he got some sense of the fight to the death that had gone on there.

"I thought he was Abbot Peregrine. He told me he was Abbot Peregrine."

"His name was Joachim," Knight said, as if it mattered. Who knew what the man's name had really been? "What did he want?"

"He was convinced I knew . . ." She stopped, looking up at him with tear-filled eyes. There was caution in her glance. Knight nodded reassuringly.

"Don't worry about it now."

"I didn't tell him anything. I let him listen to the tape but I didn't tell him anything."

"I'm sure you didn't."

"I didn't know any more, but he wouldn't believe me. He wanted to kill me."

She shrugged and then began again to weep. It seemed the best therapy and he encouraged her, holding her close, murmuring as he might to a child. But this was a woman who had held off a killer and in the end killed him. That was something she would have to live with for the rest of her life.

He said, "He was one of those who killed the cardinal."

She stopped crying, thinking about it. She wept again but it was different now. He had given her a way of accepting what she had done, what no doubt she had had to do if she were going to remain alive.

2 9 3

He realized that she was pushing something against his side. A microcassette. He took it from her. She looked at him significantly. "I took it from his pocket. Afterward."

"Good girl."

What a remarkable woman she was. He hugged her close again. Despite the horror, she'd had sense enough not to let Cardinal Fergus's last tape become part of a police investigation.

When he got through to Washington, he found that Laura was on her way. She had left her office two hours before, meaning that she might arrive at any minute. Lipscomb waited for him to finish phoning.

"What the hell do you know of what went on here, Knight?"

"I was just going to ask you."

"The guy she killed? He was dressed as a priest. Roman collar, black suit."

"You're kidding. You figure he was pretending to be one or what?"

"You haven't any idea?"

"Me?" Knight laughed. He ranked it about four on a scale of sincerity. Lipscomb made a face.

"How come you know the lady?"

"She's a friend of a friend. Here she is now."

And Laura arrived. He had a moment with her before Myrtle realized Cardinal Fergus's niece had come.

"Myrtle's all right? Thank God. And thank you so much for coming."

She wore black leather gloves and when she gripped his hand tightly he had a sensation of dangerous intimacy. Gratitude glistened in her eyes as she looked up at him, and it took a deliberate effort not to lean forward and kiss her. She seemed to sense this. She squeezed his hand more tightly.

"I'll go to Myrtle now." She said it in a whisper. When Knight turned, Lipscomb tilted his head to one side and lifted his brows. "A friend of a friend," he repeated.

Knight was grinning like a boy when he went downstairs. He wanted a public phone from which to call Roger.

"You've got the tape?" Roger said, after he had absorbed the news. "Good! Are you coming right back here?"

"I better go back upstairs and see if I can be of any help to Laura. And Myrtle."

"There will be plenty of time for that. For now, come home. We have to wrap this thing up."

Roger banged down the phone. Wrap it up? The sight of Joachim in a rubber bag had given Philip the sense of an ending, but of course Roger was right. He had not been hired to see that an end was put to Brother Joachim. What Harry Packard wanted was the name of the treacherous bishop. And Roger had spoken as if he knew how to wrap it up.

It was dark when Philip Knight got home to Rye and he was surprised that Roger had not turned on the yard light. He was more surprised when he noticed that the house too was dark. He reached forward and pushed a knob on the dashboard, extinguishing the headlights of the van before continuing slowly down the county road past the house. Thirty yards beyond, the road dipped sharply and turned eastward. He ran the vehicle onto the shoulder, and turned off the engine.

He eased open the door and did not close it tightly. He kept to the road as he started back toward the house. The fallen leaves would announce his coming like a riffle of drums. He walked on the balls of his feet. Caution seems foolish until we know for sure it is called for, but the dark house worried him, the worry connecting to the struggle that had taken place in Myrtle's apartment. Irrational? It was impossible to tell.

At his own property, he thought of removing his shoes before leaving the road but decided it was not heels and soles that makes leaves rustle. He let each foot settle slowly, muting the noise, and went almost silently across the lawn in the direction of the garage. When Either and Or sensed his approach they would bay it to the world, and he wanted first to silence and reassure the dogs.

No bark or growl or muzzled sound met him as he approached the kennel.

The hurricane fence was ten feet high. The outside kennel gate was locked. But the dogs lay crumpled on the concrete. Dead. Their throats slit. How? He must have gotten to the animals from the garage. Knight stopped in his tracks.

His present position formed the apex of a triangle whose base was the walk from the garage to the house. Unequal sides led to the endpoints of the baseline. He was closer to the garage. But it was the house he had to reach.

Myrtle had fought successfully for her life. Either and Or were dead. He would not let questions about Roger form in his mind, but it was impossible not to be assailed by images of his brother's ineptitude, his physical vulnerability. All that goddamn weight.

In a rage, Philip ran crashing toward the house. What difference did it make if he could be heard?

The back door was not locked. It was not even closed tightly. In the kitchen, Knight moved quickly out of the doorway and pressed against the wall beside the door. His ears seemed as sensitive as a dog's. Nothing.

"Roger!"

"Is that you, Phil?"

The voice came from the study. Knight ran toward it. Roger sounded elated, not frightened. The lights went on as he dashed through the living room. Knight came to a startled halt in the doorway of the study.

Roger sat in the revolving chair, turned away from his computer. He held a shotgun, directing it across the room at the man in the chair. The man wore a light topcoat and he held his upper arm with one hand. Blood seeped through his fingers and stained the topcoat. He looked with wary indifference at Knight.

"Hello, Father Lewis."

And Knight took the weapon from Roger and aimed it at the priest.

8

HARRY PACKARD WAS RELUCTANT to admit that Philip Knight had done what he had been hired to do, and Laura was appalled.

"His brother was almost killed and you have the nerve to question their bill?"

Harry picked up the slip of paper, then let it flutter to his desk. "Have you looked at this thing? They want me to replace their dogs."

"You should!"

"Laura, I hired Philip Knight for a very specific purpose: to find out what American bishop is a KGB agent.

What do I get for my money? Two Trappists, one dead, one alive, both of them KGB, the live one repentant and soon to be installed as archbishop of New York. I have a murder in Kentucky, another in Wisconsin, and two dead dogs in White Plains. It is all very exciting, but I do not have what I hired him to do."

"You have Father Lewis."

"Yes. There is Father Lewis."

The .45 found on the odd young priest was the gun used to murder Cardinal Fergus and five other people. Father Lewis had been in Rome at the time. There was a strong case and if it could be successfully pressed, Harry Packard could claim credit for apprehending the assassin. How on earth could he possibly balk at the Knights' bill?

"Oh, I'll pay the damn thing. I'll even buy them some dogs. But I won't sleep nights until I know who the traitor bishop is."

"Can't he figure that out?" Roger asked when Laura brought the check to White Plains. The Knights had taken in Myrtle Tillman until she could recover emotionally from the horror in her apartment. She would have to be in good condition to take over as Archbishop Peregrine's secretary after the installation. The Trappist had flown to Rome where he had been ordained bishop by the pope himself. The two men, Polish pope and Russian Trappist, had been closeted for two-and-a-half hours of private conversation.

"You know who it is?" Laura asked.

"Of course. Surely you do too."

"Tell me."

"Think about it."

Laura noticed that Myrtle and Philip leaned forward too, so she wasn't the only one in the room who did not know the name of the bishop. Roger looked at his brother and Myrtle and could not fail to notice the blank looks on their faces.

Philip said, "Explain it, Roger. What have we missed?"

The events between the assassinations in Rome and the apprehension of Father Lewis, which had seemed just random occurrences as recalled by Harry Packard, emerged as related episodes in a logical plot line as Roger reconstructed them.

Why was Cardinal Fergus killed?

"He was the victim of Italian terrorists; at least three groups claimed they did it. And there was the Latin American connection." Philip was assuming the role of *advocatus diaboli*.

Roger shook his head vigorously, causing his jowls to sway. He pressed his eyes shut as if in pain.

"Father Lewis," he said. "Father Lewis. Keep your mind concentrated on him. He was in Rome, the assassination weapon was in his possession, he killed Cardinal Fergus."

"And the others?"

"And the others. Their presence confused the motive so long as it was unclear that Lewis had done it. With his guilt clear . . ." Philip tried to interject, but Roger waved him off. "With his guilt clear, the motive is clear. The archdiocese of New York became vacant and the plan was to fill the post with a traitor."

"Peregrine?"

"He disappointed them. Furthermore, he had revealed his identity to Archbishop Rossi. From that moment, the apostolic delegate's life was in danger. Joachim dispatched him on the way to the airport, feigning an accident. Peregrine has explained the technique to me.

It is foolproof and would have been even if the dashboard had been padded. In this case, the vehicle was a pickup truck. Death would have been swift and painless.

"Peregrine, it was thought, could be brought back to his senses, by threats, by a reversion to his former convictions, by blackmail. They were quite willing to take the risk.

"They were not willing to have Cardinal Fergus's last dictation remain available."

"Roger, that tape is all but innocuous. Cardinal Fergus gave public talks almost as inflammatory as his last message. He had been all but discredited before he was killed. Why should the tape bother them?"

Roger smiled. "You say that because you know what's on it. They did not. The unknown. It is always far more intriguing, and menacing, than the known. That was the wedge I had with Father Lewis. I telephoned him to convey the dreadful news of what had happened at Myrtle's apartment. And then I set the trap." He brought a glass of diet pop to his lips and drank thirstily. If the delay had been due to anything other than food or drink, Laura would have suspected Roger of a dramatic pause.

She said, "What was the trap?"

"I told him that it was lucky Myrtle had not kept in her possession Cardinal Fergus's revelation of who the bad bishop was. You will appreciate that this is not a lie." Myrtle made a reproving noise. "I told him that I had that name written down in a sealed envelope, which I was prepared to turn over to the proper authorities. I suggested Cardinal Carey."

"So you did lie," Laura said.

"Certainly not. I had written down the name and sealed it in an envelope and I am still willing to give it to Cardinal Carey."

"What did Father Lewis say?"

"He said the matter was of such importance he would send a messenger. So I prepared myself." Roger's expression became bleak. "It never occurred to me that I was endangering Either and Or."

"You suspected Father Lewis?" Laura asked.

"Of course. He was the link. Ask yourself why the bishops met in Kentucky. Father Lewis. Ask how an impasse occurred and who was responsible for the name of Peregrine going forward. Father Lewis."

"You don't *know* either of those things," Philip protested.

"There was still an element of conjecture," Roger agreed. "My trap was needed to remove all doubt. And it worked."

Myrtle said, "You are lucky to be alive."

"And who is not, Myrtle? Who is not? You and I may know we ran a risk, but everyone's life is constantly endangered in unknown ways. There is nothing unique about the two of us."

"Roger," Laura said. "Whose name did you write on that paper?"

In the fireplace, a log collapsed, sending a shower of sparks up the chimney. No one in the room was distracted by it and again Laura took comfort from the fact that she was not the only one who did not know what Roger Knight knew.

"Archbishop Deegen's, of course. He is the man whose identity Cardinal Fergus had discovered. Father Lewis was his instrument."

"And not the opposite?"

"I thought of that," Roger conceded. "But it is inherently implausible. Deegen would have had to be such a dupe, so unconscionably stupid, that the hypothesis fell of its own weight. Besides, I must confess that he

301

intrigued me as a candidate. His cover was imaginative. Why, it was almost as if Cardinal Fergus himself had turned out to be a double agent."

An unwise remark and one that robbed Roger's performance of an approporiate denouement. Myrtle was incensed at the suggestion, and she wanted to enlist Laura in her protest. Roger apologized, waddled to the kitchen, and returned pushing a tea cart heaped high with snacks.

"I hope I won't have to eat alone," he said.

But there was a certain wistfulness in his tone.

Epilogue

PAIR AFTER PAIR of prelates preceded the newly installed archbishop of New York down the main aisle of Saint Patrick's cathedral as the great organ swelled and the huge church seemed to pulse with the rhythms of Bach. "Jesu, Joy of Man's Desiring." Seldom have men of such eminence been so thoroughly ignored. Every eye in the church strained to see the tall, mitered figure of Archbishop Peregrine as he followed the long procession through what was now his church.

There are parts of the world where a church would be filled with cheering on so festive an occasion but in North America such Mediterranean lack of inhibition is not the custom. Nonetheless, there was a palpable current of affection between the people and their new archbishop. Hanratty gulped air and blinked his eyes, damned if he would cry, but he just could not restrain himself. Nor was it sufficiently comforting to see that Neal Admirari's eyes were misty too. Lulu van Ackeren, her fingers twisted tightly in Admirari's, looked with shining countenance at Peregrine as he passed, happy tears streaming down her cheeks.

"Better red than dead," Admirari said, a feeble effort to make fun of Peregrine's vestments.

"Too bad he's such a reactionary."

Admirari sighed. "Ah, you Trotskyites."

Annoyance rescued Hanratty from sentimentality. If Admirari or anyone else resurrected that nonsense of Fergus's parting shot, they would have Matthew Hanratty and the power of *The New York Times* to contend with. The point now was to work on Peregrine, make shameless use of their old connection, and ease him toward enlightened views.

Cardinal Carey had pride of place just in front of Peregrine and he aimed his seignorial smile right and left as they went down the aisle. Behind him Peregrine would be directing blessings at the crowd. Maybe it was the ham in him, but Austin Carey continued to get a kick out of the panoply of his office. Yet there had been a considerable reduction in pomp and circumstance after Vatican II. The thought could make him long for the good old days. Had cardinals ever been carried as the pope had been? Peregrine was going to be all right. Thank God. He could have made a big fuss over Lewis.

It was the state department that came up with the saving suggestion. Extradite Lewis to Italy and let him stand trial there. The pope gave his okay and so long Lewis. Peregrine had been no trouble at all.

"You owe me one," Liberati said, but he didn't seem to mean it. It was hard to imagine dealing with someone who did not think in terms of such time-honored quid pro quos.

"I will extend a helping hand to Peregrine," Carey said unctuously, watching Liberati wince. "I know the two of us will work well together."

Oddly enough there seemed no need to head off Deegen. The archbishop of New Orleans should have had a running start with their new colleague. And of course it was only a matter of time before Peregrine became cardinal. Given the ex-monk's easy acquiescence to the Lewis solution, Carey had been somewhat surprised when Peregrine selected him as one of the concelebrants of his installation Mass. The hope that he might have acquired an improbable ally permitted Cardinal Carey to forget his aching legs.

The reception was strung out through three rooms of the archbishop's residence but Roger took up his station by the food. Philip sipped punch and tried not to watch the havoc Roger wrought on the trays of hors d'oeuvre. His own receptive smile drew a middle-aged cleric whose high Roman collar seemed especially immaculate. He introduced himself as Monsignor Barrett.

"We're journalists," Roger said mushily, licking his fingers in apparent preparation for a handshake. The fastidious monsignor plunged his hands into his pockets.

"Actually we're private detectives," Philip corrected. Barrett was if possible even more alarmed.

"You don't say. Are you working?" His eyes flitted to Roger, who was stacking a new supply of minuscule sandwiches in the palm of his hand.

Barrett settled for the Myrtle connection, in fact seizing upon it as a plausible explanation for the presence of the Knights. Philip asked Barrett what he did. The response to his question was not brief. While he listened, Philip watched Roger move away from the table and cross the room, his progress reminiscent of a tug in the East River. His destination was clear. Archbishop Deegen stood in a corner, holding a cup of coffee, looking with benevolent sternness at the gathering. He acknowledged Roger's arrival with a nod.

"Naturally I am at the disposal of the new archbishop," Barrett was saying.

Deegen bent with a puzzled smile toward Roger. In a moment he was erect again. He glanced once icily at Roger, then moved rapidly away from him, into the center of the room, swimming in the sea of the people.

Roger's return to the food was direct. He had the look of a man who had just completed a job and was about to reward himself.

RALPH McINERNY has written several novels, including *The Priest,* which find their themes in the groves of academe and the often comic, sometimes tragic, commotion that plagues the post-conciliar Church. He is also the author of the very popular Father Dowling mystery series.

Since 1955 McInerny has taught at the University of Notre Dame where he is Michael P. Grace Professor of Medieval Studies and Director of both the Medieval Institute and the Jacques Maritain Center.